MW00816607

DON'T LOOK AT ME

Kathy,

Great to

See you

again!

Always,

Charles

CHARLES HOLDEFER

Thanks to Anna Lipinska, Geoff Pitcher and Andrew McKeown

Portions of this work, in different form, appeared in *Aethlon*

© 2022 by Charles Holdefer

All Rights Reserved.

Set in Sabon with LATEX.

ISBN: 978-1-952386-35-0 (paperback)
ISBN: 978-1-952386-36-7 (ebook)
Library of Congress Control Number: 2022933364

Sagging Meniscus Press
Montclair, New Jersey
saggingmeniscus.com

I'm Nobody! Who are you?
Are you—Nobody—too?
Then there's a pair of us!
Don't tell! they'd advertise—you know!

How dreary—to be—Somebody!
How public—like a Frog—
To tell one's name—the livelong June—
To an admiring Bog!

E.D.

Contents

DON'T LOOK AT ME

ONE

FRACTURES

"Have you ever had a standing O?"

He leaned in. She took a sip of wine. Now that they'd almost finished their second bottle, she saw him in a different light. She almost trusted him. It had been a surprise when Philip Post invited her to dinner and, in spite of his reputation, a part of Holly was pleased. Philip was undeniably handsome. His ruffled hair, his accent, the crisp British inflections, his attentive manners, all contributed to his seductiveness, and he surely knew it. The overall effect was such that it was sometimes easy to forget what Philip was actually saying. Holly's mind had wandered, just seconds ago. He'd asked her a question, hadn't he? My, this was too much wine! She'd been thinking: *I could tell him about the letters. Yes, I could!*

She wanted to impress him.

Philip pinched at the table cloth. "Come on, Holly, tell me. I have my suspicions. I reckon you've had a standing O."

His voice was confidential, coaxing. Why did he want to know? Looking into his eyes—a mix of hazel and blue—she considered how Philip would appreciate the significance of her discovery, unlike her family and friends; he could understand her delicate position, and might even be of service. Holly nodded.

He smiled. "I knew it."

"Those days are past me now."

"That I can't believe."

"Philip," she began, with a playful wave to change the subject, "you know I work in the Special Collections archives, right? They've assigned me to the war letters? Well, something peculiar has happened. It was an accident. But I think I've discovered something important."

He shifted in his chair, his eyes darted upward—the briefest flicker—but Holly caught it. Oh, she'd seen it all her life, this nervous reflex! Philip had done it at least three times this evening, and on this occasion it was followed by a movement around his mouth, a tiny tensing of his lips. Holly was six feet, nine and one half inches tall. Even when she was sitting down, people were always sizing her up. They couldn't help themselves. And Holly couldn't help registering every instance.

"How exciting." His voice a conspiratorial whisper. "I love peculiar accidents, especially important ones."

Holly paused. Was he mocking? Philip specialized in media theory and it was often difficult to gauge how serious he was about a subject, even if his jokes (he would argue, his eyes merry, letting you in on the secret) served a serious point. His manner was contagious, too. Philip referred to their college town as "Grainball City" and Holly, though impatient with outsiders who made ironic remarks about the Midwest, caught herself mentally using the term. The way Philip said it wasn't exactly scornful; it was like a form of recognition from someone sophisticated. It felt flattering to be teased. He also referred to the university as "Grainball U." If Philip could mock this town and their employer, well, so could she! But she would never let him mock *her*.

"It's a difficult subject," she said, cautious. "I could be mistaken."

"Tell me about it."

He didn't avert his gaze. Maybe she wouldn't tell him yet, because revelation was also a confession, a form of exposure, which she could withhold and use to tease him back. She could assert her own kind of superiority. A short time ago she would've said that she no longer cared about the opinion of Philip Post and his ilk, but suddenly it mattered how he might perceive her. She was a Master's student on the verge of dropping out; her basketball scholarship had long since expired. Unlike the more promising graduate students who'd been granted fellowships and teaching assistantships and were already burnishing their CVs, Holly subsisted on loans and part-time jobs. In the library she worked alongside undergraduates, scanning old letters from the Civil War onto basic software so that they could be transcribed into a digital archive. It was a repetitive task that wouldn't have intellectually challenged a ten-year-old. As far as Philip Post or anybody with a promising academic career was concerned, she'd been exiled to Siberia. All this was true, but it wasn't the whole truth. Because they didn't know what she'd discovered.

The waiter approached their table and put the check between them.

"I'll pick this up when you're ready." He stooped closer. "Or can I get you something else?"

He'd hovered over them the entire evening, unctuous and clingy, as if he longed to sit down and join them.

"Please leave us," Philip said.

He backed away.

Philip pursued, "I bet you've had *lots* of standing Os."

Reaching for her purse, Holly wondered: why is he stuck on that subject? She doubted that he was a basketball fan. Did Philip even know anything about basketball? Had he seen her play? The warmth in his eyes no longer struck her as seductive; he appeared . . . well . . . *puppyish*. Impressing him was beside the point. She recalled a circle of graduate students gossiping about Philip Post in the office cubicles, and the burst of laughter when someone said, "Can't you imagine spanking him? I sure can."

"*Hol-lee! Hol-lee! Hol-lee!*"

The din had been deafening, more than 18,000 spectators on their feet, clapping and chanting her name. Even people who, seconds before the final buzzer, had been rooting against her and cheering for the other team. Now a victory had been seized, a slice of history was complete. The crowd rose as one, roaring its approval. The acclaim was tremendous. The building shook. She was the cynosure of their desires.

She had suffered being The Tall Girl. For years she'd endured the stares and remarks and outright insults. *Can you see my house from up there?* and *Look! It's Queen Kong!* Worse, this growth had come early. She reached six feet tall when she was twelve years old. Part beanpole, part flamingo, with stick-thin arms and legs, Holly was all pointy knees and elbows. She remembered with special bitterness her sixth-grade teacher who'd exclaimed, when Holly stood against the wall to be measured for a classroom chart, "My goodness! You might never stop growing." In an agony of self-consciousness she hurried with hunched shoulders to her desk in the back of the room (strategically placed so as not to obstruct her classmates' views), fighting tears and, for the moment, literally believing what she'd heard (the words of her teacher, an *authority*): she might never stop growing! She was in sixth grade—by next year, in seventh grade, would she be *seven* feet tall? In eighth grade, *eight* feet tall? The future—her future—seemed positively monstrous.

"Are you raising your hand?"

A question in class, and Holly knew the answer, but she decided not to admit it. How could you raise your hand and duck at the same time? She hated being looked at.

"Me? No."

That same year she'd lost her mother, a blow crueler than any she could've previously imagined, a change which made her look apprehensively at the world and suck her teeth. In her mind Holly replayed and scrutinized everything that happened that day. Anita Winegarten had been taking the family cat, an aging castrated tom named Pirate, to a pet clinic in Alliston, a town nine miles away, where there was a veterinarian with a good reputation for small animals. (The local vet in Sheridan served the nearby farmers and their large livestock; a sickly cat ranked low on his priorities, and probably he would suggest a measure that the Winegarten family didn't want to hear.) Her mother had loaded Pirate, who was limp as a dishrag but mewing feebly in protest, into a travel cage. "Don't worry, honey," she reassured Holly. "Everything's going to be all right." She put the travel cage in her car and drove away.

And that was the last time Holly saw her.

Early that evening, a trucker spotted a car in the ravine on Highway 62, several miles west of Alliston. There was a corner and the ditch was steep, and the undergrowth, a dense patch of ragweed and orange tiger lilies, was thick enough to conceal an automobile. Other passersby had driven by this spot and noticed nothing. But the trucker, from his higher perch in his cab, had seen a glint of sunlight reflecting from what looked like a windshield. When police arrived on the scene, it had been nine hours since Anita Winegarten had left the house. When they found her, she was still breathing. But she succumbed to her injuries on the following day.

Holly didn't learn the details of her mother's death until much later. Her memory of events was a wash of emotion punctuated by images, such as the moment her mother put Pirate in the cage. *"Everything's going to be all right."* And afterward, how their father hadn't brought home the smashed car but had returned with some of its contents; the travel cage, now empty (the police said they'd found it that way—where was Pirate?); the car's registration papers; her mother's purse. One day before the funeral Holly sneaked into her parents' room while her father was upstairs explaining events to her little brother, and she opened the purse, which looked and smelled as it always did, a jumble of items scented with spearmint. This time, unlike earlier instances of snooping, she wasn't playing with her mother's compact mirror or looking for dimes and quarters. She was just . . . *thinking.* Eventually she helped herself to a piece of chewing gum (her mother always carried gum and offered it around) and folded the stick into her mouth, slowly chewing. How could she be gone? How was it possible?

Even before the accident, Holly's thoughts about her family were often mournful, centered on a question: what went wrong with us? Her father, Art, was a tall, balding man with long arms and mittlike hands; he was the high school social studies teacher and baseball coach. In his younger years he'd been a stand-out center fielder with dreams of making the major leagues; he'd played college baseball on full scholarship and later joined the navy, serving on the *U.S.S. Niagara.* While stationed near San Diego he met Anita, a short, busty woman who was working on a degree in speech-language pathology. She had a pert nose and wore her hair in blow-dried flicks and in early photos, she appeared rather glamorous. Later, when Art convinced her to come to the Midwest and they'd settled in Sheridan and started a family, she was motherly and plump as a pigeon. She worked as the high school guidance counselor and was popular in the community, appreciated for her friendliness and ease in conversation. In a town of this size, where public school life and sports teams were the main interest and source of local pride, Holly's parents had been important figures, and much respected.

But their children, Holly and Honus? It was as if a mix-up had occurred and their lines of inheritance had gotten crossed. Although she had her mother's pert nose, in every other way Holly was very much her father's girl. Long and sinewy, and then some, after her astonishing spurt of growth. Whereas Honus took after his mother: he was short and pudgy in atypical places for a little boy. Five years younger than Holly, he was just as sensitive to the gaze of others. He had cried when some kids had jeered at them—"Hey, it's Laurel and Hardy!"—and this was before he even knew who Laurel and Hardy were.

And his name! What had Anita Winegarten been thinking when, in a moment of weakness, she'd consented to Art's enthusiastic plan to name their son after Honus Wagner, the legendary German-American shortstop whose prodigious throwing arm had first been spotted by an alert scout watching a ragged youth fling rocks? (How many times had Holly heard *that* story?) Holly recalled the summer vacation when the family had piled into the car and driven to New York City, where they stayed in a cramped hotel and saw skyscrapers and the Statue of Liberty, and their father took them to a baseball game (of course), their mother took them to a Broadway musical (unable to get tickets for *Cats,* they saw *Lubed,* where the word "fuck" was said forty-three times—young Holly had counted) and, on their last day, they went to the Metropolitan Museum of Art where, after breezing by the Egyptian mummies and the Temple of Dendur and paintings by Rembrandt and Picasso, her father finally found the corridor leading to an oak-paneled room of long tables covered in glass, which contained a collection of the earliest, and most prized, baseball cards. "See that one!" he'd said, taking his son in his arms and lifting him to look, "that's *Honus Wagner.* That card is priceless. That's who you're named after."

Honus peered, interested, while Holly and her mother waited listlessly, shifting on tired feet, eager to go out for ice-cream.

On the long, tedious drive home, which took two and a half days, Holly shared the back seat with Honus and, to amuse herself, teased him. She pretended that they were being followed by sinister strangers. She pinched his arms and legs, whenever he fell asleep, and when Honus protested, she feigned innocence and said they were "spider bites." She called him Honus-Wonus, which made no sense, but it seemed to annoy him so that was its own reward. And when her parents overheard their bickering and told them to cut it out, Holly resorted to more subtle means. She didn't touch him, she didn't speak. She looked at him. Stared with bugging eyes. "Stop looking at me!" Honus cried. Holly turned away, watched the world rush by her window. A few minutes later, she moved her head and silently bugged her eyes at him again, and when Honus noticed, he insisted, *"Don't look at me!"*

"What's going on back there?" her mother asked.

"I don't know," Holly said.

"She looks at me."

"Holly, leave him alone."

"How does that hurt him? *Looking?*"

"You heard me. Leave him alone."

Thereafter it became a sly contest, stealing glances at Honus, pretending to look straight ahead, but screwing her eyeballs to the side. Eventually Honus became so exasperated that he exclaimed, "Fuck you, Holly!"

The car veered.

"Hey!" her father shouted.

"See? If you weren't so cheap about theater tickets," her mother snapped.

On the way home they also visited several Civil War battlefields, because Art Winegarten was a history buff and liked to show his children maps and monument markers and muddy creeks while they stood in weeds and sweated and swatted at gnats. Holly wondered if her mother was right, that her father also enjoyed this sort of thing because you didn't have to pay. At one of the battlefields Honus fell to his knees and threw up his lunch—the less said about *that*, the better—and her brother's struggle continued when they got home to Sheridan.

Honus tried to devote himself to his father's dreams. Art loved baseball and fantasized about his son following in his footsteps; but Honus just couldn't make it work. In Pee-Wee League, because of his squat build, he got put behind the plate as a catcher. But he wasn't good at catching, though he worked hard to block the ball or knock it down with his body. The elastic straps of the protective equipment chafed his tender skin and led to a nasty rash that he nervously scratched into bloody stripes which, when they began to scab and heal, itched terribly, till he scratched them raw again. He ended up on the bench after a foul tip zinged off his bare hand and broke two of his fingers. Art consoled him that it was all right, accidents happened and there was no shame in watching from the side, but Holly knew her little brother well and could see how relieved Honus was, even thankful as he leaned back on the bench and deliciously rubbed his rash against the wire mesh. How *glad* he was to have broken his fingers!

Later that same summer, Anita Winegarten had died, so anything to do with baseball was forgotten, trivial. Holly recalled how, the night they got the news, she'd sat crying at the foot of the stairs. Honus had just been put to bed and her father came down and wrapped his arms around her. Sobs surged through Holly, she began to choke and hiccup, and Art ran his hand through her hair, speaking softly until Holly exhausted herself and breathed more easily. Then he lifted her in his arms and began to carry her upstairs. She clung to his neck and started sobbing again. Her father hadn't carried her to bed like this since the old days, when she was a small child. That seemed so long ago. She held him tight, pressing her face against his chest.

Art managed her weight without difficulty, but maneuvering her length was another matter. After two steps he paused, wobbling slightly, and Holly lifted her eyes and watched as he tried to angle her sideways and attempt several more steps. Despite his best efforts, her feet banged against the banister and the spokes beneath the handrail.

"Ow!"

"I'm so sorry, Holly, I'm so sorry."

"Hol-lee! Hol-lee! Hol-lee!"

She became the star center for the Sheridan Trojanettes. They had ruled their sports conference of rural schools, but at the state tournament the team faced much stiffer competition, and the weakness of the rest of the squad became apparent, so it was up to Holly to carry them, on both offense and defense.

And she did—she dominated the tournament, leading all scorers and setting a new state record for blocked shots. And the final game had been a turning point in her life.

Because on this night, after already scoring forty-four points while being triple-teamed by the defense, she found herself at the free throw line in front of 18,000 screaming people with two seconds left, her team trailing, seventy-six to seventy-five, and her father, now the varsity girls basketball coach, watching her from the bench in pained wonder. What was Holly thinking? Certainly not of her mother, not now. Not *yet*. She could barely stand. How did a person get through such a situation, in front of so many eyes?

In her younger years, she'd resisted encouragement from others to play this game. Holly was slow and uncoordinated, a prisoner of her stature, and basketball seemed like yet another way to call attention to the aspect of herself that she liked least. Why seek out an audience? To trot back and forth like a giraffe in shorts—the idea made her cringe.

But, as time passed, out of anger and boredom, she'd embraced the game. Mainly anger: that was the trigger. In the summer of her fourteenth birthday her father had married a virtual stranger who was also named—oh, how stupid irony could be!—Anita. Just like her mother. *Anita*. She was a paralegal at a law firm on the town square; she had a big nose and wore big earrings and pink workout suits. Holly so thoroughly resented seeing this woman moving into *their* house and sitting in the same chairs once occupied by her mother and showering (*naked!*) in their bathroom that Holly spent most of that summer outdoors. First she hung out with her schoolfriend Caitlin but then Caitlin left town to be a counselor at a church camp; while Holly's other main friend in those days, Kyla, had attracted the interest of Tyler, a grinning boy with an incipient moustache. Kyla plucked her brows and her arms were soft and plump, and she liked to sit on Tyler's lap. They spent hours giving each other hickeys in a garden shed where Tyler put his hand up Kyla's shirt and tried to take off her pants.

"Do you think I should let him?"

Holly pondered. Did she mean the hickeys? Putting his hand up her shirt? Unbuttoning her jeans? It was all sort of embarrassing, not to mention endless. She didn't answer quickly enough.

"Never mind," Kyla said. "See you!"

She left to spend time with Tyler, and Holly no longer saw her.

Meanwhile, back at the house, Honus, in a shocking display of disloyalty, had fallen in love with his new step-mother. He was worse than Holly's father! He accepted every overture from the newly-arrived Anita, who cooed and petted and spoiled him by letting him drink as much soda as he wanted. Honus soaked up attentions and soon he was cheerfully submitting to almost anything Anita said. He became her adoring slave.

Rather than witness this disgusting spectacle, but having no friends available and nowhere to go, Holly boycotted the house and went out to the driveway. (She didn't want to go away too far, lest it seem she was renouncing her rightful place in the household.) She retrieved a basketball from the basement and started shooting at the hoop attached above the garage. It was a pretext. It allowed her to appear occupied. She shot for one hour. Two hours. Three hours.

"Aren't you coming in for lunch?" Anita called through the screen.

"No, I'm not hungry."

"Of course you are."

"I'll eat it out here."

Her father Art was away all day, supervising a summer baseball camp, but when he returned in the evenings he insisted that Holly come inside and join them at the table for dinner. After the meal, though, she went back to the driveway and shot baskets till after dark. Between the pud and thud of the bouncing ball, and the rattle of the backboard, she could hear the sounds of the television through the screen windows.

She could picture the others sitting on the couch and sometimes heard them laugh along with the television, the canned roar of the studio audience. Riotous applause! They were all in it together. No, she didn't want to go inside.

Holly's skills developed slowly, sometimes unconsciously. Her first real pleasure in the game came the following year, when the Nichols family moved in, just two doors down her street. There were three Nichols boys and soon Holly found herself in demand to fill out their number for basketball games of two on two. The Nichols' driveway was larger and offered a better playing surface. In the beginning there was a temporary awkwardness due to the fact that Holly was a girl, but it was quickly forgotten as they grew absorbed in their contests, which lasted for hours, and sometimes, as their imaginations imposed new twists and exceptions and overtimes, a game went on for *days*, with fantastic scores like 315 to 313. Scott, the eldest Nichols brother, teamed with Danny, the youngest, while Holly's partner was Mickey, the middle son. Holly quickly developed a crush on Scott. She admired his confidence, his easy laugh, his muscular little butt. He was a natural athlete and games consisted of his mighty efforts to make a team with Danny who, as the youngest, was unable to accomplish much on the court. The sides were evenly matched, as Holly and Mickey assumed the middle. Once the Nichols boys became used to her, and she to them (these boys were so *loud,* they used bad language, and they were always scratching their nuts), the arrangement seemed to have existed forever.

In the early years Holly lumbered and was a poor dribbler, but the summer she turned seventeen, something changed. She'd reached her full growth at fifteen, or fifteen and a half, and now, as if overnight, her coordination caught up with her musculature, and everything gelled: suddenly she could make her body do what she *wished* it to do. Her jumps were well-timed; she dribbled comfortably with either hand; she was no longer slow and in the heat of the moment her reach was explosively quick. She remembered the first time she blocked one of Scott's shots. He was a year older than she, and he started for the boys' varsity team, but she leaped and let fly a long arm and swatted away his attempt at a lay-up. Surprised, Scott laughed, but she noticed a strain in his face after that moment, an added intensity to his play, a determination not to be shown up. A short time later, Holly did it *again*. Scott had stolen the ball from Mickey, dribbled twice and turned, assuming he had a clear shot—and Holly was already there, anticipating, jumping as he released the ball. She slapped it back in his face. "What the fuck!" he shouted, losing his temper, as his brothers howled with laughter. His upper lip was already swelling, and blood shone red on his teeth.

"*Wasn't on purpose.*" It was all Holly could say.

She was sorry for his lip, yes . . . but a part of her was also proud. By then she was intensely in love with Scott, a secret she harbored in isolation because he was dating someone in his own class, Lacey Ryerson, one of the prettiest girls in school who belonged to a circle of other very pretty girls who didn't mix with Holly. They belonged to the Dance Club and performed a routine called "Strut Your Stuff!" Holly hadn't even considered joining the Dance Club; she didn't want to wear leotards in front of gawkers; she most definitely didn't want to *strut her stuff*—the very phrase made her recoil. ("Stop slouching!" Anita frequently reminded her.) But now, a change had occurred, and in some ungraspable way Holly had just shown Scott her affection by slapping the ball in his face. It was a declaration of love. If only he could understand. Why couldn't he see it?

That winter, when the basketball season started at school, Holly was completely in command. For the first time, the organized league games became as fun as the ones in the neighborhood. And the approval of the crowds was a tonic. The cheers! For her! This was no strut, no affectation: this was *game*. She loped down the court, experiencing a surge of exhilaration as she left opponents behind.

That was the same season her father Art became the varsity coach of the Sheridan Trojanettes. For his entire career, baseball had been his abiding interest, while helping out in other sports was merely a professional duty. But when the previous coach retired, he threw himself into the job and, with his star daughter, an exciting new chapter in life began. Suddenly he and Holly had a new relationship, sharing hard work and hopes, sharing success. They were a team within a team.

"Box-out drill!" Art called, clapping. "Let's go! Let's go! First time, no hands!"

Players ran toward the basket, thundering down the floorboards. Holly was always first or second to arrive.

Of course, it could get awkward having her father in this role. All the other players called him Coach Winegarten, but she couldn't bring herself to say *that*; she couldn't call him Dad, either, not on the court. So she avoided calling him anything because there wasn't really a word to describe what passed between them, this new intimacy. At home, their relations shifted, too. She started referring to him in the third person as Art. "What's Art going to show us tomorrow about defense?" At first she said it archly, as if it were a private joke between them. He accepted it with a shrug and a grin. He seemed to like it.

Up in his bedroom, Honus played his parents' old vinyl records on a turntable that the first Anita, his mother, had brought to Sheridan from California. He'd rescued it from a box in the basement and found a replacement needle at a garage sale. He wired up the big block speakers encased in lacquered plywood and you could hear him singing along behind his door.

Lookin' at the devil
Grinnin' at his gun
Fingers start shakin'
I begin to run . . .

Honus took scissors to the album covers and cut them into pieces which he rearranged on his wall, inventing imaginary duets, experimenting with possibilities. He got into trouble for that. "You should ask first! That's no way to treat those records."

"But they were just sitting there," Honus said.

"Some of them might be collectible."

"Collecting dust. You weren't listening to them. I'm making something out of them. Don't you see?"

"Hol-lee! Hol-lee! Hol-lee!"

Senior year, the last game of her high school career. She'd already signed a letter of intent to enroll on a full sports scholarship at the state university, which had one of the strongest women's basketball programs in the country. This is how she found herself at the free throw line in front of 18,000 screaming people with two seconds left to play. Just moments ago, trailing by one point, Holly's teammates did what their opponents and every single spectator knew they would do: they passed the ball to her. It was up to Holly, to do the job and win for them, one last time. She caught it at the far corner of the court, feinted left, then dribbled in close to the basket. But, before she could get a shot off, she got clobbered.

It was intentional, but not exactly vicious. Basic strategy dictated that fouling Holly made sense, instead of letting her take a clear shot at a short distance. The odds were better for the opposition to send her to the free throw line.

But there were accidental factors, too. As defenders converged on Holly and they all fell in a tumble, Holly's right foot was planted, then wedged against another player's leg. Her upper body fell first, but her leg was inadvertently held back. The strain—she felt it—while thinking: *please, let me fall.* But she couldn't, not swiftly enough, and that fraction of a second was enough to break her leg.

The pain was amazing. For several seconds she was actually blinded by a sort of explosion in her head and she couldn't see. She heard the roar of the crowd, the referee's whistle. More pain shot up her side as her opponents disentangled from the pile. She cried out and rolled onto her other side, a spray of her game sweat casting droplets on the varnished floor. "It's OK, Holly, you're OK," called Kat Myers, one of her teammates, standing over her, reaching down to help Holly to get up. It was sort of encouragement they always said to each other when someone fell. Kat was excited, caught up in the moment and Holly, in her confusion, mechanically responded, taking Kat's hand and finding her feet. She took three strides to the foul line. Each time, a terrific pain shot up her leg and into her spine, like a charge of electricity. In the general melee and because Holly had responded fairly quickly, the referee didn't call a technical timeout for injury. The other team had used up all their timeouts, otherwise they would've called one, in order to create a delay and add to the psychological pressure on Holly. At the Sheridan bench, everyone was standing, Art was pacing out of bounds, his tie unknotted and his shirt dark with perspiration. The din in the auditorium was deafening. Art still had a timeout but he hesitated to use it. He could see that something was wrong but stopping the action might indeed play into their opponents' hands and put more pressure on Holly. But still—he moved towards the scorers' table. He had only seconds to decide.

At that moment Holly looked over at the Sheridan bench and saw where her father was heading. Her long arm made an abrupt, chopping motion in his direction. He caught it in the corner of his eye and stopped, turned to her, and she repeated the gesture, in front of thousands of witnesses. Art went no further, and the din intensified. Was the player commanding the coach? Was the daughter ordering her father? Or was it just a heartfelt expression of individual will?

She held the ball now. She was panting from the pain, her mouth hung open, a trickle of drool edging out of one corner and making its way to her chin. The backboard, basket and net began to blur in front of her eyes. She blinked and tried to focus. *Put it in,* she thought. *Put it in.* Maybe she didn't have to see. Maybe it could be just like another lonely summer night when she refused to go into the house, when she shot in the dark . . .

It went in.

The roar intensified, she heard the muffled voices of teammates beside her, encouraging her, and now the ball was in her hands again. One more. One more. She'd maintained almost all of her weight on one leg but lifting her arms required a slight shift in balance and a momentary pressure on the other leg. The pain shot up her spine, excruciating, and for a moment she actually forgot where she was and what she was doing. She saw flashes of blue and then green, and it seemed as if somehow she was outdoors. Not playing basketball but simply standing and waiting. The blue was pieces of sky and the family was on summer vacation and her father had taken them to a hot grassy field where something terrible had happened. Her mother Anita stood nearby. Holly wobbled and felt the pebbled rubber of the basketball in her hands, her heart beat wildly. There was the basket. Put it in. Put it in.

It went in.

"*Hol-lee! Hol-lee! Hol-lee!*"

She could not walk off the court as the nearest bleachers emptied and pandemonium ensued. She left the auditorium on a stretcher. The ceiling was spinning. From the floor level to the highest rows of the arena, a standing ovation. "Oh Mom," she gasped. "Look at me. I'm broken."

April 12, 1863

My dearest,

I do not mock the demise of Union—do not doubt my devotion—beyond the obstacles of war—to you.

A love so big it scares. You rubbed my Stomach (my breast not covered with the Bed-cloaths) and bid it ease us.

I want to see you more—Sir—than all I wish for in this world.

You can and must NOT doubt me—

Yours lovingly,

Emily

"So tell me about it," Philip said.

When paying with his credit card at the restaurant, Philip had split the total exactly in half. They left a cash tip and his portion was light so Holly had topped it up, upon which Philip asked, "You know the waiter?"

"No. He was a strange fellow, though, wasn't he?"

"Used to be one of our doctoral students," Philip said. "Specialized in the Vorticists. He was in the running for a Randolph Fellowship but when he didn't get it he cracked up and shaved his head and sent menacing messages to the Dean. Utterly lost it. Never did finish his dissertation. One of *those* cases."

Holly nodded knowingly, though she was uncertain about his allusion. In a college town like this one, you found ex-students and hangers-on in every niche. Bus drivers were extremely polite and helpful because many of them had master's degrees in social work. In front of the restaurant, Philip went to the rack and unchained his bicycle. Together they walked out into the night.

The air was soft. They strolled along tree-lined streets under a platinum moon, Philip pushing his bicycle, an old-fashioned model with upturned handlebars and an oversized frame. ("My faithful steed," he called it.) He wore a smart leather shoulder bag in which he kept his laptop and pedal clips. The street was largely empty of traffic but the neighborhood pulsed with activity. In lighted windows of two-story houses that had been converted into student accommodations, you could see young people in front of computers leaning toward their screens and typing. On front porches, housemates sat on lawn furniture and sipped tall cans of beer, chatting and joking. In one yard a drunken boy slipped on the grass as he was trying to pound in a sign with the latest anti-Bush, anti-war slogan, and a porch erupted in hilarity as he lay on his back with his face in a rictus, feigning death on a battlefield. Further down the street, music throbbed spasmodically from a larger structure, the brick mansion of a fraternity house whose front lawn was illuminated by spotlights for a swelling circle of revelers. The party had begun.

"I turn here," said Holly, pointing to a side-street.

They cut the corner and continued in the leafy dark, their arms almost touching. "Philip, have you ever heard of Michael Donahue?"

"No, I don't think so."

Since Philip concentrated on media theory, she wasn't surprised by his answer. American literature wasn't his specialty. Earlier in the evening he'd described himself as a "memester." But at least he didn't pretend. So many professors bluffed and dropped names. They protected an aura.

"Well, he's a pretty obscure figure that only a few people will remember. You see, I'm working in Special Collections at the library, in the Civil War archive?"

"Right. There's something peculiar and important, you said. Sounds sexy."

Holly stopped walking. Now they stood in front of her house, a mustard-colored hatbox which she shared with her landlord and another renter. The windows were unlighted. "You might not have heard of Michael Donahue, but how about *Emily Dickinson?*" She smiled down at him. "There's a connection, see, we're talking about one of the greatest American writers, if you care about that."

"I thought you were going to tell me about your standing O."

He pushed back a lock of hair from his forehead.

"Geez, Philip, what is it with you?"

"*Over there,*" he hissed, pointing to the shadows of the neighbor's garage. "*Against the wall.*"

"What?" Holly turned quickly. Had he seen someone lurking?

"We could do it against the wall."

Holly replayed the words in her mind and turned back to him. "Are you nuts? Did you just say what I think you said?"

"Or *there*." He pointed. "Up against a tree! Standing Os for both of us. You like it standing, you said you did."

"I said no such thing!"

"Come on, it'll be great, Holly. Will you do it for me? *Please?* I've always wanted to be dominated by a giantess."

"You—you," she sputtered. "*Go!*"

She flung out her arm and Philip reeled back. She glared at him and then, with an exaggerated shrug, he gave his bicycle a push and climbed on, rolled off silently into the night.

❁　❁　❁

Holly was on friendly terms with her housemate Chelsea, who was also her landlord, though there were many things about Chelsea that she didn't understand. There were two bedrooms upstairs, one where Chelsea slept and the other which she used as an office, where she conducted most of her business. Holly lived downstairs with her own bedroom and the kitchen, which Chelsea never used. The basement was rented by a large young man named Wayne who worked night shifts delivering pizzas. He had his own entrance and they rarely saw him, though they found his empty pizza boxes in the trash and often heard him thumping down below. They called him the Troll.

Holly had never seen Chelsea cook anything or rarely even use a dish. When she'd first moved in and Chelsea told her that she would have the kitchen to herself, Holly assumed it was the typical exaggeration of a landlord; but it was true. Chelsea never prepared food. She had a cup and a spoon, maybe two spoons, which she kept upstairs, with an electric tea kettle. She drank tea, or sometimes ate dry cereal out of the cup; but otherwise she ate in restaurants or ordered carry-out. Once she'd accepted an apple from Holly and then stared at it in her hand; Holly wondered if she'd forgotten what to do with it. How it *worked*. (She never got to see Chelsea eat it, either, because a phone rang in the office upstairs and Chelsea put down the apple and ran to answer it.) Nor did Holly understand Chelsea's job. Chelsea was an independent consultant, specializing in subsidiary systems consolidation, which she'd explained to Holly several times though it still wasn't terribly clear what it was all about, so Holly had stopped asking. Chelsea also sold fresh flowers over the Internet, or had some role in facilitating their distribution and delivery, via the cloud, and she owned or had mortgages on several other houses near the campus, renting them out to students. This augmented her cash flow. She hired the Troll for casual labor such as moving iron radiators or fixing toilet floats. She also paid the Troll, when needed, to play the Bad Ass whenever a foolish student was late with the rent.

The morning after Holly's dinner with Philip Post, Chelsea asked her, "Did you go out last night?"

"I don't know why I bother!"

Chelsea blew on her tea. "Oooh, touchy. What's that supposed to mean?"

"I'm not so naive, am I?" Holly spooned yoghurt onto some cereal. "Maybe I flatter myself. I used to be very naive but am I really so clueless, anymore? I'd thought I'd seen a few things. But God, now I wish I were more naive. Chelsea, there are so many CREEPS!"

"You might have to help me out here."

"Oh, let's drop it."

"Your call." Chelsea took a sip. "We'll keep this a creep-free zone. Fine by me. But you're OK?"

"Sure I'm OK."

Chelsea watched her for a moment and seemed on the verge of another question. Then, "Well, I'm gonna get a shower. I have a conference call in twenty minutes."

After Chelsea went upstairs, Holly's cell phone rang. It was Philip Post.

"I think I owe you an apology."

"I think you do, too."

"I'm sorry, Holly. It was a misunderstanding. I sincerely thought we were talking about the same thing. And so then I assumed . . . well, that I could hang from your shoulders. You see what I mean? But there was no harm intended. And no harm done."

"You think? Bullshit, Philip. Why would I talk to you like that? Listen, if you have issues about—about all that stuff—it's not my problem. I don't want to hear it. Understand?"

Philip chuckled.

"Issues? Such a lovely American expression, that one, it covers so many things. You mean difficulties? Or perhaps unresolved conflicts that I'm supposed to confess in counseling? Make myself a better person? Most amusing! Maybe I could get some prescription medication, too. That would be an experience in self-improvement."

"You're a smug shit."

"No, it's not so simple, Holly. If only life were reducible to such formulae. I'm just being honest."

"And so am I!"

Holly hung up.

Will you prepare a sturdy box
for my ravishing—mind—
with holes allowed—so we can breathe
in kind?

Holly had come to literature by accident. It was like learning a foreign language, this language within the language. Her college plans had revolved around basketball, even after her serious injury in her final high school game. After surgery and spending months in a cast and several additional weeks with a support brace, using crutches and undergoing physical therapy, Holly resumed her training. That fall, at the university, she was redshirted for her freshman year in order to preserve her future eligibility. But this period was nothing like a respite. In fact, Holly worked harder than ever, going to the sports medicine clinic, rebuilding her leg, staying in shape, doing her best to maintain and improve her skills while waiting for the healing process to be complete.

Academically, she'd declared herself as a pre-business major but her first two years of classwork were mainly devoted to general education requirements, with courses in English composition, earth science, psychology and comparative civilization. Most of her study depended on her schedule for basketball practice and physical therapy. There wasn't much time for the luxury of intellectual curiosity.

And friends?

The university was a lonely place. Holly was homesick, an irony not lost on her because the entire summer before leaving Sheridan she'd made it clear to her family that she was eager to run away, even with a brace on her leg. She painted her toenails alternating magenta and royal ruby gloss (how many hours could you stare at your elevated foot?) and spent afternoons outside on the driveway balanced on a crutch or sitting on a lawn chair within range of the hoop and playing dull games of

H.O.R.S.E with Danny and Mickey Nichols, usually winning, though she relied on them to chase down the ball.

Hanging out with Danny and Mickey was just a pretext, of course, because in truth she was waiting for Scott Nichols, hoping, every day, every hour, every *minute* that he might descend like an angel and join them. This happened rarely. Scott had already been off to college for a year, on a football scholarship at a small Lutheran school in the north of the state, and now that he was back in Sheridan for the summer he spent his days catching up with other friends and, most piercingly to Holly, other girls, rapturously reuniting with his high school sweetheart Lacey Ryerson, and then less than two weeks later, dramatically breaking up with Lacey in order to fall into the delighted arms of another cutie, Stef Pruitt. Holly knew all about these developments without even leaving her driveway, because she extracted excruciating details from Danny and Mickey and, when possible, additional agonizing tidbits from her brother Honus, who was in the same class as Stef Pruitt's younger brother. Clearly, shooting baskets with Holly was not a priority for Scott Nichols. He had other things on his mind. Other *girls*.

Holly was aware that people thought she was aloof, and that this notion had been reinforced by her recent celebrity. Her introverted side, as much as her height, supposedly explained why she hadn't dated in high school, why she spent so many hours by herself shooting hoops, why she watched old VCR movies alone in the primitive rec room in the family basement instead of coming upstairs to join Art and Anita and Honus in front of the new flat screen home entertainment center, and why, though this was never said aloud, she was a virgin.

Holly's features weren't strikingly pretty but they were pleasant; she had a decent sense of humor, at least her teammates thought so; she didn't always shun the company of others. But, for boys, an inescapable barrier existed, independent of her personality: it was, of course, her height. In the crude economy of youthful affections there were few boys as tall as Holly—basketball players, generally—and these boys preferred to date smaller girls, prettier girls, girls with shapely figures.

"Hey, need a ride? I'm going your way."

"How do you know it's our way?"

This conversation took place between a male voice from a car window and a group of girls on a grassy strip behind the gym exit. But not the group, exactly. It was understood who the voice was really addressing: an attractive girl named Clara in low slung capri pants. She responded on cue, flirting in kind, and though she said "our way" as if she were speaking for the group, Holly and two other girls hung back, knowing their place. They'd turned as one toward the voice, but Kristi (whose blotched complexion looked like a bad encounter with a cheese grater), Magda (a chunky girl with mismatched scrunchies and lopsided pigtails) and Holly (in a warm-up suit and size fifteen running shoes), let Clara speak for them.

Holly despised this arrangement, the presumptuous tone of this male voice which she'd come to think of as The Voice, and she hated the thought that *this* was the future, *this* was more "grown up." Answering to The Voice. In that case, she wished she were small again, back in the world of elementary school and the simple games she'd made up with her cat, Pirate. There was nothing inferior about that time. Quite the contrary. Small was better.

Now, irreversibly *not* small, Holly also seethed at how people assumed she was "above" all sweet talk; by considering her aloof, they underestimated her feelings. Why *wouldn't* she want to fall in love? Why should her stature disqualify her? The fact was—and such feelings had nothing to do with The

Voice, as far as she was concerned—Holly was particularly susceptible to the tug of romance. *"I'm going your way."* That could mean so many things! She craved to be with someone who was going her way. She couldn't help it; it caused her to suffer and she didn't know why. And it had started when she was small, back in the simple world. At four years old, she'd spent an entire summer making drawings of a fat-cheeked boy named Darren, her pre-school pal, and she'd stuffed them in the back of his T-shirt while he squirmed and laughed. Even after he moved away she covered a bedroom wall with colored pencil renderings of his face. Childish stuff, to be sure, but the beginning of a long parade of classmates and teachers and television actors and imaginary composites who inspired dazzling crushes, known only to herself, because she'd been too shy to share her feelings, especially after her spurt of growth. She ached all the more intensely because she couldn't share; she possessed this need, and it possessed her, alone.

According to the magazine,

You can work wonders for your well-being if you learn good posture. Stand tall! Slouching can cause lumbar pressure and painful side effects. When you slouch you appear insecure to others, which creates a negative impression. Boost your confidence: stand tall!

As a going-away present before college, Art surprised Holly with the gift of an old Ford Comet that he'd had fixed up and repainted a robin's egg blue. It was a small car and she had to push back the driver's seat to the limit, but it would certainly come in handy. Holly was pleased by the car but she was also distracted. Those final days of summer—she was eighteen, legally an adult—Holly spent her evenings hiding in the air-conditioned basement, more than ever violently in love with Scott Nichols. She simply couldn't stop thinking about him. She felt all clenched up inside, every waking hour, desperate to see him, to be with him. Why didn't he stop by, just to say hello and inquire when she would shed her leg brace? She entertained fantasies of Scott admiring her, of Scott *adoring* her. (Walking hand in hand near the boat dock at Lake Nasqua . . . watching movies together, laughing and leaning closer, their shoulders touching.) These weren't passing images, but elaborate scenarios played out many times in her head, with long heart-to-hearts and personal confessions and variations in dialogue, setting, incidental details—all of it, though, adding up to a glorious, free-flowing bliss . . .

A week before she left home, Holly climbed into her Comet one night to pick up some carry-out pizzas from a local restaurant called Angelo's. Her leg brace had been removed a few days earlier and she was wearing crisp new jeans that she'd bought online, from the same source she'd shopped at for years, because it had always been difficult and embarrassing to try on jeans in stores, since she had to prowl around the Men's Department to find her size. In junior high school she'd found the right brand of jeans from a supplier in Wausau, Wisconsin (free deliveries on orders of $100 or more!), from which she developed her formula, her Personal Holly Uniform: jeans and T-shirts, or jeans and sweaters, depending on the season, with a few variations, which she renewed from year to year, with scientific precision. Her latest shipment of three pairs of jeans had arrived, in anticipation of her departure from Sheridan, and though she'd calculated the inseam perfectly, to her dismay she found the jeans rather snug in the hips. She'd finally stopped growing taller, but now there was this added issue. Maybe she wouldn't be able to buy from the Men's Department anymore. When would it ever end? She couldn't see a solution and it wearied her to think about it. She squeezed on the jeans in the hope that she could break them in. That evening, standing at the cash register to pay for the pizzas, she heard a voice behind her.

"Hi Holly."

She turned and it was Scott Nichols. Smiling at her.

For a moment she simply stared at him. Then she choked out, "Hey Scott."

Then her mind unfroze and swiftly concocted an image of Scott and Stef Pruitt having dinner in an intimate booth in the back of Angelo's, where the tables glowed with red candles. Holly saw it very clearly, because she'd already been there with Scott, in her fantasies.

"You're looking really good," he said.

Speechless, she nodded in reply. (*He'd actually just said that. It wasn't a fantasy!*) She was aware of his eyes. It was a forward remark, no doubt about it, but it was also different coming from Scott than from someone else, since they knew each other so well; they'd played together since they were kids. It wasn't The Voice. And Holly's nod in affirmation, instead of appearing tongue-tied, for the moment gave her a poised air, asserted a confidence that she did not remotely feel.

Scott's parents, Ted and Eileen, emerged from the main dining room. "Hello, Holly! How are you?"

They conversed for a minute as Holly realized that Scott wasn't having a romantic evening with Stef Pruitt, he was spending time with his parents. He, too, would be leaving Sheridan soon, to start his sophomore year in college. This was a special occasion for them. Holly recovered her composure.

"I've been hanging out some with Danny and Mickey," she said. "Just the usual stuff. You should come by, Scott, before you go. It would be fun."

"That's what they told me. Sure, I'd like to do that."

Ted Nichols put in, "How do you like your car? Your dad told me about it."

Holly pointed out the window to the parking lot. "I've only driven it a couple of times because I just got my brace off. I think the color is kind of cool. If you come by, Scott, I'll give you a ride."

She surprised herself with her boldness. Scott laughed. "Sure. Why not?"

"See you."

And the following day Scott did come by, with his brothers, and they shot a few baskets, chatting, with some mild goofing around. This meeting was a little stiff, but not too stiff.

"Once your leg is back to 100%, you're going to be a star," Scott told her. He sent her a swift pass, and she shot the ball. Swished it.

Holly smiled. "I don't know about that."

Every word, every second, was precious.

Soon it was over. Scott looked at his watch and announced that he had to go. It was only 5:30. He didn't mention going for a ride. His last words: "I hope you have a great year, Holly. You're going to a big-time level, not like me. We're really proud of you. You know that, don't you?"

His brother Danny nodded, and Holly tried to smile. "Bye!" Mickey called. He'd arrived on his skateboard and now he rattled down the sidewalk. "Bye!" Then they were all gone.

Holly didn't go inside the house. She sat on the bottom step at the edge of the driveway. Her Comet was parked in the street—it had been waiting there in plain sight the whole time—but she didn't want to look at it. She bounced the basketball a few times, *pud pud pud*, and then stopped. She gently rolled the ball under a rose bush.

"You OK?"

She looked up. It was Danny. He hadn't left, after all.

"Sure I'm OK. Damn it, Danny! What's that supposed to mean?"

"Just asking."

He stood by in silence.

Eventually she added, "Is Scott going out tonight?"

Danny shifted on his feet. "Yeah, I think so."

She felt a quiver coming to her nostrils. She knew that Danny wouldn't lie. After all, he'd been informing her of Scott's movements all summer. She and Danny had a special relationship, of sorts. He'd been her date for the senior prom—one of her rare social outings in high school—though it had been a mistake from start to finish, a rash choice, the result of her profound confusion. For her junior prom, Holly almost hadn't gone, but at the last minute she was escorted by Rodney Wheelen, a sincere Christian and not a bad-looking fellow but whose denomination didn't allow him to dance and who spent the evening trying to bring her to the Lord. For the senior prom, Holly was resigned to the idea that she wasn't going to be asked, and at first she tried to pretend that she didn't care, the whole ritual was stupid, but a week before the big night, she panicked and asked Danny, who was four years her junior. She knew that he was very immature, even for his age, and that he would've been more pleased if Holly had asked him to spend an evening playing video games. But his greenness also made him pliable and, as she expected, he accepted the invitation of his neighbor pal. (Naturally, in her fantasies, she imagined arriving at the prom arm in arm with Scott, but he was off in college, unattainable; while the middle brother, Mickey, now a high school junior, already had a date; so who else could she turn to?)

That night, Danny sang along with the radio on the way to the prom. Since he didn't have his driver's license, Holly drove her parents' car. Danny wore an ivory tuxedo and had put gel in his hair, which stood up in spikes; when they had their picture taken under the entrance arch, as was the custom for each couple, he reached up and put his arm around her waist and tilted his head against her shoulder. Later in the evening, on the dance floor, he spun and clapped and, though he was actually a decent dancer, Holly had expected Danny to be somewhat shy or even intimidated by all the upperclassmen; she wished that he would show more restraint; it embarrassed her when he laughed and yelped.

When they drove home that night, she parked in her own driveway. Danny lived only two doors down the block; he could walk the rest of the way. But, as she turned off the ignition, he wormed out of his seat and slid toward her. She had no intention of kissing him and, as she reached to open her door, his hand darted out and cupped her breast. "Not much there, but it's sweet," he said.

Holly snapped. In a blink she clamped her arm around Danny's neck and squeezed him into a headlock. It was a technique she'd used many times over the years on Honus, when he got on her nerves, but it wasn't how she'd intended to spend the night of her senior prom. Now she spoke to him and he wiggled and whimpered and she clenched her free hand into a fist and applied it with force to Danny's scalp and rubbed away the spikes that had annoyed her all evening.

"*Don't do that and don't talk like that! You hear me? And don't you ever, ever tell anybody that I was the one who asked you out tonight. It wasn't me, it was you. You asked me. You got that?*"

"Yisss," Danny squealed.

That was then.

Now Holly sat on the bottom step and Danny watched her with his hands in his pockets as first one tear, and then another, leaked out and rolled down her cheek.

"I'm sorry, Holly. I wish Scott was with you."

"Thanks, Danny."

"I won't tell nobody."

✿ ✿ ✿

A slot in front—where words—come
Out into the light—you sense
Within—one blink, my dear—
the box will fall through skies

Philip Post left a message on Holly's phone, two days after his first call. "If we could just talk, that's all I'm asking," he said. "There are things I'd like to tell you. You can always reach me at this number."

She deleted the message.

The Special Collections Department was located on the third floor of the university library and its shelves were subject to extra security measures. Unlike the rest of the facility, where patrons could wander among the stacks and pull down any volume, Special Collections housed items considered too precious or fragile for public access. Although the university couldn't boast of a Gutenberg Bible or a Shakespeare first folio or some other big ticket fetish of bibliophilia, it possessed some choice morsels. These ranged from rare first editions by Wordsworth and Coleridge to seventeenth century maps of early Portuguese colonies. Recently they'd added several shelves of television scripts from a hit sitcom of the 1980s that had been donated to the library by a Grainball U alumnus who had worked as an executive producer. The scripts ended up in Special Collections after a librarian discovered that they were being pilfered from the general film archive and sold at startlingly high prices over the Internet. To consult a work in Special Collections, you had to present a photo ID and fill out a form with your "statement of purpose"; then you left your bag at the front desk and were escorted to a reserved area where you were allowed only sheets of white paper and a pencil for note-taking and, depending on the item, you might be asked to put on a pair of protective nitrile gloves. At no time were you out of sight of a librarian.

Holly worked in a cubicle in a windowless purgatory between the locked shelves and the consultations area. She was one of a handful of student employees involved in drudge work while the professional librarians focused on more serious matters. The head of Special Collections was a harried woman named Inez who was usually out of the office. She travelled around the country in quest of donations and was also responsible for appraisals and purchases. One day she might be negotiating for an original hand-pressed bicycle catalogue by the teenagers Wilbur and Orville Wright; the next day she might be politely declining a gift from the estate of an alumnae. ("We don't want your Grandma's fucking *National Geographics*!" she exclaimed after she hung up the phone.) Holly quickly learned that librarians didn't correspond to a staid, nerdy image; they were sharp and opinionated and there were probably as many tongue piercings here as in the English department, whatever that meant. Her immediate supervisor was a chinless, ponytailed man named Merle. Next to his desk he kept an aquarium, which was a source of in-house fighting because bringing pets to the workplace contravened university rules.

He was in open revolt and recently had threatened to bring in a turtle. (Well, maybe there *was* something peculiar about librarians.) Merle was in charge of the Civil War archives, a large trove of personal letters, diaries and photographs of soldiers and their families. There were tens of thousands of documents, often fragile and crumbling, stored in acid-free cartons. These holdings were difficult to catalogue and they represented painstaking work for historians who turned to them for primary sources. Most were handwritten, often in nearly indecipherable scrawls that defied computer recognition software. It would've required an army of library workers to transcribe them all, which was out of the question, at a time of budget cutbacks from the state capital, particularly for higher education disciplines that appeared to offer nothing more than knowledge for its own sake. What was the cash value of history?

Merle's brainchild had been to crowd-source the task, and to get unpaid volunteers to transcribe the letters. Retired high school teachers, Civil War buffs, in fact anyone who was interested could enroll in a program to download images of old documents and type up a clean transcription for the library. The result would be a vast, searchable digital archive of precious testimony posted online for free. "We preserve what's special," Merle enthused, "but what's special belongs to everyone!"

Every few days, he asked her, "Where we at, Holly Holly?"

For reasons known only to himself, he always said her name twice. He seemed to like the sound of it. Holly scanned the documents in the acid free cartons so that he could upload the images onto a special secure site for the crowd-source transcribers. "I'm at PBL 246," she might reply, "January 1863."

"Goody goody!"

The morning she deleted Philip's phone message Holly walked to work on her way to July 1863. Today the air was heavy, promising rain in the afternoon. Her route took her past an apartment with an American flag on the balcony railing. The flag was upside down, limp, faded by the weather.

It had been draped on this balcony for years. Holly could remember when its colors were fresh, back when she was an undergraduate, but it still hung upside down in protest. The same wars dragged on. Approaching the library, observing a squirrel which hopped on the sidewalk in front of her as if showing the way, Holly considered how going to work in July 1863 wasn't so odd, after all, in a nation still divided by war. She realized how little she understood, and it was like turning back the clock on her own life, to a time before she entered graduate school, before the pressures of basketball or even her worries of how others perceived her. The innocent days before her mother's death.

Ting! Ting!

In the street Philip Post rolled by on his bicycle. When he saw her notice him, he rang his bell again.

Is he following me? she wondered, hastening up the steps.

> *Inside your head. Are you the same*
> *Apart—from me—I couldn't say*
> *since I'm not free—yet*

College basketball had changed Holly's way of seeing. She'd thought she understood the game, playing so much of it in Sheridan, commanding the post, dominating the boards and running from baseline to baseline. It didn't seem like a complicated sport. But at this higher level, goaded by the presence of top players and by the shrewd remarks of Coach Vivienne

Booth, Holly realized that she still had a lot to learn, more than well-intentioned Art, for all his devotion to the high school team, had been able to teach her. In addition to rehabilitating her leg and getting in better shape, Holly began to appreciate more elusive nuances, a geometric creativity of swiftly executed passes in a moving environment where opportunities opened or closed in fractions of a second. Lying in bed at night, she rehearsed these permutations, saw the possibilities unfold in her head with the precision of shifting shapes in a kaleidoscope. They were formally exquisite.

"The center *must* move," Coach Booth insisted, and you really couldn't argue with her. It was an ongoing challenge. But later that same day, Holly might hear a witless voice: "Hey, do things look different from up there?"

This was at the cafeteria, as she faced a grinning university employee who swiped her card. He thought he was being clever, as if she hadn't heard this line before. Holly gave a small nod and then pushed her tray down the railing.

Fact was: things *did* look different from her perspective, though not in the way that he meant. One of the things she'd absorbed since leaving home and running the gauntlet of the eyes of others was a keener awareness of a contradiction, a realization that however much people stared, they couldn't see *her*. Not the real her. They saw a long sinuous figure to which they attached their own agenda, while Holly became persuaded that she possessed an invisible and resolute self that was independent of anyone's gaze and, in fact, beyond anything they might fathom. This self existed of its own accord. It was the main feature of her life. The rest was dross.

"No no no!"

Shoes squeaked, players stopped, the ball caromed off the rim and rolled away.

"*Think!* We're not just throwing it up there! You can't count on those chances. That's how you lose. It's gonna take at least four passes, and if you make a cut on the second pass, you can set up a close shot with the fourth pass. But if you don't *think*, you're never gonna get to the fourth pass! Drop step, then inside pivot. Let's try it again. Winegarten, it's not that hard."

"Sorry."

"Don't apologize. Just show me what you can do. Get your head out of the clouds."

Obviously Coach Booth wasn't making a crack about Holly's height. She was stressing, yet again, the primacy of footwork. Holly ran through the sequence correctly the next time, and the time after that, feeling the heat of scrutiny. Coach Booth couldn't see her true self, either, but she was quick to note any inconsistency in her outward behavior, to observe a lack of concentration when Holly was on the court; Coach Booth zeroed in and it was unnerving.

For the next two years Holly made adjustments; she had little time off the court for study or romance. Occasionally she thought of Scott Nichols and fantasized that he would telephone her out of the blue, but such reveries had lost their immediacy; Holly didn't fret about them. She wasn't interested in the guys she saw on campus, loud frat boys with backward baseball caps or moony stoners advertising their aw-fuck-it attitude. Fellows of that sort had no clue about her secret self; they saw only her stature. In her sophomore year, Holly was healthy again, competing fiercely for a position on the varsity squad.

Then the center shifted when she met Jérémy Ndao. She wasn't prepared for what awaited her.

Jérémy was a Senegalese graduate student in post-colonial literature in the French department. A tall, lean African with a bright smile and a little pink tongue that Holly found, frankly, fascinating, he'd approached Holly at a party she'd attended with Sherelle Burton, a teammate on the basketball team. Most of the people at the party were African American; they were part of a small but lively social bubble that existed in this very white university town. In an earlier conversation, Holly had heard Sherelle complain of how her boyfriend Carl had cheated on her "with this little white girly-girl." At tonight's party, when she met Carl, he'd immediately begun to flirt with her as soon as Sherelle was out of earshot. He stood very close and rarely averted his eyes from hers as they conversed. Carl probably wasn't serious, moving in with his big shoulders, but his approach made Holly uncomfortable. It wasn't nice to Sherelle. Holly took a step back but Carl took another step forward. A minute further into their conversation, it happened again. She began to worry: what if he *was* interested? Holly didn't want any trouble, so she ducked out of the conversation as soon as she could and retreated to the kitchen on the pretext of filling her glass with ice. And that was when Jérémy approached her.

"I don't know you," he said. "What brings you here?"

He was only a little shorter than Holly and wore wire-rim glasses. He spoke with an accent that she couldn't identify.

"A friend," Holly said.

"Ah," he replied, with a lilting laugh. "A *friend.*"

She hadn't said anything funny but part of Jérémy's charm, Holly soon learned, was that he never seemed bored and was often amused by his surroundings. The world was always renewing itself. There was nothing sulky about him. Instead of shying away as Holly was inclined to do, or seeing awkwardness in another person and trying to press it to his advantage, as Carl had just done, Jérémy treated a situation as part of a larger spectacle which was absurd but also very entertaining.

He invited others to share in his pleasure. "We all need friends, don't we?" he added, smiling. "Sometimes I'm as lonely as a tree. My name is Jérémy."

Dzheramee.

And that was how it started. He was very polite, and he invited her to the Bijou, the local art cinema, to see a Korean movie. Holly enjoyed the novelty and the following night they returned and saw an Iranian movie. Afterward they went for a bite at a quiet bar and he wanted to discuss the films. He wasn't pompous and he seemed curious about Holly's opinions. He could converse about a movie for longer than the movie had lasted. It was the first time she'd socialized with an intellectual.

After their second outing, she was in love and knew that she would agree to have sex if he wanted to, a situation which very soon presented itself. It was her first time and it wasn't terribly pleasant but afterward she felt quietly smug to have lost her virginity with an interesting man like Jérémy. She had always wondered if her initiation would be yet another embarrassment, but now that it had finally happened, she was relieved. A hurdle had been successfully cleared. Later, when mulling over the event, it struck her that sex was more interesting to think about after the fact than it had been when it was actually *happening*. But turning it around in her mind made her want to try it again. Since junior high days she'd occasionally masturbated (though she didn't like that word, associating it with sniggering boys); sometimes her dreams took an unexpected erotic turn that left her yearning when she awoke. But this was different. Certainly no dream. Her next opportunity with Jérémy came shortly thereafter, and was followed by others in quick succession, and each time the experience got better, till on the fourth time with his arms pressed round her (a very pleasing sensation, this pressure) and she reached down to help him enter her, set it right, she was suddenly wracked with a slow convulsion of such astonishing intensity that it briefly frightened her—where did *that* come from?—a question promptly replaced by a thought: *so that's what the fuss is all about.*

"You are the most beautiful girl I've ever been with," he said.

"I don't believe that," she told him. Still, she liked hearing such words, and when he repeated them on other occasions, she no longer contradicted him. Previously she'd avoided makeup, skeptical of the trouble and thinking that it made her look bug-eyed and alarmed; but now she sought out complementary shades of shadow and accentuated her eyes. Holly's hair was long and straight and brown and for years she'd done nothing to it, simply pulled it back behind her ears or, while on the court, braided it into a rope; but now it was very long, halfway down her back, and she took new pleasure in its weight, in tending its gloss.

She also began to entertain a delicious thought: if her true life was a challenge to pursue alone, it would be better and actually *truer* if she could share her invisible self with someone else. How she longed for this intimacy! Wouldn't that be wonderful? *Shattering.* It would make her burden sweet. And she would let the other person share his invisible self, too. She could be trusted. She knew how hard it was. The loneliness of each would be banished and replaced by love.

Soon Holly was entertaining fantasies of a future with her cosmopolitan husband, driving him back to Sheridan in her Comet and showing off her brilliant African man to the shocked envy of small-town gossips; later, they would have gorgeous children, and (this was a riotous fantasy, and she knew it, but her mind was afire) she saw herself in Paris where Jérémy had studied, walking hand in hand past fountains and down the boulevards, laughing in conversation at sidewalk cafés; in another fantasy Holly wore colorful robes in Africa in the company of towering Watusi women, a stately procession of dignity and beauty, long slender hands clapping, a synchrony of sisterhood. No longer cramped by the world, she was breaking out!

"No, no." Jérémy laughed heartily when she inquired about the Watusis. "Those are not my people. You should know better, my darling."

"You're still seeing him?" Sherelle said, when Holly let drop in a conversation her plans for the coming weekend. She and Jérémy were going to see a travelling exhibition of Inca gold jewelry that had just arrived at the university's museum of anthropology. She hadn't been able to conceal the pride in her voice. Sherelle hesitated, and then said, "Be careful, Holly."

"What do you mean?"

"Oh, he talks plenty smooth, all right. But he still owes DeeDee money."

"What?"

Diana Davis, or DeeDee, was the starting forward on the basketball team. She was an intense competitor, and somewhat mean on the court.

"She fell hard for him, and she ended up paying his rent for two months. He doesn't make much money as a graduate assistant and he has expensive habits. He keeps saying he'll pay her back but nothing happens. She was all in love with him but he has a wife back in Dakar, you know."

"A *wife?* He has a wife?"

"You didn't know, did you? I was wondering. I guess we couldn't expect him to tell you."

Holly burst into tears on the spot. Sherelle was shocked at this spontaneous reaction and, with a frown, she put a hand on her shoulder. "Hey, hey. I guess I should've thought of this earlier." Holly was crying so hard that she couldn't talk, and was hiccupping, gasping for breath. Sherelle was embarrassed and didn't know what to do. "*Come on, Holly*. This shit happens. It's bad but it's not like we're fourteen years old anymore."

But that was where Sherelle was wrong, because in her heart Holly *was* fourteen years old, still working through emotions she'd been denied as a girl while growing so much in other ways. She was catching up, violently wrenched into a harsher world.

That same night she tracked down Jérémy in his teaching assistant's office and confronted him. She found him typing into his computer. "I know you're married! How could you not tell me? How could you?"

He looked up, blinking, still partly enmeshed in his thoughts. He saw her standing over him, her hair spilling around her shoulders. Nervously, he laughed.

"What's so funny? It's not funny, Jérémy. There's nothing funny here."

"No, you don't understand. I'm not laughing at you," he said, laughing.

She raised her hand to slap him across the face but then hesitated. Not because her emotions changed but because of his wire-rim glasses. Irrationally, she didn't want to hurt those glasses, which looked fragile. It was the briefest of pauses but time enough for Jérémy to pedal with his feet and push his chair back on its wheels, putting himself out of reach.

"You owe me an explanation!"

And Jérémy gave her one, nodding at her. He admitted that he was married and claimed that he'd been meaning to tell her all along. It wasn't a secret. The fact that Sherelle and DeeDee knew about his situation proved his point, didn't it? And there were two sides to the story about DeeDee and her money . . .

"Never mind DeeDee! I want to know about *me*! What you think of *me*?" Holly demanded.

"What do you want to know?"

"I've been a fool, haven't I?"

"I would never say that. I've never thought that." He paused. "But Holly, I'm not going to be somebody's trophy."

This riled her all over again. "Is that all there is here? That's too easy. Is that how you dismiss me?"

The conversation see-sawed for more than an hour before she let him take her in his arms, run his hand through her hair. She was still upset but he was her only comfort, too. Calm was restored. He began to kiss her neck. Then the conversation took a disastrous turn when Holly tried to put aside her anger in order to declare her devotion to him. "Divorce her and I'll marry you. Take me, Jérémy. You belong with me."

The ensuing silence was terrible.

As he looked at her, at first she thought he was searching for words, then she realized something else. He was bored.

She left his office.

After this conversation, Holly was physically ill for several days. Her mind raced so fast that her head throbbed, and if she tried to eat, she was afflicted with stomach cramps. Sleeping was difficult; she stared into the darkness, at the mercy of her thoughts. She cut classes and basketball practice. When she returned to her routine, everyone noticed a change, the rings under Holly's eyes and her reckless, aggressive play on the basketball court. "What's *the matter* with you?" Coach Booth reproved after Holly hacked a teammate badly, a girl named Suze, knocking her to the floor. Suze jumped up to her feet immediately, cursing, on the verge of flinging the ball in Holly's face. "That doesn't impress anybody, kid," said Booth. "Where's your professionalism?"

But Holly wanted punishment, and the surest, quickest means were self-inflicted. Two days later, still playing like a person unhinged, she turned swiftly in order to make a crazy burst in pursuit of a ball that was going out of bounds. In the last two years, she'd acquired the habit of favoring her right leg, because of her previous injury, and once again, she put full force on her left leg as she twisted and pushed for speed. But, this time, her knee crumpled, suddenly, completely, audibly, with a sickening sound like stepping into slushy ice. She crashed to the floor. Pain shot up into her lower spine and she pressed her nose and forehead against the varnished wood, gasping, trying to deflect the pain and make it go somewhere else. She couldn't really think straight except for one realization which hovered above her while the team trainer knelt beside her and spoke in a faraway voice. The trainer was coaxing Holly to change her position, turn her body around. Holly knew, then, without a doubt, that *it's over, it's over, this game is over for me.*

Surgery. A return to crutches. Going to practice or working out was impossible; that spring she also quit attending classes, taking "incompletes" in order to avoid flunking out entirely. She spent her days alone, her leg propped up on a chair as she surfed her laptop or watched television. Holly didn't want to talk to anyone.

In June, instead of returning to Sheridan, she rented a room near the campus and attended summer school, trying to finish her incompletes. She explained to Art on the telephone that this was necessary in order not to lose her basketball scholarship. Although her playing days were over, she needed the medical coverage and she could squeeze out one more year of tuition waiver, if she stayed off academic probation.

"Well, sure, you have to do your studies," Art said. "But won't you come home for a visit?"

"Yeah, I will. I just don't know when."

Holly pictured the house back in Sheridan, with its "Player of the Year" statuette prominently displayed in the living room, and the hallway of plaques and framed photographs, all celebrating her success, her status as a star. The image oppressed her. She couldn't spend time in that atmosphere. The house was a goddamn Museum of Holly. Now it would seem more like a mausoleum.

"We want to see you," her father persisted. "We should spend some time together."

Holly wished she could strip the walls and the shelves and throw all that crap in the trash. But Art would object, wouldn't he? He'd probably give her a pep talk about making a comeback. *Stand-tall-and-proud,* all that bullshit. He believed such words would be good for her, a comfort, even. And as for stripping the walls of the house—well, it wasn't her house, and this paraphernalia was also about *his* pride.

"I'll let you know," she said.

☼ ☼ ☼

"How do you feel, Holly?"

Two weeks into the summer session, she'd stopped returning phone calls. Art drove up to see her and now sat in Holly's room, his forehead wrinkling with concern, while Holly scratched a cuticle and avoided eye contact. She loved him as much as ever but she wished he would go away. This was impossible to say.

"I'm OK," she mumbled.

"Really? I don't think so. I don't believe you."

Eventually she looked up. "Daddy, it's over. It's all over. I'm not going to be a star. It was always just a dream and probably wouldn't have worked out even if I hadn't gotten hurt. But now I *know*. It's over. We don't have to pretend."

Saying these words felt like an act of defiance. They also brought a sense of relief.

Surprisingly, though, Art didn't contradict her. "Sweetheart, you're just beginning. Your life isn't over. Please don't talk like that."

"Now I have to be me," Holly said slowly. "But who's me?"

There was a respectful silence, and then Art replied, "You already have the answer. But it's like anything else. It doesn't come automatically. Being who you are takes practice."

The rest of their conversation was more circumspect. Safer. He took her out to lunch, throwing her crutches in the trunk of his car, and they spoke of life back home. "How's Honus?" she asked. "What's he up to this summer?"

"He's working for Talbot's again, he's earning money but he'll make himself deaf. Normally I don't believe in chiropractors but he still has pain, so we might go down that road."

Talbot's was a lawn service company in Sheridan, and Honus was a summer pilot, operating a riding mower. While working, instead of wearing protective covering for his ears, he preferred to put in ear buds and blast his favorite music over the engine noise. Honus suffered from sciatica that a local doctor had said was due to his wearing his skateboard pants so low. He counseled Honus to give up this fashion, an opinion seconded by Art and Anita (and probably everyone else in Sheridan) who sincerely wished that Honus wouldn't wear his skateboard pants so low. So far, though, he hadn't compromised his style.

"Art, can I ask you a favor?"

"Shoot," he said. "Fire away."

"All those pictures of me around the house . . . could you take some of them down? I'd appreciate it if you did. Why don't you put up more pictures of Honus?"

"Well—don't think you can erase the past, Holly. You shouldn't want to, either. You've got so much to be proud of."

"Could you at least put up more pictures of Honus?"

He nodded. "Yes, of course. We can figure that out."

"Thanks, Daddy. I'm not trying to erase the past. But it's time to turn the page."

If you hear me—moan or shout—
Please—ensnare my mind
Keep me in—to let you out

Later that same afternoon, after Art said goodbye and got in his car for the drive back to Sheridan, Holly unstrapped her leg brace and sprawled over a chair to study, her exposed ankles dangling over the armrest. The visit with her father hadn't gone badly. Necessary words had been said. But now she had tasks to address, reading for a required course that she'd left incomplete. The course was entitled "Major American Voices" and for the next morning's session there were poems by Emily Dickinson. The name wasn't unfamiliar; in high school she must've read something by this person, but nothing she could remember, nothing that had stuck. The first poem was strange and morbid. It began,

The soul has bandaged moments—
When too appalled to stir—

The poem went on to refer to a Goblin and Fear, and to a Felon in shackles. Whoa, Holly thought. This stuff is messed up. But the first lines spoke to her: the injuries she'd sustained on the basketball court and from Jérémy were deeper than physical or emotional: they'd touched her very soul. For several months they'd paralyzed her, and left her *too appalled to stir*.

But, upon reading these lines, just as in making her confession to Art earlier in the day, she felt something budge within her, a necessary stirring. Perhaps the bandages could come loose, and she could move again.

She flipped through the pages of the course anthology and lingered over another poem. The beginning made her smile.

> *I'm Nobody! Who are you?*
> *Are you—Nobody—too?*
> *Then there's a pair of us?*
> *Don't tell! they'd advertise—you know!*

Yes, exactly! she thought. I am not a star and I will not strut my stuff. From now on, I refuse! She inserted her finger to hold her place in the book, jumping ahead to other pieces, which she read with growing fascination. Often the meaning was far from obvious; she couldn't say that she fully understood this person. Rather, it was the inverse. As she read on she experienced an uncanny sensation of *being understood*. It was a relief, such a relief. Who was this wise, scary stranger? My God, she thought. She knows me! She knows all about me.

Impossible, of course, but some of the words felt as if they were written specifically for her. Solitude was dissolved, and she felt as if the barriers of space and time no longer existed. There was a different world present which she and the writer shared, a richer kind of intimacy than she'd ever anticipated. Holly flipped back to the earlier poem, which continued:

How dreary—to be—Somebody!
How public—like a Frog—
To tell one's name—the livelong June—
To an admiring Bog!

Holly laughed. "Where next, sister?"

TWO

APPRENTICESHIP

Holly surfed the Internet for what she could learn of Emily Dickinson. The story intrigued her, of the talented daughter who lived with her parents and spent much of her life as a recluse in an upstairs bedroom, speaking to others while hiding behind her door. On the rare occasions when she showed herself to outsiders, she dressed entirely in white. Like a bride? A ghost? A mental apparition? Even more strange, people around her didn't grasp the range of her imaginative life, because it was only after her death that her family discovered, locked in a trunk, a vast cache of hand-sewn notebooks with hundreds of poems. Wide-ranging, from dense to playful. Poems that were now considered classics of modernist literature, hailed for their formal innovation and original thought.

Holly shook her head. *Some kind of screwball!*

Dear Holly,

(said the postcard, which bore a cartoon image of a giant ear of corn being pulled by a tractor),

your email bounces back maybe its my typing but the BIG PEOPLE (Mom and Dude) want to see you, ok? So do i. Come home.

Your wonder bro,

Honus

Holly began reading outside of her assignments and spent two months immersed in Dickinson's poetry, while completing her other summer classes and working part-time at Stoddard's Family Restaurant. (No alcohol was served and every weekend, the menu promised "all-u-can-eat tater tots.") She did food prep for the salad bar, a task that didn't pay as well as waiting tables because there were no tips but which she preferred because she wouldn't have to approach strangers and ingratiate herself with small talk while listening to their remarks.

Holly found it best to read the poems singly, and repeatedly, instead of consecutively, because their compactness required concentration, even though the language was generally simple and the stanzas were short and easy to memorize. She could learn a poem and mull it over throughout the day as she went about her business. She applied dressing to a three bean salad and silently repeated the sixteen lines and 112 syllables of "*I heard a fly buzz—when I died—*." Poems like this fed Holly's morosity but also bemused her with a cagey wit, a geometric shifting of sense and rhythm like a swift succession of perfect passes on a basketball court. Holly rehearsed the lines and felt her mind growing more agile. It wasn't really that the poems made her smarter or taught lessons about life or explained the world; rather, they made the puzzling experience of life in this world burn brighter before her eyes. Its difficulties became limpid.

That fall, she left the basketball team and switched her major from pre-business to English.

"Really?" Art said. "You want to teach, Holly? Do some coaching?"

She detected a hopeful rise in his intonation; she'd called him on a Sunday night when she knew he'd be closed off in his study, marking papers and devising practice sheets, getting ready for the coming week.

Holly didn't know what else to tell him. She didn't want to teach or coach. To stand in front of a classroom of whispering, snickering teenagers; to clap and holler at players on the court? Relive those years—no way! Those were precisely the experiences she was fleeing. She told her father, "I just think literature is very interesting, that's all."

A pause. "So that's your plan?"

"Well, yes."

She waited for him to say something (it was his turn, wasn't it?) but he was silent. It was as if she was supposed to explain herself. She added, "It's something I've got to do. Listen, I better go now. Time to get ready for next week. I have a lot of reading in front of me."

She plunged into her new plan. She soon discovered that not all of her required reading was interesting, in fact some books assigned by the English department were as appealing as cold lumpy oatmeal, but Holly forged ahead, mowing down reading lists, turning pages for most of her waking hours, sometimes devouring several books in a day, a hungry giantess gorging herself in the solitude of her cave. Always she was haunted by a fear that she needed to catch up, that she was at a disadvantage compared to other students in her courses who were already conversant with a world of ideas that was unknown to her. Because it wasn't only a matter of reading books: there was a certain way to *talk* about them. Sometimes it wasn't immediately obvious (at least not to Holly) what you were supposed to say. In literature classes people spoke of hegemonic discourses or changing paradigms or neo-subversive marginalities. Holly took her seat in the back row, as was her habit, and she listened.

After class, she made trips to the library to retrieve additional books or she searched electronic journals for related articles and downloaded them. She didn't hang out in bars or socialize in coffee shops like so many of her classmates, who were arty and jokey and snarky and favored off-brand clothes and dreads and tattoos. Her basketball days were behind her but she retained the habit of discipline, a focus and drive that left no time for idling. Respecting a regimen was actually a comfort, a protection against the world. She had immediate likes and dislikes but was unsure what they meant. She admired Willa Cather and Edith Wharton and some of Zora Neale Hurston but found Kate Chopin stuffy, and was unimpressed when Edna Pontellier drowned at the end of *The Awakening*. What a yawn! She adored James Weldon Johnson's *The Autobiography of an Ex-Coloured Man* and, upon finishing it at 2:30 a.m., immediately began to reread earmarked passages, marveling at the chiseled prose, pondering the narrator's problematic invisibility and her own desire, for different reasons, to be invisible. A semester later, *King Lear* was a bruising experience that somehow fortified her, while Dylan Thomas left her both hot and cold. Hemingway's characters were campier than Oscar Wilde's, as far as Holly was concerned, though this contradicted what the professors said. The Beats bored her, as did most contemporary poetry she encountered (often presented with performance video, featuring many hand gestures for added *insistence*). Holly's developing tastes were an odd smorgasbord but her favorite writer remained, always, Emily, her secret friend and fellow Nobody.

By the following summer, Holly was a changed person. More sophisticated in some respects, less vulnerable, but not kinder. She still wore her uniform of jeans and interchangeable T-shirts; she still walked with long, sloping strides, her chin lowered and watching the ground in front of her as if searching for a path. Anybody could see that this young woman wasn't bursting with happiness. On the other hand, they couldn't know that she was less unhappy than before, that the exercise of her mind had rewarded her. Sometimes her synapses positively crackled at the approach of a new metonymic connection; she snatched her pencil to make a note. In quieter moments, she fell into her reading as into a reverie. Like a pool of still water, it calmed and soothed her. Literature wasn't escapism, a way to flee reality; it was an escape *into* reality, a way to go beyond the complacency of everyday life, its superficial rituals and hypocrisy.

In early June, Art passed through town en route to a baseball camp and he invited her out to lunch. Holly had assumed they could go to Da Nang Pho, a Vietnamese restaurant that she enjoyed for its big bowls of Pho soup. She loved the hot beef broth, the fresh mint and sprouts, and fishing for tasty beef strips with chopsticks. (She'd left soup stains in several library books because she always went to Da Nang Pho alone, reading as she ate.) But Art surprised her by announcing that he'd made a reservation at Bartini's Bistro, an upscale eatery that she'd never entered. They walked there and along the way they passed the apartment with its upside-down flag on the balcony railing. Art frowned. "Why are they doing that?"

Holly hesitated before answering. "Oh, it's probably a statement about Iraq."

"Well, it's bullshit."

She knew she should tread lightly. Her father was a patriotic man. In 1976, when Art was Holly's age, he'd been in the navy, and he'd celebrated the nation's bicentennial by running 1776 miles on the deck of the *U.S.S. Niagara*. He embraced the symbolic number. He measured an open section on the deck where he was allowed by his superiors to run a mini-lap of 162 yards, and he calculated that he would need to run 19,295 laps to attain 1776 miles. He began on New Year's Day and, averaging nine miles (or 98 laps) every day without exception, he finished, as planned, at sunrise on the Fourth of July. He'd run on the deck in all weathers, in blistering heat and on rolling seas, as the massive stern of the *U.S.S. Niagara* cut its way through the thick warm soup of the Indian Ocean. He was proud of this achievement, and every fall shared his story in the classroom with his social studies students.

Holly didn't want to argue with her father about politics, so she tried to apply some of the things she was learning in the English department. She was eager for his approval of the new ways she was growing. She told him, "It's a matter of semiotics, you could say. Upside down—the symbol of distress, right? That's what you're experiencing now, isn't it? So actually you don't need to feel alienated by this display, even if you don't share its ideological premises. It can work for you, too. Play with the paradigm, and you can appropriate it as your own."

Art sighed. "Oh Jesus. Can't you just talk like a real person?"

Her father's lack of interest in polysemantic semiotics probably colored what happened next. At Bartini's Bistro, they took a table and cautiously unfolded the starched linen napkins, looking at each other over the stemmed glassware. Holly wondered when was the last time her father had taken Anita to a place like this. When she saw the prices on the menu, the thought repeated itself. She felt as if they were on a date, and there was something bizarre when they agreed to order the duck breasts and quinoa. They spoke guardedly until Art finally came to the real subject, the reason, she realized, that he'd made the trip and brought her to this place.

"It's nice to do something sociable. Don't you think? I'm glad we could. Wouldn't you like to do more of this?"

"You mean come here? At these prices?"

"Don't joke, Holly. I'll put it to you straight. When are you coming home? You don't work every weekend, do you? You can't live in books. It's important not to miss out on life. You have to make time to be sociable."

"Sociable?" said Holly. "I'm sociable. Are you saying I'm not sociable?"

"No, that's not what I—"

"You can't pressure someone into being sociable. That in itself is not sociable. If you really want to talk about sociable."

The conversation went on in this vein. It wasn't a cheerful lunch. But she agreed to return to Sheridan to get the Comet serviced by a trustworthy and cheap local mechanic. That would provide an occasion for a family visit. Two Saturdays later, Holly drove around a bend of highway which took her over a hill and afforded a view of her hometown. She'd been down this road countless times, seen the vast upflung sky over the prairie houses which seemed to cling to the earth. A nostalgic feeling ebbed through Holly, a wistfulness. It surprised her. Yes, this had been home. This place meant a lot. But she was in no hurry to admit it.

"Dinner!" Art called. "Table time, everybody!"

Holly sighed and uncrossed her legs and put down her book. Honus came crashing down the stairs.

Anita chimed: "I made your favorite potato salad, Holly."

Favorite? Three or four years ago, she'd complimented Anita on her potato salad, in order to please her. She'd been trying to mend fences and get along with her step-mother. *Be pleasant.* Now she would have to eat it for the rest of her life. They sat down at the table.

"So . . . what are you reading, Holly?" Art asked, his voice peppy as they passed around the dishes.

"Book."

"Ketchup!" Honus grunted, and Holly passed it over. He didn't say "please" but Holly knew that it was pointless to insist. Honus had scraped a huge amount of potato salad onto his plate and, with food in front of him, Honus was incapable of thinking of anything else, before he had his ketchup. He needed his ketchup, pronto. It was a law of nature. He shook out fully one-third of the bottle on top of the potato salad.

"Holly, you hardly took any!" Anita remarked.

"Uh, I don't eat so many carbs now."

Art smiled at Anita and shrugged vigorously. "Except for quinoa. We ate quinoa a couple of weeks ago, didn't we, Holly?"

"What's quinoa?" asked Honus, his mouth a bloody hole.

After lunch, Holly retreated to a corner of the basement where she could be alone and still catch a Wi-Fi connection. She was typing into her laptop when Honus sidled up, swinging a brass ring on a chain. "Whatcha doin'?" As far as Holly knew, the ring wasn't for anything in particular; it was just one of a number of rings on chains that Honus possessed, and wore around his neck, in some kind of fashion statement. Recent photos of Honus on the walls revealed his predilection for chains.

"Writing a paper," she said.

He watched in silence for a minute while Holly pounded the keyboard. Eventually he said, "You're making it up?"

Holly looked up. "What?"

"It's cool. You're fast."

She wished that he would go away, but she saw that he was trying to be friendly, so she took time to explain. "Come here. Let me show you."

He peered over her shoulder while she clicked away from her document and opened several online tabs.

"See the dogs? Like that one? And that one? There are all these dogs and people like to dress them up in clothes. They post these pictures and they film them, too. Look at this one."

She clicked a link and played a short film of a Corgi in a blue pinafore, standing on its hind legs and turning a circle while a soundtrack played "Bolero." Then Holly clicked on photos of a boxer dog dressed as Elvis, and then other photos of Chihuahuas in pink bibs with matching caps. They were waitresses. Honus snorted.

"Looks funny, right?" she said. "But what does it *mean?* That's an interesting question, isn't it? This stuff is all over the Internet because people love to dress up their pets and share the result. That includes a portion of the queer community. They have fun with this, too, you know."

Holly paused, waiting for Honus's reaction. She thought it would be instructive for him to hear about this.

"Uh huh," he said.

"So you could argue that this is a valid expression of identity, of finding a space in which you can express difference, right? Your pet is an extension of you. You could argue that."

Honus looked back at her. Not arguing.

"Or, on the other hand," Holly continued, "you could consider something other than the purely human perspective, the anthropocentric, and wonder about the dogs. I mean, in some of these photos, they look like they're being used. Do you think they really *want* to wear clothes? That's a consideration. There's plenty of power at play here, clearly: one species dominating the other. It definitely looks speciesist."

Honus frowned and cupped his hand under his chin.

"But on the other hand, check out this one." She clicked a link where a terrier in a purple jacket danced and yapped, danced and yapped, its little mouth so animated. "He's having a blast! Doesn't he look happy?" she asked. "Sure, he is.

Happy! And this opens up a third space, a place of alternative. Look at him!" The dog danced. "He likes it! Pretty obvious to me."

Honus watched till the end of the clip, and then he cleared his throat.

"Holly, I thought you studied Shakespeare and shit."

She closed the tab.

"Well, that too. But this is metaliterary media theory, it's for a new class I'm having this summer. A person doesn't only read books. You have to make sense of the world. We live in a never-ending continuum of cultural expression. In fact, the entire world is a text!"

Hearing herself speak, Holly felt a twinge of unease. At the university these matters sounded vital, an important insight across disciplines. Now, though, in the family basement in Sheridan, beside the chipped ping-pong table and storage boxes of Christmas ornaments, where the air smelled of humid carpet and Anita's pine-scented freshener, she sensed that she was not only explaining to her little brother but trying to convince herself, too. *Of course* she wasn't expending hours of intellectual energy on something trivial. Power, identity, our relations to other creatures—these were important questions! She didn't want to do them a disservice. But somehow a necessary oxygen had leaked away. Her strangling feeling was exacerbated by the fact that Honus remained silent, patient, even, before he excused himself and went upstairs. Was he humoring her?

Later that afternoon, Holly reclined on the couch, reading another book. Anita came over and stood by the window. Holly was aware of her presence, but kept her eyes on the page. Recently Anita had cut her hair short and added professional slicing highlights; she looked much younger. Over lunch she'd wanted to discuss a recently released movie that was definitely anti-racist. Now she seemed to be waiting for something. Holly didn't look up. Eventually Anita said softly, "Nice day."

Holly thought: *For God's sake can't you see I'm too busy for banal conversation about the weather and if you think you can tell me to go outside and play as if I were some little kid you'd better think again!*

Holly said: "Um."

"It's balmy but not so hot we need the air conditioning. Don't you like it like this?"

Holly looked up. "Yes."

"But it's not going to last. It'll get so hot that we'll have to put on the air conditioning. Summer days!"

"You truly think so?"

Holly kept her face perfectly neutral when she said this, and Anita looked back warily.

"What are you reading, Holly?"

"Some Eagleton."

"What's that?"

"Literary criticism."

Anita pursed her lips. "Well, I think it's better to have a nice thing to say."

The screen door slammed and Holly found herself alone.

That fall semester marked the first time she saw Philip Post, a new recruit in the faculty. Actually, she *heard* him first, a sharp clip-clopping in the Crewe Building. She turned and saw a handsome young man striding down the hallway. She spied his cowboy boots, the source of the sound, and then looked up to take in his black jeans, his snowy white shirt and, dangling from his collar, an untied black bow-tie. It hung out casually, or at least that was the effect. It invited questions. Had he this morning been on the verge of dressing very formally for class but at the last second decided, *What the hell, I'll let it all hang out,* in a cheekily subversive appropriation of the black tie convention? Or maybe he'd been up all night at a party and was coming in to teach directly after his revelries? Still giddy with champagne? Gliding on his bicycle with jacket-tails flapping in the wind? In the hallway, heads turned. "Hallo!" he called out to a colleague, some colorless individual instantly vaporized and rendered irrelevant. Philip turned abruptly and disappeared into an office, leaving only an after-image, a post-dazzle impression. *Who was that?*

Holly tried to register for his class entitled "Metaliterary Applications: a Post-Gutenberg Practicum." The course she'd taken over the summer with another instructor was the necessary prerequisite, so she had the right to enroll at the next level, but she was too late. Philip Post's class was already full. She tried again the next semester, but the same thing happened. Enrolling was like getting tickets to a hot rock concert. Post, she was told, had arrived from Cambridge and accepted a dual appointment in the Communications Department and the English Department. As a new hire, he was still untenured and outranked by all the senior colleagues, but he was easily the most popular professor across several disciplines. Among undergraduates, he was a sensation.

By then, Holly had achieved a sure footing in the traditional literature curriculum, her grades consistently A or A minus. It felt like a respectable niche, and life itself didn't grate on her, especially when she was immersed in a good book. She was certainly less of a mess than a year ago. She found it easier to laugh and to enjoy simple, everyday things. A juicy orange. Mint tea. The feel of the sun through her clothes. She was gratefully aware of sun-like rays within her, too, a sense of well-being. A newfound confidence. Late nights while her peers were bar-hopping and meeting new people, Holly was closing down the library, also meeting new people. She cruised the stacks on the fourth floor, the main site of literature holdings, and pulled down volumes at random, reading a few pages here, a few pages there, flirting with authors and sometimes lingering longer to make an acquaintance. It was like surfing the Internet but more serendipitous because there were no links, just random reaches off the shelves. The texture and smell of the book added to the experience, the quiet crack of the spine, the inky library stamps. Some volumes hadn't been checked out in forty, even sixty years—they probably hadn't even been *opened* until this instant her eyes met the page. Moving promiscuously this way through the stacks she made some welcome discoveries, new friends: Henry Bashford, Józef Mackiewicz, Emily Carr. Each was interesting in different ways. Carr's *The Book of Small* instantly caught her attention for its title; she pulled it down and wrapped herself around it. More than once she looked up from her reading and playfully imagined seeing a figure in white at the far end of the stacks, a fleeting presence, slipping silently around the corner. "Don't be jealous," she whispered. "No one's going to replace you." For a class where she was allowed to do an independent study, Holly wrote a paper entitled "Humor in Emily Dickinson," focusing on some of the quirkier poems. Her teacher, a squeaky-voiced man named Tibbets, commented in green ink: *"Very original, and convincing in your chosen corpus. You know, I'd always considered Emily a sourpuss!"* He added a smiley face, and circled her grade: A plus. Holly took special satisfaction in this paper, because it was the most personal work she'd ever done.

Because of her spotty academic performance during her basketball years, though, Holly lacked a few credits at the end of the spring semester, and she needed one last summer class to graduate. She was still working at Stoddard's Family Restaurant, so the most convenient slot was an 8:00 a.m. course called

"Fundamental Readings" taught by Professor Borden. It was the only course that fit her work schedule. She knew that Borden wasn't popular, but a summer course lasted only six weeks, so she wasn't too concerned.

For the first class, Professor Borden showed up with traces of scrambled eggs in his moustache and took attendance by calling out the roll without making reference to anyone's first name: he said "Mr. Esteves" or "Ms. Melton" or "Ms. Winegarten." He told them that in future classes they must sit in the same chair, to avoid any confusion. After lecturing them for forty minutes about how Ralph Waldo Emerson was a major thinker, a formal innovator and the Grandfather of New Age Quacks, he took out a cigarette which he sucked on, unlit, rounding off his lecture with a few more remarks, concluding, "this man still has much to tell us!" Then he looked at his watch—the hour was over—and scuttled out the door.

A spontaneous discussion broke out in the room about whether this hasty exit was due to Borden's need for a smoke or because he had (according to rumor) bladder issues.

Holly stuffed her notes in her book bag and sloped off to Stoddard's to prep the salad bar. It had been a strange morning. After the first few class sessions, though, she became reconciled to Borden's idiosyncrasies. As long as she didn't look too closely at his jowly, sallow face, which was distractingly doglike (a basset hound, Holly thought, the only thing missing are the floppy ears), she found Borden fairly interesting. He rarely looked at his notes, always addressing them formally, with a perceptible southern accent and unribboning sentences that sped up and slowed down like a train passing through small rolling mountains. A convenient development was that he allowed students to pick the topic of their research paper. ("You are your own master," he intoned—a very Emersonian sentiment—"but are you up to it?") Since Holly had taken on extra hours at Stoddard's in order to make more money, she didn't have time to cook up a new topic, so she decided to recycle her A plus paper from the previous semester with Tibbets. There seemed no harm in this and it would save her a lot of trouble; it was an Ace up her sleeve. She read through the paper once, made a few minor changes, printed out a fresh copy, and turned it in.

The next week, Professor Borden handed back the student work. "I'll give everyone a few minutes to read my comments," he said.

Holly was shocked to see her paper spattered with red ink, with lines and arrows and bracketed phrases. She flipped to the last page and found her grade: C plus.

Her first reaction was embarrassment: Borden must've found out that she'd taken a short-cut, and he was penalizing her for it. Maybe he was on friendly terms with Tibbets, and somehow her name had come up. (*"You know the one— the tall girl?"*) A flush of shame rose up her neck. But, as she returned to the first page and read though Borden's markings, and looked at the second page, and the third, the slashings and rips all the way to the end, she found no mention of this issue.

Now her embarrassment shifted to anger. What was going on here? This was a bloody defacement of her writing! Of her thinking! OK, there were a couple of typos that she'd missed, and that Professor Tibbets must not have noticed, either (his returned version was pristine white, apart from a few approving checkmarks and his final compliments); but these minor lapses weren't such a big deal, were they? And it was downright perverse how obsessed Borden seemed with her punctuation, applying and rejecting commas, writing *[SPLICE!]* in all capitals, as if spitting out his reproach. Worse still was the way he crossed out words or entire lines—how presumptuous!—or circled repetitions and connected them with accusing arrows.

In his margin comments, he wrote things like "*dubious*" or "*develop?*" Sure, Holly had understood weeks ago that Borden wasn't exactly a smiley face kind of guy, but come on, he didn't have to be insulting. There was nothing uplifting in his comments or remotely friendly, only a final statement in crabbed handwriting beneath the C plus: "*Potentially interesting but lacks rigor.*"

Holly's jaw pulsed. There was a buzz from students around her, who also seemed unhappy with their grades and who'd begun to whisper and compare their results.

"Never mind that," said Professor Borden. "Someone else's grade is not your affair. Your grade concerns only myself and you and God. In that order."

He went on to explain that his assessment, however, need not be final. "If you rewrite your paper, I will reconsider your work. If you refine your thoughts and your expression of them, you will have another chance. On each paper I've made some suggestions for improvement that you could pursue."

After class, on the way out of the building, students immediately resumed their conversations and comparisons of grades. In addition to C, there were also D and F grades. No one had as high as C plus. When asked her grade, Holly became shy and answered, "C minus." She made herself smaller.

"This is like, total bullshit," someone said.

"And bullying."

"He's getting off on this pompous pose, this little power trip. What a loser!"

"He's a prick."

"He's a dick."

"It's not just *his* class," said a dyed-blond boy named Randy. "It's ours, too. We all have a stake. He's running down everybody's G.P.A. for the sake of his narcissism."

"Exactly!" said a girl named Jessica. "I've always had As, only a few Bs. What allows him to judge? I'm going to grad school. This guy has no credibility. It's like he's trying to be the cliché of the stern professor that everybody fears and respects but, obviously, *nobody* respects him. He doesn't scare me. He's not even a good cliché. Fuck him!"

The grumbling continued over the next two weeks but Holly knew that she wasn't the only one to accept the challenge of rewriting her work. Students were rattled. For Holly it was, above all, a matter of pride: she didn't want a C plus and it irked her that Borden thought she deserved one, that he believed that she wasn't clever enough to notice the typos and repetitions that he'd circled with red ink. She *could* see them, but she just hadn't gotten around to fixing them, that was all.

Soon, however, as she tried to address the margin comments about the content of her work, it became more than a matter of pride. She lost herself in the task. It was absorbing. She believed that she was right about Dickinson's humor, that some of the poet's ruminations about solitude or even death, which many readers found daunting, were expressed with cunning asperities that were the verbal equivalent of a sly grin. Seriousness didn't rule out sensuous delight.

> *I felt a Cleaving in my Mind—*
> *As if my Brain had split—*

This poem was fiendishly abstract; it dramatized the human thought process. The struggle to construct meaning. Yet it registered this struggle physically, even cartoonishly, in the subsequent lines in which the speaker unsuccessfully tried to reassemble the pieces of her brain, "Seam by Seam," only to conclude:

> *But Sequence ravelled out of Sound*
> *Like Balls—upon a Floor—*

Was this what it felt like to lose your marbles? You had to *hear* it in order to *know* it; now Holly needed to show it, in prose, by firing off a neat set of passes that would bring her ball closer and closer to the goal. Fortunately, she wasn't alone, she had teammates. Borden had queried her about sources, and with research Holly discovered that as early as 1913 *The Atlantic Monthly* had referred to Dickinson's "transcendental humor," and that in France, in 1977, the *Revue française d'études américaines* had published an article called "Emily Dickinson, Jester." There were also poetry aficionado websites where contributors made wry allusions to some of the same poems. The web writers were an odd bunch, and some used unfortunate pseudonyms like Woodtick and BigButtLover, and their posts might include paranoid politics or vacation selfies; but there were reasonable voices, too, such as a retired geologist in New Zealand named Malcolm whose remarks on "It would have starved a Gnat— / To live so small as I" were quite useful to Holly. She was reassured that she was not the victim of some personal delusion. She just needed to make her case more thoroughly, more forcefully. She felt a growing excitement in the conviction that she, more than anyone so far, would make it *better*. She worked hard on her second draft, which she further revised, layering on argument, examples and nuances; the morning she turned it in to Professor Borden (by now, it was the fourth draft), after having stayed up till three a.m. to finish it (but still feeling wide awake with mental electricity), she forced herself to adopt a neutral expression. She felt like grinning. Here, you old dog, she thought. This'll show you!

A week later, on the last day of class, he handed back the paper. The grade: B plus.

This time, instead of lingering behind with the other students as they grumbled and compared their results, she pursued Borden down the hallway. He'd made his usual hasty exit, but Holly's long strides soon caught up with him.

"Professor Borden, I need to talk to you!"

"Yes?"

"About my paper."

"Yes?"

"Do you have a minute?"

"Let me guess. You want an A."

He'd started to climb the stairs, and now he turned and faced her. At this angle, they were on eye level. When Holly hesitated, he added, "Ah, a lucky guess, yes?"

But she didn't falter.

"Not precisely. What I really want to know is why I didn't get an A. What it takes to get an A."

Borden nodded. "Shall we go to my office?"

She followed him to the top of the stairs, into a little cranny below the steam pipes. He invited her to sit down, excused himself and left her to ponder the interior, its sickly ficus plant, the untidy desk and some books stacked on the floor. She was tempted to kneel and check the titles, but she didn't want Borden to come back and find her snooping. So she waited. (Must be true about his bladder, she thought.) Eventually Borden bustled into the office and closed the door.

"OK, I'll give you an A. You just need to rewrite it again. Let's go over it. Your transitions aren't so hot."

Holly fumbled with the zipper of her book bag to extract the pages. "But—but it's the end of the session. What would be the deadline? To tell the truth, I graduate next week. This is my last class. There's not time. I can't take an incomplete."

"That is purely an administrative matter. I couldn't care less. We shall have a contract, Ms. Winegarten. I'll give you the grade now, you'll get your A, and you will work on this project until you get it done properly. That could be a few

weeks, months . . . I don't know. Next year? It's all the same
to me. It's up to you. You will have to hold up your end."
  "Based on . . . what?"
  "Honor."

❀ ❀ ❀

That was a surprise. Holly felt her real education began that
summer, after she graduated, rewriting the same old paper.
And it wasn't for the subject itself, which was rather specialized, but for the seriousness of approach, the ear for excellence,
the constant questioning. She was groping but, at another level,
she understood the enterprise. She grasped why she must grope.
It was its own reward. She wouldn't have used the creaky old
word "honor" but she responded instinctively to what Borden implied. Honor was the opposite of strutting your stuff.
It served something else, expressed a kind of faithfulness. It
was about the beauty of the work, not about you.
  She met with Borden weekly, and she produced not one
but two more drafts of her essay. He whittled at her prose
and picked at her thoughts, sometimes emitting short woofs
of laughter or smiling with his snaggly, yellow teeth. "*I see, I
see.*" He encouraged her to disagree with him. "Contradiction
is a chance to learn something. Show me!" He wasn't unre-
ceptive to questions of identity and difference but he literally
hissed when she tried to use the phrase "hypervisible praxis,"
which she'd heard in another course but which he considered
jargon. "My ears are bleeding. Goddamnit! Repeat it aloud,"
he said. "*That* is not in the least felicitous." Once she bumped
into Professor Borden downtown, coming out of a bank. They
spoke briefly, their first non-literary conversation. "The teller,
some kid with a goatee I've never seen in my life, addressed me

as Bob. *Bob!* We live in a slobocracy!" He threw up his hands and walked off.

Holly found it hard to figure him. He was a serious man but he was also a performer; he was sincere in his opinions but he also seemed to savor the expression of his outrage. He reveled in his adherence to certain forms. (This discernment didn't apply to the way he dressed: no ties or vests for Robert Borden; he wore scuffed brown shoes and corduroys and a plain, button-down white shirt, stretched tight across his pot belly.) Yet he also seemed to be aware of the perils of his position, of being a ham, and in his office Holly sometimes had the impression that he toyed with his role of professor in order to amuse himself, purposely exaggerating or flirting with her in a highly obscure manner (an unwelcome thought, no matter how highly obscure). The most fruitful exchanges occurred when Professor Borden was so engaged with a subject—for instance, Dickinson's use of animal imagery—that Holly's contract with him seemed entirely forgotten. He was only interested in her idea, tapping the page, repeating a line aloud, his dogface in full bloom. Here he was dead serious, not performing—unless it was the performance of an abstract athleticism, a demonstration of concentration. It wasn't even "her" idea anymore; it had become a phenomenon as impersonal as the melting temperature of platinum or the rings of Saturn, available to anyone to observe. Language—and *consciousness itself*—were part of a natural grain of things, available for scrutiny.

That was the beautiful thing, the honorable thing, the reason Holly kept coming back. Because in the end it had absolutely nothing to do with her. In a sense she had disappeared: not into a void, but into something larger, something shared.

April 16, 1863
    My dearest
    I cannot undo what has been done, nor do I wish to. My
brain—boiling! I came down to finish the baking, before din-
ner, talking to Vinnie, with your face—in my mind.
    "What's that?"
    Sister reached to my hair.
    Found a straw!
    "Where did that come from?"
    So I continued—to lie.
    "I don't know."
    A bird does not carol all the time—to prove the cost of
Music.
    Emily

"I've decided to apply for graduate school," she announced
in Borden's office. "It's too late to try the PhD program here
but they accept late entry applications for the M.A. I'll be on
probation till they get my G.R.E. scores but I can still do it!
Will you write me a letter of recommendation? They say I need
three letters of recommendation."

She couldn't hide her excitement and she'd assumed that he
would approve. After all, didn't they share the same passion?
But Borden's face froze and he started straightening things on
his desk.

"Oh dear," he said eventually. "You've thought about this?
You want to do it?"

"Sure."

"Yes. I'll write you a letter. No problem."

They spoke of a few practical details, but Holly could
hardly hear herself because now she was confused. She'd intended to tell him about an upper-level graduate seminar that

was going to be offered in the fall. "Emily Dickinson: Exemplar or Avatar?" It had just been posted on the departmental website and Holly was excited. (*I have to be there for that! I can't miss it!*) So excited, in fact, she made up her mind on the spot. Yes, she would go to graduate school.

Now she asked Borden in a choked voice, "Do you—do you think I'm ready for grad school? Please be frank."

He smiled with his lips. "Yes, Ms. Winegarten. The real question is, is graduate school ready for you?"

This answer didn't satisfy her. It felt phony and fulsome, especially for its contrast with his usual skeptical tone. It created a chill, and instantly changed their relationship. By now her paper was finished; she'd respected her contract. She'd earned her grade. Holly saw him only twice after this conversation, the second time for less than a minute when she retrieved the letter. (Borden had chosen not to upload a secure form onto the university intranet system, and instead gave her a sealed envelope with his signature across the flap.) Holly was sorely tempted to rip it open and see what he'd said about her, but she carried it dutifully to the Admissions Office.

Why should I doubt? she asked herself.

He'd given her an "A", hadn't he? Wasn't an "A" from Borden worth much, much more than an "A" from Tibbets? (She'd asked for a recommendation from him, too, and from another instructor, Molly Wu of "Early Modern Alternatives" who'd also given her an "A.")

I'll be fine, she told herself. *The center must move. Find the ball.*

When she phoned Art and informed him that she was staying in school and going further into debt to pursue her interest in poetry, he didn't sound thrilled. But her mind was made up, and she tried to mollify him by adding that as long as she remained enrolled, she could retain the health insurance that had originally come with her athletic scholarship. (A recent court ruling about a brain-injured football player now forbade the university to renege on its incapacitated athletes; Holly had seen this damaged student on campus, toggling an electric wheelchair, a sad figure who'd paid a high price for her health perk.) Art, for his part, attempted a different positive spin on her news. "If you're still gonna be in school, Holly, you can keep an eye on Honus."

"Well . . ."

It was true. Honus had graduated from high school and was entering the university in the fall. How fast time went! It was difficult for Holly to imagine her brother as a Little Scholar, toiling late nights at the library. (No matter: Honus probably couldn't imagine it, either.) Art and Anita had dropped alarming hints that brother and sister could economize by sharing a place together, but that idea went nowhere. Holly pretended to be deaf, and Honus insisted on getting a room in the dorm. "Hey! I wanna be with *normal* people."

April 17, 1863
  My dearest,
  Do I repine? The straw that Vinnie took from my hair—she put it in the waste with pottage peelings. When she turned her back I retrieved it. Smouched it, as the children say.
  I hold it like a lightning bolt in one hand.
  I write you with the other.
  Now I kiss—lightning.
  Yours lovingly,
  Emily

Due to her late application or perhaps due to her overall grade point average (her final two years of diligence couldn't completely blot out her earlier performance), Holly wasn't offered financial aid in the form of a grant or a teaching assistantship. She took out a student loan for $10,000 and, though she had spartan habits and benefitted from in-state tuition, this wouldn't cover all her living expenses, so she looked for an additional part-time job to supplement her income from Stoddard's. This was when she started working in Special Collections.

She registered for three courses and this time, it felt different from earlier years. More auspicious. High flying, even! She was a bona-fide graduate student. One was a required course on "Introduction to Research Methods," which offered an overview of bibliographic and electronic resources. It was reputed to be dull but easy. The second was a course on the Victorian novel, taught by Professor Jefferies. He was a man with irritating tics but it was a strategic choice for Holly, since she'd already read much of the reading list, and this would give her an edge. She knew Professor Jefferies from an undergraduate lecture course where he'd excelled at tautology. He said things like, "And there's another point, and that point is" or "to come to this understanding, you must understand that . . ." Once you noticed it, you couldn't stop noticing it. It was contagious.

A student raised her hand.

"Yes?" said Professor Jefferies. "You have a question? What question do you have?"

"The line about the dying soldier in the wagon, the dying soldier in that line . . ."

"Yes. '*Like a devil sick of sin! A devil sick of sin!*'"

"Is the allusion biblical? Biblically, is there a reference . . ."

Holly wanted to slap her forehead. But she decided to put up with Professor Jefferies in order to give herself as much time as possible for her course on Dickinson. It was an upper-level graduate seminar. She would be elbow-to-elbow with doctoral students. She wanted to be in top form.

The seminar room on the third floor of Crewe Building offered a different atmosphere from other classrooms. Holly couldn't head straight for the back row; instead, she joined three other students at an oval table. Professor Muller, whose thick mass of gray hair cascaded in long, leonine tresses, introduced herself by saying, "Well, you all know who I am. Just call me Rosemary. But let's complete the picture. Tell me about *you*."

So they went around the table. A girl named Penelope Chang started, and told everyone that she was working on a PhD in literary biocriticism. "My emphasis is on post-anthropocene satire and 21st century science fiction." Then a pasty-faced young fellow with large puffy lips named Dalton (he didn't share his last name) told everyone that for his PhD, he was bringing Gilles Deleuze to pre-postmodern texts. "I want to sneak up behind Emily Dickinson, you know, that's why I'm here, to do that kind of thing." Then he stared at his hands and laughed in an uninflected monotone. (Holly wondered if he was on medication.) Next came Courtney Davies, who talked for five minutes non-stop. She told the group that she was working on dystopian narratives with an emphasis on Margaret Atwood and that Rosemary was her thesis director and she loved what she was doing and where her research was going and she hoped that this seminar would be as super as it sounded in the course description. She'd found a terrific article on the Emily Dickinson Museum website about young Emily leaving Homestead for Amherst that she wanted to share with them, *right now*: she unsnapped an enormous blue book bag and removed a pile of hand-outs and began to pass them around. With a rising panic Holly tried to piece together a way to introduce herself. She didn't have a research period or a methodology or a dissertation subject. When her turn came, she said, "I'm Holly. This is new to me, my first graduate class ever. I'm here because I admire Dickinson." She squeezed out a smile.

Oh, if she had stopped there, everything would've been fine! The eyes around the table weren't unfriendly. Sure, she could feel them looking up and down, gauging her height, but that was nothing new. She was used to that. No one was being snotty or dismissive. Their gaze was just about to shift away, and the conversation to move on, when Holly added as an afterthought, "Professor Borden recommended me."

It just popped out. She hadn't planned to say this but as soon as she did, Holly knew why. She wanted to make an impression. She wanted to sound *smart*. These people surely knew who Professor Borden was. His severe manner, his reputation as a hard grader. She was trying to show off. She couldn't help herself.

Now the eyes returned and this time, they weren't looking at her height. Courtney Davies frowned, Dalton looked up from his hands and blinked at her, his lips looking very chapped and dry, and a question hung in the air. *Who ARE you?*

Rosemary cleared her throat. "Well . . . let's begin."

How could Holly know? It was only in later weeks that she was able to piece together the story, or at least much of it, of Professor Borden's notorious status in the department. There was plenty of gossip among graduate students on the subject.

How in an email to another colleague he had described a vis-
iting female poet as a "lightweight memoirist" and had written disparagingly of "ladies book club fodder" and "clit lit";
how, when this colleague had shared the email with other colleagues, who shared it with Rosemary Muller (who'd invited
the poet and introduced her at a university-sponsored event),
Rosemary had filed a complaint, accusing Borden of violating
the university ethics code against abusive and discriminatory
language and, more specifically, of sexual harassment. Borden
had to appear for a disciplinary hearing and, though the harassment charge was dropped, the rest of the complaint was
upheld and Borden had received an official reprimand from
the dean. Thereafter, he'd embarked on a misguided attempt
to defend his cause, sending feisty emails to the entire department in the middle of the night—many teachers suspected that
there was a correlation between closing times at bars and Borden's flaming correspondence—in which he complained of lax
standards and intellectual groupthink. To the amusement of
the graduate assistants and adjuncts who were on the same
mailing list, he quoted published articles of senior colleagues,
exposing what he considered bad prose and muddy reason-
ing in a series of messages with the subject heading: "Translated from the English." These achieved a minor cult status
and earned him another disciplinary hearing on the accusation
that he was creating a hostile work environment. For instance,
a tenured specialist of the Raphaelites, Alexander Pearson, had
described literary interpretation as "a paradigmatic condensa-
tion within a diachrony" and he'd been very unhappy when
Borden translated it as *"texts mean something when you read
them."* Pearson hadn't been able to refute Borden's rendering,
but he'd managed to get him disciplined for other remarks of a
personal nature. (Borden had asserted that his translation was

not only an improvement on the original but also captured perfectly the vacuity of the source.)

Holly learned much of this from her classmate Penelope, who worked as a teaching assistant and had read the emails. "This crazy guy is your friend?" she asked. "This dinosaur? Is he really drunk all the time? That's what I heard."

"I know him just a little," she said. "He wasn't a bad teacher. I've never seen him drunk."

"They asked him to take early retirement, they want him to go away. He's a loose cannon and they don't let him teach graduate level courses anymore. He's stuck mainly with crappy freshman composition classes like they give us T.A.s. His translations were funny but T.A.s don't like him because he grades so hard that students are scared of him so they come running to us, which causes overcrowding in our groups. The guy must be needy or have a screw loose, if you ask me."

"I don't know," Holly said, "it's hard to say. Maybe less a screw loose than—well—he's pretty wound up?"

Holly felt that she was being disloyal but she couldn't bring herself to defend him much further. Borden could be obnoxious, there was no denying.

"He's hardly published," Penelope said. "You think a guy like that could get a job nowadays? Not on your life! It's so much harder now."

This side of things had never occurred to Holly but, in the short time she'd been in graduate school, she'd heard frequent allusions to publishing. People were always checking up on who had done what. They were highly competitive, going to conferences and giving papers, speaking with awed tones about the annual convention of the Modern Language Association, where thousands of specialists gathered to participate in panel discussions, to see and be seen, where freshly-minted PhDs hoped to make an impression and get recruited for one of the shrinking number of tenure track positions or, failing that, to grab a one-year adjunct contract at a subsistence wage with no health insurance. ("The meat market," they called this winnowing process.) Graduate students were like a nervous pack of wolves, circling and sniffing the air for a career.

The previous summer, Holly had been so busy trying to win Borden's approval of her paper that it hadn't crossed her mind to question *his* written output. The same day as this conversation with Penelope, she consulted the library catalogue and the M.L.A. Index. In the last thirty years, Borden had published a single monograph and a handful of articles, all on Ralph Waldo Emerson, with the exception of one piece on Thoreau. (A crank writing about other cranks, Holly thought.) She printed out the reference and searched the library stacks and retrieved Borden's book. It was a slim volume, published twenty-four years earlier by the University of Indiana Press. Holly slipped into a chair in a study carrel and began to read. She recognized the arguments instantly, because she'd heard versions of them in Professor Borden's course. They were very clearly put forth, which was a great help in understanding some of Emerson's more gnomic pronouncements. But—and this was the strange part—their clarity made them unostentatious, so unlike his hammy persona in the classroom. She felt that she was encountering a piece of disembodied thought, hovering on the page. If she could switch off that booming voice in her head—well, it could've come from *anybody*.

The biggest scandal in the department, though, wasn't Borden. That dubious honor went to Philip Post. As an undergraduate, Holly hadn't been aware, but now she was privy to eager gossip in the T.A. cubicles on the fifth floor of the Crewe Building, a hot-house of rumor and innuendo, where teaching assistants

stuck ironic *New Yorker* cartoons on the walls of their cork-
board kennels alongside pastiches of Renaissance courtly love
poetry and bawdy rhyming parodies of "Jabberwocky." The
atmosphere here was more self-consciously clever than in the
workaday world of Special Collections, with Merle's bubbling
aquarium and Holly's tidy workspace with acid-free containers. It was also shabbier and inhabited by thin skins. Holly
remembered her basketball days, when gripes had been that
the women's facilities had fewer whirlpools than the men's,
and the alumni-funded juice bar wasn't always stocked with
mango-peach, the most popular drink. Conditions were luxu-
rious compared to T.A. cubicles, where there weren't enough
chairs and there wasn't even a coffee machine and a broken upper window was patched with plywood. This place had all the
charm of a litterbox. What graduate students lacked in ameni-
ties, though, they made up in incestuous entertainment, in in-
trigue and tittle-tattle.

Philip Post, she learned, had been having an affair with
Courtney Davies, the same Courtney who shared her Dickinson seminar. She wasn't one of Philip's students, so their dal-
liance was technically not a violation of policy. Courtney had
fallen hard for Philip but she'd become suspicious of his loy-
alties, so she hacked into Philip's email, where she discovered
a highly personal correspondence with another young woman
who *was* one of Philip's students. Courtney was disgusted. Not
only disgusted—outraged, and eager for revenge. She hurried
to the English department to confront him. She intended not
only to break off their relationship but also to embarrass and
discredit Philip Post at his workplace. Why not? Sleazeball had
it coming! She waited for him at the door of a classroom on the
fourth floor of Crewe Building where he was lecturing sopho-
mores on reception theory. She accosted him as soon as he
stepped out, and a heated argument ensued, to the bewilder-

ment of students and passersby. It degenerated into a shouting match and an exchange of expletives that soon grew so loud that people began to open their doors and peer out, in order to see what the fuss was about. Courtney and Philip stood toe to toe, oblivious to their surroundings.

"Stop it! Please!"

This was Rosemary Muller, from the end of the corridor. She hurried forward and interposed herself between them.

"This must stop *now*!"

There was a hush as Courtney and Philip paused, glaring. Then Rosemary gave another order.

"We're going into my office."

It was like a school principal with misbehaving children. They followed her. Holly knew these details because she'd heard them from Courtney herself, one afternoon when she was hanging out in the T.A. cubicles. Courtney had shared the story with everyone present in an attempt to rally other graduate students to her side. "I want people to know the truth!" Her relationship with Philip Post had started casually the previous Christmas and when it grew more serious, they'd kept it a secret because Philip had convinced Courtney to embrace discretion. "Even if you're not my student, you wouldn't want anyone in the department to think that you were currying favor, would you? We have to look out for your interests." But later, as they sat in Rosemary's office, everything changed. Rosemary asked, "What's this all about?"

"He's been fucking a student, that's what it's all about. I have *proof*, that's what it's all about. And not only fucking, he's been . . ." Courtney took a breath, and then spat out: "spanking!"

Philip silently shook his head.

"Don't deny it! I've read those emails! You simply cannot sit there and tell me you haven't had sex with Stacia Barnes."

She turned to Rosemary and added, "I've downloaded screen-shots, so if he tries to delete them, it's too late." She turned back to Philip. "Buddy, your ass is grass!"

"Courtney, please!" Rosemary said. "Let's not raise our voices anymore. These are serious charges and they must be handled in a professional manner. Any proceedings will have to originate from a formal complaint which will be submitted to the Disciplinary Committee." She turned to Philip. "As a member of the committee, I personally guarantee it. You know very well our policy about teacher-student relations. It was part of your signed contract. There are also rules about appropriate usage of university email accounts. And if there is suspicion of violence or any form of assault, that, Mr. Post, is a criminal matter, which will be reported to the police."

"This isn't right," said Philip.

"What isn't right?" asked Rosemary.

"Did you or did you not have sex with Stacia?" said Court-ney. "I dare you to answer that question in front of a witness!"

Philip nodded.

After a pause, Rosemary said, "Could you verbalize, please?"

"Yes, we did. Have sex."

"See!" said Courtney.

"But she wasn't my student. She was a consenting adult over whom I no longer had any professional responsibility. If you look at the dates on those emails, I don't believe you'll find any correspondence of a sexual nature prior to May 22." There was a silence during which they stared back at him blankly. "That was the date she graduated. Stacia was no longer a stu-dent. As for the appropriate use of university email, it would seem to me that the idea of one colleague hacking into another colleague's account ought to concern you, too. I'm sure that violates university policy, doesn't it? It might've been worth mentioning. But in this case, it's none of the university's concern, because it was my Gmail account."

There was a silence.

Rosemary asked, "Is this true, Courtney?"

"It was Gmail. I'll have to check the dates to make sure. I bet he waited till a minute after midnight for her student status to expire. He's that calculating, Rosemary, I swear he is! Tell me, Philip, why do you like hitting girls? Why does that get you off?"

"I like neither your tone nor your insinuations," Philip said. "And it should go without saying that my proclivities are none of your business. But I will tell you this much. You are jumping to inaccurate conclusions about who was spanking whom."

Then he got up and walked out of the office.

"You gonna come see us at *Dead Freddy's*, Holly?"

"Well, I'm pretty busy. I've got a paper deadline for tomorrow."

"It won't take up your whole night," Honus pleaded. "You should bring some friends, too."

Holly hesitated, gripping the telephone and looking over at Chelsea who was painting the doorframe of Holly's bathroom. The bathroom interior was finished. Recently the Troll had planted new shrubs in the middle of the night. Holly went out one morning, and suddenly bushes were there. All these home improvements concerned Holly. Would she have to pay more rent?

"I'll see what I can do, Honus. But I'm not guaranteeing anything."

Honus was excited because he'd joined a band and they were playing at a local music club. It was a monthly slot on Monday nights when *Dead Freddy's* stopped serving alcohol from seven p.m. to nine p.m. and offered entry to kids and bands who were younger than the legal drinking age. Holly's mid-term research paper for Rosemary Muller was due the following morning. She'd spent weeks stewing over the project and taking copious notes without attempting to impose some order on her thoughts. This was a classic blunder, she knew, but she couldn't help herself.

She didn't even consider recycling her humor essay, one more time. It was a point of honor, to be sure, but she also sensed that this subject would be out of place in Rosemary's seminar. It would sound unserious. The discussions so far had been accessible, and Rosemary's tone was friendly, but the interpretations of Dickinson were unremittingly sober, emphasizing her radical difference, her incipient subversive feminism, and her decentered critique of slavery and religion during the Civil War. None of it was unreasonable, but that, too, was a problem. Where to begin? Among the topics that Holly was invited to choose from, she'd opted for "Representation of Otherness." She had plenty of ideas, but she didn't know where to start. Maybe Rosemary would extend her deadline? Holly couldn't bring herself to confide in anyone about her difficulties, least of all Professor Borden.

"Hey Chelsea," she said. "You ever been to *Dead Freddy's?*"

She'd feared that the bar would be empty but *Dead Freddy's* was jammed, mostly with people younger than the university crowd. High schoolers or even, by the looks of them, junior high kids who'd flocked to the opportunity and now squeezed around tables, laughing, talking shrilly. Holly and Chelsea found a space near the back of the room and ordered Diet Cokes, waiting for the show to begin.

"It's not too late to sign up!" an emcee announced. "Keep your spot under ten minutes." Presently Holly spied Honus and another young man, pulling trolleys toward the platform.

The first two acts were solo hip-hop with pre-recorded backup sound. The first performer got more applause, though Holly preferred the second, a girl who'd let her bangs grow over her eyebrows like a sheepdog, who punctuated the rhythm with her own foot-stomps. Honus fidgeted by the edge of the platform. Soon the emcee approached the microphone. "And now" (he looked down his clipboard), "Honeybunch!"

A smattering of applause, but nothing much happened, because it took them several minutes to set up. There was a guitarist with an amp on a trolley, and a drummer with a snare and bass, also on wheels. There were problems getting the amp plugged in correctly. Holly noticed that the drummer had only one arm. Eventually Honus approached the microphone. "I'm Honey. This is my bunch. It's all over."

The guitarist thrashed out three chords, forward and backward, forward and backward, a chainsaw sequence, and the drummer pumped the foot-pedal to the bass and cracked the snare with one hand, and Honus began to sing:

We mock the doom
of even the stars.
Youth bleeds truth
Youth bleeds truth!
Cyanide pills, candy bars.
Youth bleeds truth
Youth bleeds truth!

Holly had heard Honus sing Christmas carols when he was a little boy, and sometimes around the house with his ear-buds in, he joined a tune with a ghostly falsetto. But she'd never heard him sing like *this,* full-throated and testing the limits of his vocal cords. He retained a high choirboy pitch, but this definitely wasn't "Hark! the Herald Angels Sing."

> *No one can say*
> *That you were right*
> *So sure of yourself*
> *Out of your head—*
> *Yet I still love you*
> *And now you're dead*
> *Now you're dead*
> *Now you're dead!*

They did two more songs, but these were more ragged, and the guitarist and drummer had trouble matching their accompaniment to Honus's singing. Still, the applause and whistles were genuine, and at the end of their set Honus held up his arms and skipped back and forth across the platform to acknowledge them. Then he helped the musicians wheel away their equipment.

"He can sing," said Chelsea. "It's not my kind of music, I admit. But your brother can really sing."

"Yeah, it's . . . it's something all right."

Holly was still digesting what she'd witnessed but she was glad for him. It was a nice surprise. Her little brother was in his element. You couldn't take that away from him. She and Chelsea were putting on their coats when Honus pushed through the crowd and called, "Hey! Hey! You leaving already?"

"It was good, Honus," Holly said. "Way to go! But I can't stay for the other acts."

"Aren't you going to introduce us to the rest of the band?" Chelsea asked.

"They can't stay. The equipment isn't ours, and we're supposed to return it right away."

"It was good, Honus," Holly repeated.

They ended up lingering at *Dead Freddy's* for a few more acts, a few more Diet Cokes, listening to Honus hold forth about music. He chattered happily, still buzzed by his performance. His bandmates, Jerz and Steve, were great guys, he declared. "We're finding a sound, there's something more every day. Honeybunch isn't punk—we're more like Skunk, see? It's a black base of sound with a white stripe on it. And we want to make a stink so loud you can't ignore it."

Holly tried to absorb this information. The one-armed drummer Steve was African American but probably Honus meant something else. The guitarist Jerz was a pale kid as young as Honus. "Who wrote those words?" she asked.

"Those are mine. It's just stuff that goes through my head. The first one I've had a long time, before I started the band. It's about Mom."

For a moment Holly was speechless. She looked around the room, let him rattle on a while longer, before interrupting. "About *Mom?* Cyanide? She wasn't out of her head. What the hell, Honus. What are you talking about?"

Chelsea quickly raised her glass, ducking her eyes.

"Why are you so literal, Holly? It's a *song*."

"It's disrespectful, Honus."

Thus the conversation ended on a tense note. And that was only the beginning of a long night for Holly: she stayed up till 5:15 a.m., writing her paper on "Representation of Otherness." She'd never been so unhappy about a piece of her work before. Why am I doing this? she wondered. Why did I *choose* this task? There was nothing wrong with the idea as such but her execution was a joyless exercise. What was the point? Unless the point was . . . well, she wanted very much for Rosemary to approve of her mind. She craved that respect.

The following morning, they gathered at the seminar table and Rosemary smiled and asked in mock innocence, "Are those presents for me?" Holly, along with the other students, handed over a stack of pages. (She noticed how thin Dalton's paper appeared, and how thick Courtney's paper was; Penelope's work was about the same bulk as Holly's.)

"This was really exciting stuff," said Courtney. "I wish I could've developed my arguments more."

Holly turned her tired head and rubbed her face. She was fed up with Courtney. This had been going on for weeks. Why don't you just climb onto Rosemary's lap and let her stroke your stomach? she thought. Let's hear you purr!

"I'm sure it's fine," Rosemary said. "I look forward to reading them all." She squared the stack of papers, and then slipped them into her briefcase. Holly noticed how everyone watched this action, bidding their work goodbye. Holding their breath. We're all the same, Holly thought. We're pining for approval. Suddenly she remembered:

> *How dreary—to be—Somebody!*
> *How public—like a Frog*
> *To tell one's name—the livelong June—*
> *To an admiring Bog!*

A silent chorus.

According to the magazine,

Try oversized accessories, like a big bag or thick arm bangles. Project confidence with a splash of color. Don't be afraid of heels, either. Heels bring sex and status to any wardrobe, regardless of your height. Stop apologizing for being tall! Don't cover up! You've got a lot of skin on your long body and you shouldn't hesitate to show it. Within the limits of your comfort zone, you shouldn't be shy about your décolletage. Or, if that's not your thing, you can rock in a backless top! Even if you feel shy at first, challenge yourself to experiment with something new.

A week later, it was slow torture in Rosemary's seminar. Everyone wanted to know the grades but had to wait till the end of the two-hour slot before she returned the papers. Today's discussion centered on Dickinson's punctuation, notably her use of dashes. There was so much to say about dashes! How they added an edge to the text and led the reader to the brink of sense. A dash could be a cognitive trigger, demanding a response from the reader, a reciprocal act of introspection. Holly thought she understood this much, but the discussion bogged down on the problem of interpretation when Dalton observed, "Dickinson's work is about herself, sure, but the self isn't consciously knowable so *she* doesn't know what she's about, which makes the work ultimately about *itself*, but since the work is internally inconsistent to the point of unintelligibility, it depends on our own ability to make sense of it, so ineluctably it's not authored by Dickinson but by *ourselves*, so it's really about us—but are we subjects or objects? Can we know?" With a shiver Dalton looked up from his fingers, and Holly felt as if she were witnessing a willed madness.

Finally Rosemary reached into her briefcase and extracted their papers. She slid them across the table to each student.

The fluorescent ceiling light buzzed. (Or was the sound in Holly's ears?) She flipped to the back page and discovered her grade.

C.

A dismal result.

Was she surprised? Not really. She'd known it was weak work. No doubt better than the prefab essays you found floating around the Internet, but that was an embarrassingly feeble comparison and was no consolation, at the graduate level. Getting a C in graduate school was equivalent to a D or an F at lower levels. It was a statement: You're Not Good Enough. Your Mind Is a Dead Battery. Who the Fuck Are You Kidding? The confidence that for a few months had boosted Holly disappeared in a stroke, leaving a horrible empty space in her chest. She raced out of the Crewe Building as if to escape the scene of a crime but that didn't help; the leafless autumn trees and ashen sky didn't sympathize. She stumbled on the uneven sidewalk. There was no comfort on the outside.

Sure, people got bad grades all the time—the campus was crawling with them—but this case was different because it was *her* grade and it was about more than just one research paper. Oh, now she longed to add her voice to the chorus! To join the show! It was one thing to reject the chorus, quite another if someone else made the choice for you.

In a panic, she emailed Rosemary to request an immediate appointment, outside of office hours. She was obliged to call Merle in Special Collections and rearrange her work schedule in order to make it fit. (*"Where we at, Holly Holly? Is it still 1862?"* She replied, *"December." "Fine, fine—no worries!"*)

Although Rosemary had never been anything but cordial, Holly discovered that she was actually afraid, her stomach flitting the next afternoon as she entered the Crewe Building. She went to the toilet before approaching Rosemary's office and, halfway to her door, Holly turned around and retraced her steps and went to the toilet again. What's the matter with me? she wondered. I wasn't this nervous before championship games. Eventually she stood before the door, took a deep breath, and knocked.

"Please come in."

As she sat down, Holly judiciously slid the chair back so that her knees wouldn't bang against Rosemary's desk. Professor Muller's office was snug but enjoyed a nice view overlooking the river and its banks of trees. The windows were closed against the autumn chill, but sounds of a marching band came through distinctly, the bray of horns, the thump of bass drums. Practicing before Saturday's football game.

"How are you, Holly? You haven't said much in class lately. Do you want to talk about your paper?"

"Yes, that's why I came." Holly removed the essay from her back pack and placed it gingerly on the desk between them like an incriminating piece of evidence. "How . . ." she began. "What can I do to make it better?" She was relieved to hear her voice come out firmly, without shaking.

Rosemary leafed through the pages. Holly avoided her eyes, observing her slim wrists, her silver and turquoise bracelets. Professor Muller spent a lot of time in the southwest, Holly knew. She had an eastern accent but she'd spoken of her love for the desert, "the luminosity that was like a patina on every object." Tan and wrinkled, her grey hair still impressively thick, Rosemary evinced a mature health, an athletic vigor to which Holly was attune. She must be a swimmer or something, Holly speculated. She was sure that she wasn't the first one to think: *when I'm that age I hope I look that good.*

"The last half of this paper is just padding," Rosemary said. "To be honest, I don't see a direct connection to the subject." Holly felt her throat tighten. This was true—toward the end of that long night in front of her computer she'd dashed off pages, pounding the keys without revising what she'd written. "So, in the end, despite the paper's length, you don't really address 'otherness' in much depth. Perhaps you haven't been exposed yet to some things you need to know. Your work seems rather uninformed by theory."

Holly knew that this was true, too, but it wasn't the complete truth. "I've read plenty of critics, actually. And I quoted R.W. Franklin a bunch of times."

"Oh, he's fine but for a subject like this one, you should've talked more about false binary oppositions and where Dickinson tries to resist them. For instance, you might've mentioned Kristeva or Cixous."

She pushed the paper back to Holly.

"What did they say about Dickinson?"

She detected a flicker of amusement in Rosemary's eyes. When Rosemary answered, her tone remained friendly but Holly had the impression that she was working at it, with the sort of polite emphasis one might use for an elderly person or a child.

"They didn't write about Dickinson," she explained. "No. But how do their ideas inform our reading of the poems? That's an interesting question, don't you think?"

Holly nodded, though in truth she didn't know, yes or no. She understood that Rosemary wasn't impressed by Dalton's manner of theorizing. You could feel it in class. She intended something more purposeful.

"I know this is new to you." Rosemary smiled. "You'll be fine."

It was time to go but before leaving the office, she couldn't resist one last question. "If Dickinson tries to avoid false binary oppositions, why should we talk about them?"

Rosemary frowned. "Because it's an important subject. An absence is itself a statement, a presence that can make itself known."

"Well ... OK ... but which absences do we choose? Which deserve our attention?"

"That's an ongoing inquiry. The quick answer, though, are the ones that matter most."

To whom? Holly wondered. To you? But she didn't utter these questions aloud. "Thank you. I won't keep you any longer. Thank you."

On the drive home for Thanksgiving Holly listened to Honus babble happily about his semester and she experienced a pang of envy. Art and Anita had been apprehensive about her brother going off to college, a kid whose spelling was SMS inflected and who didn't even know how to do his laundry. ("I'll have to use coins? They don't take cards?") No one, in contrast, was worried about Holly in graduate school. Oh, everyone knew: Holly was *serious*. But look what had happened: she'd floundered and made a mess of things while Honus had blossomed. When Holly picked him up at the dorm, he'd literally pranced toward the Comet. Her brother could shave now, and he sported new pencil sideburns. She'd never seen him so chipper. Holly doubted that he'd done much studying this semester, since all he talked about was Honeybunch and the gigs they were getting, the parties. They were even going to be paid for a performance after Christmas. Never mind the books. "One hundred bucks!" enthused Honus. "This is only the beginning!"

They stopped along the interstate to fill up on gas. Honus held the pump to the side of the car while Holly fished in her purse for her credit card.

"Aren't you cold?" she asked.

Honus wore his usual baggy black shorts and black T-shirt. No coat. It was barely forty degrees. He shrugged, and then the phone rang in his pocket. He extracted it, glanced at the number. "Sorry. Gotta take this."

So Holly finished pumping the gas while Honus paced around the station area, talking animatedly and sawing the air with his free hand, ignoring a chill wind that gusted off the highway and nearby stubble of harvested fields. When he eventually returned to the car, he glowed and clenched his fist as if in victory.

"What's that all about?" Holly asked. "You get another show?"

"No," he said with a prim smile. "It was my girlfriend."

Holly didn't catch herself in time, and blurted, "YOU got a girlfriend? *Really?*"

But Honus didn't seem offended. "Yeah, her name is Jenn. Met her at one of the gigs. She's cool. You know how it is. You get attention, you get perks."

Holly thought about this as she drove away from the station and merged back onto the interstate. Her little brother was channeling The Voice. "Perks? Come on! You're talking about a person."

"Hey, I don't force her when we do weird stuff."

"Oh my God. Honus, if you've learned anything in life, it's that you'll keep it that way. Promise?"

"Geez, Holly. *Stop the freakin' lecture!* I'm not mean."

Now he was irritated and defensively took out his phone and began scrolling through messages.

"Sorry. I shouldn't have said that. I know you're not mean."

Silence. The car bellied down the road. Minutes passed. Eventually, Holly teased, "Does she call you Honus? Or does she call you Honey?"

"Cut it out."

During the drive, Holly mulled over her conversation with Rosemary Muller for the fortieth time. She'd resisted it at first, but she could see Rosemary's point. What a person left out

spoke volumes. An absence could be a presence. Glancing at
Honus, she found herself thinking of her mother. Dead now
for fourteen years, she would still be at the Thanksgiving table with Holly. The memory of her opposite her father. Her
silk blouse under her apron. Her voice. How much did Honus
recall? She looked at him again, noticing a resemblance in the
jawline, and felt a spasm of grief so intense that her wrists
jerked, the car swerved momentarily out of its lane. "Fuck's
sake!" Honus barked. "Keep your eyes on the road." Quickly
Holly corrected their trajectory. But she had no desire to shut
out the sadness—quite the contrary. She couldn't erase her
mother's absence and create a blank. No. Art and the rest of
the family, surely they felt her, too.

Not long ago she'd dreamed about their lost cat, Pirate,
who'd disappeared in the accident but had popped up incon-
gruously in her sleep—a nightmare, really—looking down at
her from the headboard. Mewing. His return probably had
something to do with the stress of an approaching deadline, a
task both urgent and incomplete, as if Pirate had escaped his
travel cage and wandered through time all the way to her room
to remind her. Eyes closed, her head on her pillow, she'd heard
his scratchy voice quite distinctly. It was spooky. So even an
absent *cat* could be present, for God's sake, jolting her brain.
How weird was that? Of course Rosemary was right to speak
of absences.

But a part of Holly revolted, too, at the thought of recruit-
ing the poet for somebody's agenda. It sounded uplifting when
Rosemary spoke of dissolving binarity and defending the spirit
of Seneca Falls and a radical commitment to life, and though
Holly believed that many poems were compatible with such
readings—sure!—she didn't like how Rosemary implied that
Emily (her professor also referred to the poet by her first name)

was talking about the world in the way they spoke in a seminar room. As if, then and now, they were on the same team.

Really? Holly wondered. This assumption, more than any particular argument, troubled her. It sounded very nice, downright flattering, but all you had to do was look around the conference table (Courtney, Dalton, Penelope, herself and Rosemary) and bluntly ask: is this true? Are we really on the same team? Holly felt increasingly unsure of many things but she was certain that most of the time Dickinson was smarter, more articulate, and more faithful to a roving, dissatisfied mind that regularly put into question its own articulateness. Wasn't it naive, even arrogant, for them to pretend that they were in the same league?

Who are we kidding? she thought. There was a difference between the fluid intensity of full court action and the circumscribed facility of a neighborhood game of H.O.R.S.E.

At Thanksgiving dinner Honus told stories about his band. Present that day, in addition to Art and Anita, were Anita's mother, Grandma Trudy, and her nephew Jack and his wife Maria and their google-eyed, drooling toddler, Strapp. Bowls went round the table and Honus promised to share live concert footage that had been posted on the Internet.

Before the meal, Grandma Trudy had asked Holly, "When are you going to give me a great-grandchild like Strapp?" Grandma meant no harm, but Holly responded by raising her shoulders and making a show of shuddering. Then, a second too late, she cast a sideways glance across the kitchen and saw Maria, who'd been reaching down some glasses, staring at her. *Shit!* she thought. Holly didn't want to offend Maria. She seemed like a nice person. But too late now! And, even after her gaffe, Holly couldn't help thinking: what kind of stupid illiterate name is Strapp? What's the matter with Jack and Maria?

At the table while passing the sweet potatoes, Holly wondered about herself. When away from home, she didn't feel antagonistic; in fact, she often entertained fond thoughts of these relatives. They were decent and likeable people. But in their presence she discovered an unexpected reservoir of nastiness. Was this something stirred up by study?

"The other guys in the band," Honus was saying, "are from outside Chicago. My guitarist Jerz is from Naperville, he's got a van we can use, and Steve, that's my drummer, he's from East Chicago, on the Indiana side. He was in the army and got sent to Afghanistan and had been there for like, five minutes, when a dude next to him steps on a landmine. Killed the dude instantly and Steve got a taste of it, too, and that's why he's like he is. He gets help and counseling from the VA and he's using the G.I. bill at the university but mainly he does music. He's in a couple of bands but I'm hoping he'll concentrate on Honeybunch."

Art inquired about Steve's army division, but Honus hadn't heard, or didn't recall, but he went on to describe how Steve was unhappy with his prosthetic arm. "He has one but says it sucks, it bugs him and he won't use it. He's under pressure to use it, because the army and the docs think it makes them look bad if he refuses." Art asked if Steve was covered by Chapter 31 for his rehabilitation. "Dad, I don't know all that stuff," Honus said.

"It's important stuff," Art persisted.

The conversation shifted briefly to the wars. At least they'd be over soon, everyone agreed. Wouldn't they? Holly thought of her Granddad Winegarten, who wasn't here today, as he and Grandma Winegarten always spent Thanksgiving with her cousins, but several Christmases ago, Granddad had surprised

Holly by siding with her about Iraq. "It ain't worth it, it's gonna be a terrible waste." They'd been watching TV footage of refugees streaming from Iraq into Jordan and Syria. "Look at 'em!" Grandad was a tall man with a big belly and two knee replacements who had seen action in Korea. He was prominent in his local V.F.W. lodge. That day, he repeated a story about his buddies taken prisoner at Pyongtaek. He'd shared this memory many times before, but they heard him out, one more time. "Who thinks about those guys now?" he asked. "You tell me." Holly was glad that Granddad took her side but he also used the word "gook" and when he asked about her team, he said things like, "In college basketball, I bet not even half the girls are white, are they? That's where all the money goes." That was Granddad Winegarten.

"Steve was invited to be in the Homecoming Parade with some other veterans," Honus said, "they wanted him to ride on a float. It was going to say 'We Support Our Troops.' But he told them to shove it. He says the university is always sucking up to people who don't support the troops and it was going to take more than a stupid parade. It really pissed him off."

There was a silence, his meaning temporarily obscured by the distraction that he'd said "pissed" at the Thanksgiving table in front of Grandma Trudy. But Art and Anita didn't call him on it. Soon they gathered round Honus's laptop, where the drummer Steve or guitarist Jerz were only occasionally visible in the clip while Honus stalked the stage, his high voice surprisingly clear. Honeybunch had definitely improved since the gig at *Dead Freddy's*. In the video, they performed "Mom" and a new song called "Rabbits."

> *Unbutton yourself*
> *Let out the rabbits!*

Much of the Thanksgiving weekend Holly hid from other people. But this wasn't her anti-social side, it was a practical necessity. How else was she going to finish reading the 768 pages of *Nicholas Nickleby*? The book was as thick as a brick and about as digestible. She'd assumed her Victorian novel class with Professor Jefferies would be no problem, since she'd already read *Middlemarch* and liked it, as well as *Great Expectations* and a couple of other titles on the list; but there remained additional novels, fantastic for the sheer bulk of pages, like gargantuan verbal slag heaps from the satanic mills of the Industrial Revolution. How did people find the *time* for such monstrosities? For Holly, the appealing poignancy of *Great Expectations* was now eclipsed in *Nickleby* by another Dickens, one she could hardly believe was the same writer, a tiresome windbag of tedious dialogue, wooden jokes, contrived coincidences and simpering, maudlin female characters. They were downright nauseating, after the Thanksgiving pumpkin pie. Why read this in the 21st century?

Holly needed to finish this brontosaurus turd of a novel so that she could find the time to focus and properly devote herself to her final paper for Rosemary's seminar. The assigned subject was "Dance in Emily Dickinson: Toward a Poetics of the Void."

On Saturday, Art asked her, "You gonna spend your entire vacation with your nose in a book?"

"I have *deadlines!*" It vexed her how no one seemed to understand that vacations did not exist for someone of her pursuits. You didn't quit after putting in eight hours. There was always another book to read, a critical article to digest, note-taking—it was never-ending! *Vacation?* "I'm totally swamped!"

"OK, OK. We'd just like to see you some, that's all."

This gave Holly a twinge. Yesterday Anita and Maria had invited her to drive to a mega-mall for Black Friday, and Holly had declined; how awful it would be to spend hours trying on clothes in front of them, feeling their gaze and listening to their advice. She knew that the invitation was for form's sake, anyway; they would have more fun without her. Art wanted nothing to do with Black Friday, either, so this would've been a good opportunity for them to do something together, but Holly spent most of the day in her room. She came out once in the afternoon to make herself a snack and found Art regluing insulation on the back kitchen door. Some strips had come unstuck. That was how he was occupying himself on his day off, with the most boring task in the universe. Honus sat at the kitchen table with a pair of scissors, cutting a news magazine to ribbons. He would put words in a bowl and fish them out as a way to generate new lyrics. He'd described this approach to Holly on the drive down to Sheridan, and she began to tell him about Dada and artistic precedents for the cut-up method, until he said, "Give it a rest, Hol." Now he had a big mess in front of him, snipping and snipping, while Art patiently pressed an insulation strip, waiting for the glue to set. She lifted the tab on a can of tomato juice—*spak!*—and her father looked at her over his shoulder, waiting for Holly to say something. She went back to her room, to her reading.

For "Dance in Emily Dickinson: Toward a Poetics of the Void," Holly undertook to please her instructor. She followed Rosemary's lead as closely as possible. She wrote about "the anxiety of binarity and the use of disparate fullness to accept and celebrate life even in the face of dualistic pitfalls." She even wrote—though she could see no pertinence—that Dickinson's rhythms were like a "jazz style." (She'd heard Rosemary say this more than once.) She also quoted a 1999 article by Rosemary Muller on how the Civil War was an inverted mirror image of a civil war that raged within Dickinson herself. She wasn't sure exactly what that *meant*, but she wrote it. For this paper she tried to join the chorus, to be a frog in a bog—very froggy, in fact, downright slimy, if need be, to find the means to improve upon her earlier grade of C.

On the day she turned it in, her paper was the thickest of the pieces submitted in their small group. (Even more pages than Courtney Davies!) There were only three students now, as Dalton had dropped out of the seminar after Thanksgiving. By chance, Holly had bumped into him in a sandwich shop the previous week and attempted small talk.

"How are you doing?"

"What?" He licked his puffy lips. The last time she'd heard him speak, he'd said that time and space were imposed by the subject and were best understood as an entropy domesticated into an infantilized commodification.

"I said, how are you doing?"

He shrugged.

"And your research?" she asked brightly.

"What's it to you?" He turned away.

Dalton didn't do small talk.

A week later, Holly returned to the Crewe Building, full of anticipation. And this time Rosemary didn't wait till the end of the discussion to return the papers. "Today we can talk more about *your* work," she told the group. Holly's throat tightened as Rosemary handed over her paper, her vision momentarily blurred. Then she saw her grade: A minus.

Relief. Oh, mercy! A minus! She had saved face. Better than that, actually, for an upper-level doctoral seminar when she was only a beginning master's student. Once she really got the hang of things, she could be a consistently A student! She flipped hungrily through the pages, looking for comments, but there weren't very many. Next to the citation of Rosemary Muller's article, Rosemary had written, "*not really necessary!*" followed by a smiley face. Yes, Holly had saved face.

But the satisfaction was short-lived. Even before that day's seminar was finished, during what should've been a victory lap, Holly looked around the room with growing impatience as Rosemary spoke of her reactions to their research. Penelope dutifully scribbled further notes, Courtney gazed raptly at Rosemary (she must've gotten an A, a big fat A, unadulterated by a minus) as Rosemary said, "We've come a long way this semester, you've shown a lot of spark." The best thing about today, Holly realized, was not her grade but the fact that Christmas was near and this seminar was coming to an end.

She thought ahead to future graduate seminars and survey courses, to the prospect of repeating this experience. The next day, in her last lecture with Professor Jefferies, he advertised his next semester's seminar, which was devoted entirely to Dickens. He blatantly tried to recruit his students. "The reading list is online, online is where you can find it." He paused, his eyes alight, unable to contain himself: "We're doing *Martin Chuzzlewit!*"

Lord oh Lord. Was that what she had to look forward to? Was that the path she'd chosen? And it wasn't just Martin Chuzzlewuzzlefuckwit and other such sad dead trees. The same doubtful question hovered even over her favorite, Dickinson, whom graduate school had sapped of her anarchic energy and robbed of her pith. Holly couldn't see herself writing about her again as she'd done with Rosemary. Courting approval, calculating which buttons to push. Pandering. It wasn't what she wanted to do. How she wanted to *live*. She'd been relieved by her A minus, but proud? No. Certainly not.

She remembered,

I aimed my Pebble—but Myself
Was all the one that fell—
Was it Goliath—was too large—
Or was myself—too small?

After Professor Jeffries' lecture, she drove to her shift at Stoddard's Family Restaurant, where recently waitresses had started teasing Holly about boyfriends, offering to set her up with a customer. "We can help you out, girl!" They'd marked her as a lonelyheart, an underachiever on the subject of romance.

Holly didn't believe that a boyfriend was the solution to her problems but she thought back to Thanksgiving and how, after she and Honus had said goodbye to their parents (Anita gave Holly a package of fancy coffee as a parting gift: "here's something to help you study!"), they'd driven past the Nichols' house. Windows glowed golden in the November dusk. Holly smelled the aroma of coffee in the car, and she pictured the Nichols family, Scott and Randy and Mickey, gathered for the holiday meal.

"You ever hear from them?" Honus asked.

It was as if he'd read her mind.

"No. You?"

"No. But I never knew them like you did."

Honus said "*them*" but he surely meant Scott; he was being diplomatic. Holly said nothing more but she wondered who Scott held in his arms now. There was none of the anguish and longing of the old days, just idle curiosity. I'm not that silly girl anymore, Holly told herself.

But today she also wondered: well, if I'm not that silly girl, who am I? She considered her experience in graduate school and she wasn't impressed with what she had become.

She knew which person she liked better.

"So, I was wrong," she told Chelsea on Sunday night as they sat drinking tea and looked out the window and watched the light disappear on newly fallen snow. "I'm not cut out for this world." With this last phrase, she wasn't trying to be melodramatic, she meant only the world of graduate study in literature, but she crossed her legs while speaking and her ankle barked against the coffee table and sent the teapot wobbling dangerously near the edge. Chelsea caught it just in time. Holly rubbed her ankle and considered yet another giraffe incident. An earlier sense of unshareable solitude ebbed within her. It was still there. It still hurt, too.

"Maybe you need a break," Chelsea said. "Save up some money, don't take out more loans. Then see how you feel. You can go back to school later."

"If you get disconnected from this stuff, it's hard to get back into it. I wish I could just drop out and travel. Like they do in novels. Go to Europe or something."

"Sounds sweet. But do you have the money?"

"Of course not. I'd have to get another job, save up first. Teaching English in Italy would be nice. There's stuff about it on the Internet. Maybe I could earn my way."

Chelsea smiled. "You speak Italian?"

Holly straightened. She knew that she sounded lost, even a bit ditzy. "It's only an idea. Excuse me." Holly rose to her feet, paying attention to the cups. "I'm going to get some air."

"Hey," Chelsea said. "Don't be mad."

"No, no. I'm not mad. Maybe a bit . . . antsy."

Holly put on her coat and scarf and a stocking cap and went out for a walk.

Christmas lights flashed in bushes; the air was chill and still, interrupted only by the metallic clang and scrape of a neighbor's snow shovel. She moved briskly and soon reached the downtown area where students gathered behind the fogged windows of coffee shops and music rumbled in bars. The temperature was dropping fast; it was going to be a cold night. She avoided the main quad and when she came to the edge of campus she saw, next to a high-rise dormitory, two bundled-up boys shooting baskets under the lights at an outdoor hoop. Never mind the bitter cold. Or maybe it was because of the cold: it made everything harder, playing with chapped, numb hands and trying to move in heavy clothes while the ball bounced badly and there were slick patches on the ground where the ice and snow hadn't been decently cleared. All that added to the fun. Holly stopped to watch as they slipped and cursed and laughed and attempted scoop shots; she respected the protocol of hanging on the periphery, waiting till the ball bounced her way and then passing it immediately back to them so that they could continue. She lingered, and the next time the ball bounced her way, she kept it, dribbled in, took a shot. She asked no permission, no one greeted her, but a couple of shots later one of the boys threw her a pass for another shot.

Now they were three, chasing the ball when it caromed, taking shots or passing it on, keeping the ball alive. "Yeah! Yeah!" one of them shouted when Holly nailed a long hook shot, impressed at what she could do, but they didn't stop to say their names, they kept working around the ball. Holly threw her cap onto a snowbank and let her hair fly in her face. For another twenty-five minutes they kept at it—huffing and improvising, impervious to the conditions, following the bounce and, before long, Holly's lead—until she said "Good night!" and left them again, headed back home, retying her scarf and putting on her hat.

"Night!" they called.

The next day, in the Special Collections department, her ears felt itchy. A taste of frostbite. Merle was in Inez's office and Holly was alone in her cubicle. She pulled down the acid free carton PBL 259 and took it to the scanner. She opened a new packet of letters. And what . . . *what in the world? Was it possible?*

THREE

EMILY AND MICHAEL

May 19, 1863
My dearest,
In the glare we would be exposed—but would we be seen?
Light has many shades.
That is why our separation is necessary. My love—will you
forgive me? My friends are a very few. I can count them on my
fingers —and have fingers to spare.
This is my Faith:
We will be known by our secret deeds. Not by name—but
by our dreams.
Yours lovingly,
Emily

It took Holly several months to confirm her discovery. It didn't
appear fully-formed like a gift in a Christmas stocking. If she
disliked coincidences in bad Victorian literature, she was even
more skeptical of them in her own life, and inclined to disbe-
lieve. Even so, on that December morning there was something
eerily familiar when she extracted that piece of paper that had
been archived for more than fifty years and unfolded it and
carefully laid it flat on the scanner. She pressed the button;
the laser swept; the machine did its work. This time, though,
instead of putting the letter aside and reaching for the next
one, she paused. Something tingled in her mind like the frostbite on her ears. Seconds earlier, she'd glanced at the page to
make sure the margins were correctly aligned on the glass. She

hadn't read a word. But now she turned it over and began to read. She couldn't say why she decided to look more closely. It wasn't part of her job. In the beginning she'd been more curious and peeked at the correspondence but soon lost interest because there was so much repetition in these letters, plain talk of weather, troop movements, food; sometimes the words were hard to unscramble, written in miniscule cursive in an attempt to save paper. She'd scanned hundreds, if not thousands of these scraps—but this one made her slow down; she hadn't yet grasped the contents but something was different. The size of the script, almost childlike, the funny-looking punctuation. Large dashes like eruptive slashes.

"The celestial vacation of thought—"

A far cry from the usual homely wishes and inquiries about crops. When Holly became conscious of the source of her hesitation, she smiled. How goofy! There was a similarity between the writing here and the fascicles of Dickinson's poetry that she'd seen online. In Rosemary's seminar, she'd learned about the problems of manuscripts. Many published anthologies made Dickinson look like a minimalist, with tidy poems of a few lines, not enough to fill a page. Early editors had naively "corrected" her punctuation in an attempt to render it conventional and at the same time to reign in the rhythms. Rosemary had pointed out the problems with this presumption, for instance when Dickinson wrote so largely that three words took up the entire line of a page. The visual effect amplified the content; the words weren't a tiny peep; a small text could be LOUD.

Holly checked the carton reference, which mentioned the non-transcribed correspondence of several soldiers: Andrew Leahy, Michael Donahue and Colum Conrad. According to the label, these men served in the 28th Massachusetts Regiment of the Union Army. Upon further examination, she confirmed that this letter belonged to the correspondence of Michael Donahue. There were several handwritings in the bundle but this wasn't unusual, because the preliminary cataloguing included letters both to and from the catalogued correspondent.

Holly paused. Well . . .

May 23, 1863

My dearest,

Tonight after I seal this I shall lie awake wondering when my words will reach you. Tomorrow I shall be asleep on my feet—but still lying, to anyone who sees me.

Why should you be my brother's keeper? No Cain—you!

Where are your arms, Michael? I could walk to Rome and find more than ruins. If only we could MEET—

Yours lovingly,

Emily

That night Holly looked up information about the 28th Massachusetts Regiment. Sure, it was from the same state where Dickinson had lived, but there were 62 regiments and the 28th, Holly learned, was composed of Irish and Irish Americans, and it had been raised in Boston. Not in Emily's Amherst. That didn't fit, not for the daughter of a prominent Calvinist family whose grandfather had founded Amherst College, whose father had been a U.S. Congressman and leading local citizen. Emily herself, aside from a brief spell at Mount Holyoke Female Seminary, had rarely left Amherst or even the family manor, called Homestead. What connection would she have with an Irishman—very likely Catholic—who, Holly learned a short time later, combing through the records, had died at the

Battle of Chancellorsville? The only reason his letters figured in the collection was because of his comrade Leahy. Leahy had also served in the 28th regiment and survived the terrible battles of Fredericksburg, Chancellorsville and Gettysburg. He'd also been present at Lee's surrender at Appomattox. Leahy had saved Donahue's personal effects; his granddaughter had donated them, along with Leahy's much larger correspondence, to the university back in 1956, and the materials had never been properly sorted and catalogued.

"Merle," Holly asked, "why wouldn't they send the letters of a fallen soldier back to his family?"

"What do you mean?"

Holly chose her words carefully. She didn't want to admit that she'd been reading instead of scanning. Reading slowed things down; reading signified that she was dawdling on the job.

She lied, "I've been doing some research on the side, for a class I'm taking? And I've noticed that some of the people who've donated to our collection have different names. Just seemed kind of funny to me, that's all."

Merle rubbed the side of his nose. "Hard to say, depends. All it takes is a marriage and names will change. Or somebody dies, they don't always know how to find the family. Especially in those days, in the chaos of the war. There could be a thousand reasons."

"Dickinson's brother, William Austin Dickinson, graduated from Amherst and Harvard Law School. At the outbreak of the Civil War, he avoided conscription by paying $500 to an Irish laborer to serve as his replacement. William became a successful lawyer and prominent civic leader in Amherst, and later served as treasurer at Amherst College. He presided over town

meetings and acted as president of the Village Improvement Association."
RICHER, Andrew, "Profile of W.A. Dickinson, 1829-1895," *Supplement of 19ᵗʰ Century Studies*, 32:2, May 1974, p. 61.

Holly felt fired up, full of purpose. The end of her first semester in graduate school had been her nadir, but now she returned to the university with renewed energy—this time, not for graduate advancement but to probe her secret. Her job in Special Collections required a student status and, following Chelsea's advice about avoiding more debt, she increased her hours at Stoddard's Family Restaurant. On weekends, she made deviled eggs by the hundreds, applying the creamy filling out of a squeeze-bag, swirling gold into egg after egg. With two jobs, working seven days a week, she kept up with expenses and tuition fees and also managed to squirrel away some savings, so suddenly the notion of foreign travel acquired a new credibility, as something more than an escapist whim. She surfed the Internet for information about visas and work permits in Italy. Getting legal papers was complicated, but it could be facilitated if she maintained the fiction of being a student.

For her classes, she took the bare minimum required by university rules. She avoided a challenging seminar like Rosemary's or a mind-numbing lecture course like Professor Jefferies', and signed up for Elementary Italian and an evening class on mythology. Neither would count toward a graduate degree, but she didn't care.

At the library, absorbed in the Michael Donahue letters, Holly felt a mounting excitement, a gratifying sensation of an intuition being confirmed. On her work-table there were always several acid-free cartons which rotated in and out from the long rows of cartons kept in storage. But now one of them did not budge; it sat there, always within reach, while others came and went. She'd broken the chronological order, created a gap. Merle didn't know or worry, assuming a forward momentum. Holly appeared industrious at her station and, most of the time, she was. She planned to plug the hole later, after she'd satisfied her curiosity. But, for now, she hid the documents in the safest place she knew: in plain sight.

The semester sped along. By March her research had advanced to the point where she was almost certain that her speculations were true. She was still trying to piece together a fuller story about the relationship between Michael Donahue and Emily Dickinson, how they had fallen in love. She looked through other letters from the 28th Massachusetts regiment, hoping for more material, but it appeared that this packet was the only source for Donahue, given his death and the circumstances with his comrade-in-arms, Leahy. So, what to do now? What was the next step?

There were giddy moments, especially in the beginning, when Holly delighted in handling the letters and holding the paper up to the light and considering each ink stroke. The objects exerted a primitive fascination. Most appealing of all was the page with the long poem that began "*Will you prepare— a sturdy box / for my ravishing—mind—*" This wasn't part of a letter but took up a sheet of its own in the same handwriting. It must've accompanied a letter, as a gift. A final, fair copy! Holly checked the *Collected Poems* and a concordance of Dickinson correspondence and found no trace of this work. It appeared to be a "new" addition to the canon, and now she held it in her hand. The only person on earth who knew it existed. She contemplated the crumbling yellow paper and took in a deep breath. Rosemary Muller had never dreamed of the likes of this! Probably no one since Michael Donahue had pondered these lines, a frozen moment reaching across time. Holly smiled. This must be how Art felt when he saw a Honus Wagner baseball card!

But this kind of pleasure in the physical object quickly palled for Holly. She wasn't of a collector's disposition, so baseball cards or their literary equivalent didn't fascinate her for their own sake. She felt a much greater interest in the words, which by the third reading had jumped from the page and taken up residence in her brain and, independent of the original traces, were now a part of herself. She couldn't have removed them if she'd tried. Now she was a vessel for these words as she went about her everyday life, walking to work or grating a carrot or lying in bed, dreaming her self into the darkness.

Her discovery gave her a marvelous feeling—oh, she wanted to share it! How could she keep this experience bottled up? Otherwise it was like laughing alone or, for that matter, crying alone. Yes, she thirsted to share.

So she was ripe, one unseasonably warm March evening when she went out to dinner with Philip Post and, after having had too much to drink, she almost told him everything. This conversation was unplanned—frankly, his invitation had been a shock. But the fact that he was so different from Rosemary Muller, so smilingly friendly, lowered Holly's guard. From a certain vinous perspective, Philip seemed a person she could confide in. He might know how to translate something vitally old into an actual form that others could appreciate. He could help Holly share her affection . . .

A momentary delusion, of course, when what he really wanted was a standing O.

"It's your guy again! Holly, come see!"

The waitresses at Stoddard's Family Restaurant had begun to pester Holly about a tall blond customer with peculiar eating habits. He always ordered the daily special, which included a trip to the salad bar. The special could vary, depending on the day, but on his trip to the salad bar he took only one thing: three bean salad. He ignored other items, which was atypical, because usually people piled their plates with a variety of food. This fellow filled his plate, too, but with only three bean salad. He was obsessed. One day two waitresses, Marcia and Kali, burst into the kitchen. "Hear it?" Marcia said. From the other side of the swinging door came a metallic scraping, the sound of someone finishing a buffet tray. They doubled over in hilarity. "What's so funny?" Holly asked. When she volunteered that she was the one who made the three bean salad, their eyes shone. Since the man was tall (his nickname alternated between "Mr. Three Bean" and "Stringbean") and since he always ate alone, he and Holly would make a good couple, right? *Obviously!* It was time to set them up!

Holly didn't find this funny at all. She knew the waitresses were bored out of their minds and hungry for any distraction, gossiping about customers and enjoying in-house pranks. That was how they got through their day. But Holly didn't want to be a character in their latest drama. One of the things she'd liked about Stoddard's was that it felt removed from the university, far enough away from Grainball U that you didn't see the student coffeehouse crowd. It was just the Ordinary World. But when Marcia and Kali joked that she would be *perfect* for Roger (that was his real name, they'd discovered), not just in terms of their height but also for his bookishness (he often read while he ate), it was an unwelcome reminder of how the Ordinary World perceived *her*. "You'd have so much to talk about! In addition to beans!" They extolled Roger's virtues, such as he always tipped 22%, which was a high rate for Stoddard's, since many of their customers were stingy senior citizens who sometimes "forgot" to tip; when Roger finished his food and his reading he took out a pencil and made a calculation on the paper placemat, and left the precise sum to the penny. "Roger is a steady guy and he's not a cheapskate, Holly, even if he doesn't spend it on clothes. Come on, girl!"

"Cut it out," she said.

Of course, when she went out to the buffet line to replenish the three bean salad, she couldn't resist taking a peek at the man. He dressed in old black jeans and a T-shirt, sometimes he wore a lumpy sweater, and his tennis shoes were very white and new. His chin was a bit pointed and protruding but otherwise his features were pleasant. Still, Holly had no desire to approach him. "I've already got a boyfriend," she lied, when Marcia and Kali quizzed her.

"What's his name?" Marcia fired back.

Holly hesitated, and Marcia rolled her eyes and obviously didn't believe her.

"Nobody's business," Holly said.

Kali, though, took a different tack. "So what? Your boyfriend doesn't need to know. Have some fun in life, Holly!"

Minding her own business, reading in Sandhurst's Coffee Shop, she sensed that she was being watched. She looked up and saw Philip Post, smiling down at her.

"Do you have a minute?"

"Philip, I've already made myself clear."

"Yes, *you* have. But I haven't. Won't you let me speak to you?"

"Are you stalking me?"

"Oh, sorry."

This last word wasn't directed to Holly but to a woman holding a tray of three steaming lattés. She was trying to get past him to a table. Philip impeded her way. He leaned to let her pass. Before he could resume speaking, an employee came pushing a cart from the other direction, so he had to lean again.

"I wanted to say—"

"Just a little more, please," said the employee, edging forward. "Excuse me."

"Oh, for God's sake, sit down," said Holly.

It was a public place, after all, so it seemed an unlikely setting for anything too creepy. Might as well hear him out and get it over with.

Philip took a chair and looked around him, as if wary of eavesdroppers.

"Why don't you like me?" he asked.

"I don't even know you," Holly said. "But I'm not going to explain myself to you. If you have something to say, Philip, say it."

He mulled, taking his time. Then his eyes fixed on her book. He recited,

"I dwell in Possibility—
A fairer House than Prose—"

Holly sighed and put down the book. He must've glimpsed the title, *New Readings of Emily Dickinson.* She replied, "How about this one?

" 'A narrow fellow in the grass . . .' "

She paused. "Maybe you know the rest?"

"Is that the one about a snake?"

"Uh huh. A snake in the grass."

"No, can't say that I remember very well." He reached over and picked up the book, trying to find her place. This annoyed her. "There are only a few bits that I recall," he said. "She's big here in America, I gather. The Ice Queen. Once upon a time, a dreary professor at Cambridge obliged me to read some of these ditties. Miss Emily had an original mind but she was rather dour, don't you think?"

"No. Actually I think the opposite."

He put down the book.

"Well then, I defer to your expertise. Are you one of Rosemary Muller's disciples? Isn't she our local Dickinson guru?"

"Yes. But—no. I'm not one of her disciples. Why do you ask? Do you have reservations about Professor Muller?"

Holly was alluding to his confrontation with Courtney Davies in front of Rosemary. The spanking episode. She couldn't resist.

"Reservations? Me?"

He shook his head, his face a study of indifference. If he was lying, he was good at it.

"I took a seminar from Professor Muller," Holly pursued, "with Courtney? Surely you remember her. Maybe by then you were no longer on speaking terms?"

"Oh, *that*," Philip said. "You're talking about *that*. You heard about *that*? Oh dear. Even so, my relationship with Rosemary Muller remains cordial and professional. No worries there. As for Courtney . . ." He lifted both palms. "I see. Maybe this explains a few things about your perception of me. So you heard Courtney assert something. Suffice to say, you don't know the whole story."

"That's none of my business, Philip. Honestly. But that night we went out to dinner, you were way out of line. I speak for myself—it has nothing to do with Courtney. She hasn't affected my perception of you at all."

This last statement was untrue and her voice sounded unconvincing even to herself. She wasn't as smooth a liar as Philip.

"You see, Holly, I'm a lonely stranger in a foreign land." His face went rubbery and he made his eyes ridiculously forlorn. He stretched the moment, displaying a clownish talent. At least he knew how to laugh at himself, she thought. You couldn't say that about many people in the department.

"Oh," she said, "I'm sure you'll bear it somehow."

"You understand me that much?"

"Uh huh."

His face recomposed itself and he looked at her steadily. "Am I really such an ass?"

His tone had changed and the question surprised Holly for its apparent sincerity.

"You truly want my opinion?"

He nodded.

"Well, I'm not your judge," she said. "But you joke so much and you're—you're slippery. And . . . oh, drop it. It's not really my concern."

"Go on, Holly. I can take it."

He waited. Holly was aware of the music in the coffee shop, the buzz of other conversations around them. A banging from the counter as an employee emptied an espresso filter.

"This much I do know, Philip. You can't go strutting around like Oscar Wilde. Nowadays it's not going to work. Maybe you have another set of expectations, but in America we have different customs."

She reached for her coffee cup and finished the dregs.

He pressed his temple, as if summoning a thought. "I have nothing to declare but my penis."

Holly almost choked, but she managed to swallow her coffee. "Yup, now we're getting somewhere. To answer your question, Philip—yes, you *are* an ass."

Philip rubbed his jaw. "I was afraid of that. It has its moments though." Again he looked around him. "Pardon me, I want to order something."

He jumped up and went to the counter. Holly stayed at the table—why should she leave? This was her place. She resumed reading her book and eventually Philip came back with a cup and began to speak of other subjects. He was placid now. The conversation felt different, less like a game. It was as if admitting he was an ass had freed him of the burden of acting like one. Like flipping a switch, everything was more relaxed.

"What are your plans, Holly? Do you see yourself working in a university?"

"No, I'm on my way out. I'm saving up to go abroad. It's time for a change."

"Excellent idea! Where would you like to go?"

At first she avoided specifics but, with his encouragement, she warmed to the subject, and he had some friendly suggestions, mentioning a colleague at an English department in France who might be a useful contact. "They hire native speakers for a year-long contract. Usually it's an exchange but they take independent applications, too. Doesn't pay much but it's a great experience. I spent a lovely year that way in Bordeaux. Drank lots of *rouge*! I'd recommend it to anyone."

Then he told an anecdote about spear fishing in Crete that had no bearing on the conversation but his telling was amusing, so maybe that was the point. "Yes, get out of town, Holly! It's a smart move. Literature departments are finished. The culture has moved on. Most of the dodo birds at universities won't admit it, they're hunkering down in their nests, but it's over.

Ten years from now, you'll see. Maybe less. The technology of the codex is dead."

He smiled as he said this. Holly thought of her professors, their entrenched habits and picayune certainties; they weren't smilers, not about a subject like this. She also thought of the graduate students, drudging and conniving, jockeying for position, eager to take their professors' places. "Literature departments are part of the institution," she said. "I don't think you'll get rid of these people so easily."

"That's an illusion. Literature has no special claim. Here in America, in big public institutions like this one, there used to be home economics departments. You know about those, right? For over a hundred years they catered to young women like you. They offered diplomas, they were serious. But then feminism comes, and that's it: they disappear, in a trice. Literature had a good run, but let's face it, fashions come and go, and people who indulge in special pleading simply don't know their history. No one bothered to study Shakespeare in university till the late nineteenth century, and even then it didn't start at Oxford or Cambridge, it was in workingman's colleges, to inject them with some official culture. It was social engineering from the start. That formula is finished now. We're moving on to other models."

"But you specialize in literature," Holly said. "Does that make you a dodo?"

He raised a cautioning finger. "*Part* of my appointment is in literature. My role is that of a sympathetic doctor, slipping that last extra dose of morphine to the unfortunate patient. There's no need to prolong the pain. I'm an instrument of something larger, and to hasten oblivion is a mercy. I'm not only talking about the tiny world of the university, either. It's so much larger. We've reached the end of the Gutenberg mind."

His eyes glowed. This prospect seemed to provide him a grim titillation. Holly thought of the letters and the poem she'd stashed at her library work-station.

"I don't think people have really changed that much," she said. "Emotions live on. So do dreams, Philip. Feelings are feelings, whatever the form."

"But the form can determine which feelings get expressed. Maybe even the feelings that get *felt*. But don't worry! I'm optimistic about the effects of digital reading on consciousness. There's a growing virtual inscape. Only now it's decided by algorithms interacting more directly with your desires, not by fusty old books and the words of some so-called genius."

Holly gathered her affairs, putting her book and notepad back into her bag. She took her coat from the back of her chair. "I'll miss those so-called geniuses."

"Oh, there'll be something else. Count on it. A medium has to be effective to be heard. Otherwise, you're back to the trite old question about whether there's a sound when a tree falls in the forest and there's no one to hear it. In that sense, I'm a pragmatist."

Holly stood up. "Well, I guess that makes me a . . . a tree." Philip laughed.

"But I'm not falling yet," she said, then left him.

"Hey Holly, can you drive us Saturday?"

"Again? You're joking!"

"We got a gig in Westlake. You don't work Saturday nights. You got plans?"

Holly avoided the question. Honeybunch was getting local attention and more invitations to play but there was a crisis because their guitarist Jerz had quit the band. He found Honus too overbearing. Jerz's guitar playing had never been anything special but the more serious consequence of his defection was that Honeybunch could no longer count on Jerz's van to drive them around. This was a big problem.

"What about Jenn?" she asked.

"Jenn's not free," Honus said. "She's working. Besides, she drove us last time."

Honus couldn't drive himself because he'd lost his license due to multiple speeding tickets while borrowing Holly or Jenn's car. And the drummer Steve didn't drive, either.

"You make me feel like a taxi service."

"Jenn would if she could! You know that."

Honus was touchy about his girlfriend.

"Yes, yes, I know."

Jenn was a soft-spoken biology major—seemed like a fairly intelligent kid, as far as Holly could tell—with corn-yellow hair pulled back in a ponytail so tight it must hurt. She had dimples and large violet eyes, and Honus doted on her. She and Honus shared the same roly-poly build and sometimes they shared clothes, big shorts and black T-shirts emblazoned with names of bands such as *Dognutz*. Honus and Jenn practically lived together in his dorm room, since his roommate had dropped out of school and hadn't been replaced by the housing services, leaving the couple with their own little love nest.

"Next time Jenn's gonna check out a video cam from the university. We're talking serious equipment like they use in the film department, we'll record the band the right way, no bullshit amateur stuff. We'll get a quality vid."

"Nice," Holly said.

"But can you drive us Saturday? *Please?*"

They made arrangements for her to pick him up in front of his dormitory. The last time she'd been up to Honus's room was a Sunday afternoon when Art and Anita came to town for a visit. They were supposed to go out for a meal. Honus gabbed on his cellphone with Jenn while Holly sat on the edge of a bed, waiting for their parents to arrive. Absent-mindedly she reached for a pink and purple package on Honus's desk. The colors caught her eye and she wondered what it was. She paused—*what?* The package contained a pair of edible panties. That's what the label said. Holly saw through the clear plastic that the pink was some kind of stretchy candy or bubblegum. A leering purple face on the package promised "Lotsa Fun!" Quickly Holly put it back down.

Honus kept talking, his telephone conversation rambled inanely. Holly didn't want to think about it but why was Honus leaving such personal stuff out in plain sight? It was bad enough when he left his socks lying around. What was the matter with him?

She didn't disapprove of Honus and Jenn as a couple, that wasn't the point. But there were certain things about her little brother that she didn't care to know. As for Art and Anita— for God's sake, they could arrive any minute! When Honus glanced in her direction, Holly pointed to the package and made a sweeping gesture. He appeared a little sheepish as he picked it up, but then he turned his back and kept on talking. "I don't know what time we'll finish dinner but I can text you . . . or you can text me, it doesn't matter, anytime is fine, but would you like me to text you? Whatever you think is best . . ." Presently he seemed to forget what he was holding in his hand.

Am I being silly? Holly thought. So what if Art and Anita see it? What am I protecting them from?

She wasn't jealous of her brother. No, she could get along fine, thank you very much, without edible underwear. But what a contrast! During her freshman year, she'd been terribly serious, focused on achieving, not fun. Training, physical therapy: making every minute count. The intensity, the *pressure* of it all! "Sure I'll miss you," Honus giggled. "Will you miss me?" Whereas Honus had come to university and merely expanded his diet, so to speak.

A knock on the door.

Holly sprang to her feet but then, annoyed at herself, she sat back down.

"Listen, gotta go. Love you!"

Honus clicked off his phone and, on his way to the door, nonchalantly stuffed the package in his pocket as if to keep it handy.

"Hello! *Hello!*"

Before a performance, Honus could be subdued, a bit surly, sipping from a two-liter jug of Mountain Dew. He wasn't inclined to conversation. For the Westlake gig, she picked him up and then they fetched Steve, loading his drum kit into the Comet. At least without a guitarist, Holly thought, there was less equipment to wedge into the car.

"How you doing, Steve?"

"Holly, you know I adore you."

"I adore you too, Steve."

Holly didn't know how to read him so when he spoke this way, she answered in kind. Steve was often a smartass. Somehow things had started badly at their first meeting. She'd attempted small talk about college life, asking what courses he was taking, and Steve laughed. Not a friendly laugh, either, but a sort of raucous cough, as if she'd said something stupid. "Oh, doing everything I can to get into law school!" he told her. "Hittin' those books!" In another conversation he spoke to her with a fake British accent, which was all the more irritating because he was good at it, and when Holly asked Honus afterward why Steve did that, Honus said he didn't know, he'd only seen him do it with her. She couldn't imagine how horrible it must've been for Steve to lose his arm in an explosion, as well as taking shrapnel in a lung and in his abdomen, according to Honus, but in social encounters Steve was always pushing, and even when joking he was pushing *away*.

The car was loaded and they were poised to go. Looking in the rearview mirror, Holly noticed that Steve hadn't put on his seatbelt. On previous trips he'd done so; he was adroit with his good arm. She hesitated; the police near the campus were strict about enforcing the seatbelt law. Holly didn't want to get another ticket. Steve had put in a pair of ear buds and was listening to music. She glanced at Honus, who was watching her, waiting. He knew what she was thinking. He moved his head, a sharp nod that said *Go*.

Holly spoke loudly over her shoulder. "Steve, could you attach your seatbelt, please?"

He tugged at a bud. "Huh?"

She repeated herself, and he said, "You worried about my safety? How 'bout you do it for me?"

"Can't reach that far, sorry."

"Well, then never mind."

"Goddamnit, we're gonna be late!" Honus exclaimed.

They could've bickered all evening but Holly put the car in gear and started out. She found the minutes long.

"Holly, I have something for you!"

She saw Philip Post chaining his bicycle to a rack in front of the library. Was the timing a coincidence? She doubted it.

"What?"

He fumbled in his shoulder bag. "Here we go." He handed her a paper with an email address and the name *Ludovic Santraud*. "My French colleague, the one I told you about. Write to him and tell him that I'm recommending you. You can write it in English. Don't forget to send your CV. I already emailed him to let him know that you'd be in touch. Ludovic might be able to offer you a contract."

"Really? A job in France? Teaching English?"

"Let's hope so. Write to him."

"Thanks!"

"No worries. You can do your bit for American imperialism. Beats dropping bombs."

August 12, 1863

My dearest—

It is so warm and today I looked out my window and watched the procession to the church yard. Another fallen soldier. When will what we know is wrong and must stop—when will it stop?

I pray for your safety. To the Roman goodness—and to my city of Grace—to any goodness—I pray. This is no time for parsers.

Write to me. Teach me to miss you less—

Your silence is too hard.

Yours,

Emily

The next day at Stoddard's, Kali burst into the kitchen. "Oh my God! He wants to see you!"

"What?"

Holly was picking through a large quantity of cherry tomatoes, prepping a tray.

"It's Roger! He wants to give his compliments to the chef."

"Right," Holly said, not looking up. "I'm sure those were his exact words. Give it a rest, will you?"

Kali and Marcia had persisted in their teasing, in regaling Holly about this customer. It was annoying. Marcia had surreptitiously filmed Roger with her cell phone and brought it back to the kitchen for Holly to watch. "See, he's not sloppy. Doesn't eat like a pig." Now Kali pressed closer.

"Well, I did tell him about you, how you're the genius behind the three bean salad, and since you noticed how much he likes it, you've started calling it the Roger Salad, in his honor."

"No! You didn't say that, did you?"

"It pleased him, Holly. He *asked* to see you. You can't leave him sitting there, can you?"

Holly sighed, wiping her hands on a towel. "OK—we'll do this, and then it's done, and then you'll have to find some other way to entertain yourself, all right?"

Kali was all smiles as Holly pushed through the kitchen door and went out to Roger's table. He was reading.

"Hello," she said. "I'm Holly."

He looked up. "Hello." He appeared perplexed, and instantly Holly understood that Kali hadn't spoken to him about her at all. She and Marcia were probably in hysterics, peering through a crack in the kitchen door.

But since she'd come this far, Holly decided to get it over with. "Some waitresses told me you liked the three bean salad, and since I'm the one who makes it, they thought I should introduce myself. They're just joking around. So . . . well . . . that's it! Bye." She turned and then she heard his chair scrape.

"I'm Roger." He stood and held out his hand and she shook it by the fingers, because the palm was wrapped in a bandage. He shyly let the hand drop to his side before explaining, lifting it again. "Had a bad encounter with a cat."

"Yes . . . a person has to watch out. Well, back to work. Bye."

In some intangible way her experience at Stoddard's Family Restaurant made Holly friendlier to Philip Post the next time she saw him. Although she'd often longed to be invisible, that wasn't the same as being disrespected, a target for jokes. Which was how Kali and Marcia treated her. Now she and Philip sat at a window table at Miüsov's, a tea-house with a Russian theme. She'd invited him here because she'd received an email reply from Ludovic Santraud, requesting that she fill out a form and attach a "letter of motivation." She wanted Philip's advice about what to say in her letter. "I'm definitely motivated." (*Just imagine: six months from now, I could be in Bordeaux!*) "But what does he want to hear?"

"This is encouraging, Holly. He must've liked your CV."

"I hope so. But if I've been lucky, I don't want to jinx it."

"It's not about luck. Don't talk like that."

He lifted the lid of their teapot and peered inside. They'd been waiting while it steeped. Now he poured, and his manner was sympathetic, not ingratiating or flirting. When Philip was like this Holly found it easier to relax. Something similar had happened their previous meeting when he'd stopped perform-ing and asked her, matter-of-factly, if she thought he was an ass. Frankness brought trust, a familiarity of friends.

They spoke about her letter of motivation and he made a few suggestions. Soon their conversation drifted to other sub-jects. His family back in Lancashire, his retired parents who entered their calla lilies in competitions and his sister who was a podiatrist in Lincoln. "I'm the only one abroad. After Cam-bridge I kept on moving."

"Why did you feel the need to leave?"

"Oh, it's school, isn't it? Some of us were always the first in the classroom to raise our hot little hands. We knew the answer! A nice feeling, to be the clever one. Remember that? Now we're not so little and we like to pretend there are serious reasons like research and all the rest, but that's only a pretext. The truth is, we're still little kids, and we like the attention."

Something in the set of his mouth made it easy to picture Philip as a little boy. Holly didn't correct him for saying "we" or attempt to explain that no, she hadn't been the first in her classroom to raise her hand. She'd been a back row person. She thought of Jérémy Ndao, how he was similar to Philip, after a fashion. The university was a safe berth for such people. Courtney Davies aspired to join them, too. It was a specific breed, the classroom performer, the pet who loved its pen.

She told him about her own family, Art's coaching and Anita's recent success in expanding the local farmer's market. (It wasn't the first time Holly had tried to assuage her uneasy conscience about being unkind to her step-mother by singing her praises to a stranger.) She also told him about Honeybunch, and said it might be interesting for Philip to see Honus perform.

Philip put down his cup.

"*Honus?* You've got a brother called Honus?"

This wasn't new territory for Holly but answering this question always required some explaining, especially for a person like Philip for whom baseball was foreign. By the time she'd finished ("and his middle name is Roberto—we have no Hispanic ancestry but another great player for the Pirates was Roberto Clemente? Do you know about Roberto Clemente?"), Philip was laughing and asking for more. He liked her stories, and Holly enjoyed having him for an audience. Suddenly, without forethought, she decided to tell him her most delicious tidbit.

"Before I leave the U.S. there's something I want to get straightened out at my job in Special Collections. Some papers that belonged to a Civil War soldier named Michael Donahue."

"You mentioned this guy before, didn't you? That one night."

"Right." The allusion to *that one night* made her pause for an instant, but she ignored it. "Philip, do you know anything about Emily Dickinson's elder brother Austin?"

He shook his head. "About as much as I do of baseball."

She poured him more tea. "You see, Austin was supposed to go to the war. He was the family favorite, their golden boy. He married Emily's childhood friend, Susan Gilbert, and the couple lived next door to Emily and her parents. The Dickinsons were a very close-knit family, they made their own little fiefdom. Everybody loved Austin."

"Something bad is going to happen," said Philip. "I sure hope so."

"Well, it got sticky later when a young married woman named Mabel joined the fan club. She and Austin had an affair right under Susan's nose, and it was very awkward in the community. Austin was no angel. But I'm talking about the war. The American Civil War. The Dickinsons were a very respectable Amherst family, defenders of the Union, their ancestors were Congregationalist clergy and they were abolitionists. They said all the right things. But Austin didn't serve in the army. In those days, you could pay for a substitute. And that's what the Dickinsons did for Austin. They paid five hundred dollars to an Irish laborer named Donahue to go in his place. This much scholars already know."

"It wasn't unusual at the time, I suspect."

"But this is where it gets interesting, Philip. Nothing much was known about Donahue. He died at the Battle of Chancellorsville. The guy's a footnote. Or he *was* a footnote, because I've got something else. Inside a packet of letters that belonged to a soldier named Leahy I found another packet of letters that belonged to a soldier named Michael Donahue. He and Leahy served in the same unit. And this Donahue was Austin Dickinson's replacement, it's almost certain. And what makes this more than a footnote is that he received letters from Emily Dickinson herself—and these letters are of a highly personal nature."

"Handwriting? You're sure this checks out?"

"Yes, I am. I've downloaded facsimile editions of her handwriting and compared them. I'm no expert but it looks the same to me. More importantly, the style—the eccentric punctuation—the *mind*—it's her all right. I know her work and I can hear her loud and clear. And there's more."

Philip clasped his hands behind his neck and smiled. "Do tell."

"Dickinson had a vast correspondence. Her letters were full of poetry. These letters are no exception."

"Really? Early drafts? New work?"

Holly nodded. "Both."

"We're talking cash value, aren't we?"

"I suppose so. And there's something else."

Holly could see that he was truly interested now, and she felt an electric tingle at being able to share, finally, what she knew.

"Yesss?" he asked.

"Well, sometimes Dickinson is cast as a nutty spinster or eternal virgin who had her heart broken by somebody. It makes her sound a bit pathetic. Everybody knows she corresponded with an editor named Thomas Wentworth Higginson, and there's been speculation about a possible lesbian infatuation with her sister-in-law Susan. There was a pastor, Charles Bowles, who she was very fond of, and a judge named Lord. After she died they found some mysterious letters she wrote to someone she addressed as her 'Master' but no one knows if they were ever sent to anyone. Some critics find them kinky, but they're an artistic pose, too. For decades, she literally didn't get out of the house. Her room overlooked a graveyard, and watching burials was a source of distraction."

"It *is* kind of pathetic."

"No, it's not so simple! Michael Donahue is a different case, that's my point. These are love letters, plain as day. My theory is that Donahue was a laborer for the Dickinsons or someone in their circle in Amherst, and that's how he and Emily hooked up. It's already known that the Dickinson family had Irish maids. For a time Austin was a schoolmaster in the North End of Boston and taught poor Irish schoolboys who'd fled the potato famine. Maybe Michael Donahue is connected to them or he was a relative to one of those servant girls, or maybe he's from the same village back in Ireland. This much I know: something happened."

Sister reached to my hair.
   Found a straw!
   "Where did that come from?"
   So I continued—to lie.
   "I don't know."
   She might as well have reached into my soul.
   Yours lovingly,
   Emily

"What?" Philip said. "They were bonking in the barn? That's what you're saying?"

"I think so. It sounds like she loved him but maybe she dumped him because he was Catholic. Or maybe she didn't dump him but he wanted to marry in the church and she wouldn't do it, so he dumped her. The question of Rome comes up in her letters. Or maybe she still had reservations about the idea of marriage itself. And then Michael Donahue goes off to the war: why? To show his loyalty to the cause? Of course there's the money and that could help his people back home, but why do it for his lover's *brother*? To prove he's worthy? Or was it another kind of statement to the Dickinson family, to puncture their high and mighty pretensions? To make them question their own worthiness? He was braver than the brother Austin. I'm still trying to figure it out."

"He could've been thumbing his nose at them."

"Exactly. But then he gets killed."

"That *is* inconvenient," Philip said.

"Of course, these unanswerable questions don't matter as much as her poetry, her *new* poetry, but you know how these things work. This love affair gives the discovery a sensational angle, right? It will attract more attention."

Philip gazed off into the air. "Hmmm. It's a neo-imperialist rewriting of a bourgeois humanist liberation narrative," he said. "An Irish mercenary is pure gold in this context. Plus there's also a subversive element in regard to first-wave feminism, which is good or bad, depending on how you spin it, though maybe it could be queered into something more transgressive."

"No!" Holly drew herself up. "You're missing the point. You're reducing all those questions to a careerist game. What else, Philip? You don't really believe in literature departments, anyway. But that's what people are going to claim, right? I mean people in universities."

Philip smiled. "Who the fuck else cares?"

"*I* do," she said. "And when I leave the university, which is pretty soon, I'm still going to care. There must be other people, too."

Philip looked at her, still waiting. "So what is it you want?"

"To save her from everything you say."

Out into the light—you sense
Within—one blink, my dear—
the box will fall through skies
Inside your head.

"So then he says, 'Two dews,' and the waiter says, 'To do what?' and Honus answers, 'No, two DEWS, in a *can*,' and the waiter says, 'Can do? WHAT? What are you talking about, dude?' "

Art and Anita pealed with laughter. Jenn was a good mimic and captured Honus's voice exactly. (In restaurants Honus preferred his Mountain Dew in a can, esteeming the taste and quality of carbonation superior to fountain versions of the drink, and since one can of soda wasn't enough to satisfy him and he'd have to order a second can anyway, which could involve an annoying delay if he couldn't get the server's attention, Honus always ordered two cans of Mountain Dew from the outset, to be safe. This, as a connoisseur of sugary fizz, was how he organized his life.) Today was the first time Jenn had visited the family in Sheridan, for a Sunday brunch to celebrate Art's birthday. Holly suspected that her parents might not be keen on Jenn's fashion sense (black fingernail polish, a grinning skull T-shirt) but Jenn held her own in conversation, chatting right along, in no way intimidated by the unfamiliar setting.

Honus slouched with his cheek on his fist, saying little. The previous night he'd played his first gig in Sheridan, and it hadn't gone well. Steve didn't make the trip and Honus had sung over an instrumental playback of Steve's drums and old tracks of Jerz's guitar from the early days of Honeybunch. The crowd, which included some of his hometown schoolmates, was restless and bored during his set, and near the end they heckled. Holly had arrived only this morning, so she hadn't seen the performance, but when she inquired about the show, he groaned. "Was the worst! People here don't get me." When she tried to console him by saying "no prophet is honored in his own country," Honus took it badly, because he thought she was being sarcastic, which wasn't the case at all. Probably nothing Holly could say would please him.

"Time for cake!" Anita announced.

"Isn't this wonderful?" said Art.

They sang the song, Honus barely audible.

After dessert, Art suggested that they plug in a DVD that he and Anita had rented for this weekend, in anticipation of family quality time.

The film was called *Desert Temptations* and it had been chosen, Holly suspected, with her in mind. Nominated for festival awards and, according to the opening credits, based on a true story, it showed a Guatemalan girl named Ester, fleeing north with her little brother to escape murderous militias and drug lords. In the desert near the U.S. border the children get separated but she manages a difficult crossing alone. After hardships and struggles, including an abusive foster family and racist parents of schoolmates, Ester rises to the top of her high school class, only to miss her final exams and the chance to graduate after learning that her brother is still alive, across the border, and in danger. She drops everything to go help him and, at great risk, they escape together, and this time they both reach the U.S. and assume a clandestine existence, working for a landscaping crew while living at an RV campsite. One day Ester finds herself using a weedeater next door to the house of her former high school principal and, screwing up her courage, she calls to him across the hedge, asking if there's anything he can do for her little brother. The principal soberly agrees to arrange a meeting. The day of the appointment at the school, he leads the young people out of his office into an auditorium, where to Ester's astonishment all her former classmates and teachers are assembled, and they burst into applause. Then they rise to their feet—a standing ovation! Even an irascible old math teacher, hesitant at first, finds his feet and smiles and starts clapping with the rest.

As the soundtrack strings oozed and slithered, Holly was tempted to exclaim, "*I could throw up!*" But it would've been rude, at a moment when Anita and Jenn were passing a box of tissues while Art and Honus, not very convincingly, feigned masculine stoicism. Earlier, Holly's eyes were stinging, too. If not for the presence of the others, she might've indulged in a few tears. Parts of the film were undeniably well-done. The actress who played Ester, a slight, beautiful girl with glistening black eyes, captivated Holly. The frightened little brother had his moments, too. So why did the director have to go and ruin it with the final scene? She'd seen versions of it in other movies, where a hero who sacrificed and suffered to do the right and noble thing was ultimately rewarded with kudos, an unconditional standing-O from the world! It was supposed to be inspiring, but for Holly it had the opposite effect. She found it brutish and disrespectful. It implied that a reward was part of the deal, a narcissistic stroke of pleasure, when the rest of the story and the reality of sacrifice suggested the contrary. Did doing the right thing mean getting noticed, getting credit?

Honus's phone chimed and he jumped up. "Gotta take this!" he said. "It's Steve." He scurried out of the room.

The rest of them stretched, turned off the TV and returned *Desert Temptations* to its rental case. Anita offered more cake. A short time later Holly found Honus by the back door, brooding, alone.

"You OK?"

He looked up.

"Steve is gonna quit the band unless we find a guitarist. He wants a meatier sound. It's an ultimatum."

His voice was hoarse, as if the air had been knocked out of him.

"Sorry to hear that."

"Maybe he's fucking with me, just to see what I'll do. You know any guitarists?"

He nervously scratched at his palm.

"'Fraid not." Holly waited a moment. "Can I ask you something? Why do you want Steve in the band? Really? What's the point? You're the irreplaceable one."

This was something that had been on her mind. She'd even spoken to Philip Post about it in the tea-house. Honus ought to be ready for this conversation.

"I know you don't like him," he said, "but you obviously don't appreciate our creative dynamic."

Honus sometimes spoke this way. She'd also heard him refer to their "sweet spot" and "interactive alchemy."

"I guess not. I don't want to sound unsympathetic about his situation and everything. But he's . . . difficult." Holly was going to say "obnoxious" but corrected herself. "I wonder why you put up with him. Really, it can't be because Steve is the best drummer out there. I'm sure there are plenty of two-armed drummers who could play better. Is it just an image for Honeybunch? Like it's cool to have a disabled black guy? Isn't that kind of condescending?"

Honus sighed. "Oh, please. Now who's being condescending?"

He pulled out his phone again and checked it, as if he could create a new message by an act of will.

"That's no answer," she said.

"Knock it off, Holly. You're trying to turn this into some of your intellectual crap. Next thing you'll be saying it's racist."

"Well, is it?"

His thumb stopped moving and he met her eyes. "OK—listen up." His tone was strained as if it pained him to witness her ignorance. "It *is* cool, OK? Steve adds something to our presence. And there's nothing wrong with that. I'm not the most handsome front man, OK? And Jerz was always a bit of a zero, you know that, he was replaceable. But Steve is different, OK? I'm not gonna apologize and neither is he. Music is part of his therapy and he can hear a tune for my words and he brings his own words, too. The rest of the world can't make him hide away in some box. He's who he is. He's difficult, sure, but you should consider the whole picture. Have you heard some of the new material? Have you heard 'Sack of Snakes'?"

Holly shook her head. She didn't remember that one.

"Our differences add up to a plus," Honus said. "It makes us happen."

"Like, limitations create a kind of rigor?"

"Go ahead and be snotty, Holly. If you don't get it, that's your problem."

"I'm not being snotty! It's an aesthetic principle. I'm trying to be on your side."

Honus stared. "You don't know how to turn it off, do you? Ever consider that maybe you could learn from us? Really. It might help you out some."

"What's that supposed to mean?"

"People like us have to find an angle, Holly. We can't run away from shit. We have to go out there and mix it up."

"People like *us*?"

"You deaf or what? You're a walking target, Holly. You're gonna get cut down."

"I don't want to find 'an angle,' " she told him. "And I don't like to be lectured by a little boy with underwear breath."

As she spoke (where did *that* come from?) she became aware of Anita and Jenn hovering in the kitchen, listening to every word. Holly looked at her watch. "I'd better go."

August 16, 1863
  My dearest—
  Your empty spot looks lonely enough—I do not love to go near the barn. But when I springle Geraniums with a Water pot—I see afar.
  Where is my messenger—my Mercury? Will you tell me your health? When I try to organize—my Force explodes.
  Yours lovingly,
  Emily

"Excuse me, can I say something?"
  Startled, Holly looked up.
  "Oh, hi Roger."
  She was unlocking her car in the parking lot, on her way home from the restaurant. In a glance she took in his cautious smile, his bright white sneakers.
  "I'd like to tell you something."
  "Yes?"
  "Your friends didn't let me in on the joke. I hope I didn't seem rude."
  Roger must've been referring to Kali and Marcia. Lately (this had definitely been noticed by the waitresses) Roger had stopped coming to Stoddard's. They'd lost a regular customer. Holly had been surprised by this development but also relieved, because it spared her further provocation.
  "No, you weren't rude."

Had he been hanging around the parking lot, just to ask this question?

"Good." He nodded. "I'm glad. See you."

He hurried away.

Climbing into her Comet, Holly wondered about his words. *See you.* Did he mean that he was coming back to the restaurant? Was he weirdly asking her permission? Or did he mean it more specifically—*you.* They'd barely spoken. But something nervy in the air made her suspect the latter.

For a week after this encounter, she expected him to pop up again. Perhaps telephone her. It wouldn't be hard to get her number from someone at work.

But her phone didn't ring, and she didn't see him at the restaurant, either. She couldn't explain his absence.

Honus first spotted the Yeti in a diner, eating a plate of pancakes. He was a big man, and very hairy. According to Honus, "This dude is just shoveling down his cakes, sitting by himself at the counter, he's got long hair and a beard, one of those beards that grows in both directions, not just out of his face but rising out of his shirt, you know, but what kills me is the backs of his hands—I've never seen such hairy hands!—and I ask myself, 'whoa, is that a dude or a yeti?' And then two days later some guy calls me about my Want Ad for a guitarist and we agree to meet up and lo and behold it turns out to be *the same dude!* Like, here comes the yeti! I felt like I knew him before we even started talking. The coincidence was a good omen."

The yeti's name was Jonathan. He wasn't a student. He worked in his family's heating and air-conditioning business. He passed the audition and Honeybunch became a trio again. Jonathan brought along his own equipment and offered unlimited access to his parents' vehicles. Previously he'd played with a band called Plumber's Butt. "It's all coming together now!" Honus enthused. "He was the missing link."

With the arrival of Jonathan—or the Yeti, a name that Jonathan gamely accepted, though he let it be known that he would've preferred to be called Doctor Groove—the fortunes of Honeybunch quickly improved. It wasn't only that he was a better guitarist than Jerz, which was no great feat; he fit into the band and enjoyed what he was doing. When he stepped forward to play a solo, a toothy grin emerged from his hairy face and he seemed to chew on the notes with relish. He also provided competent background vocals for Honus, which gave the group another layer of sound, and he rigged a better microphone for Steve's drum. Holly was thrilled to be relieved of the role of chauffeur, but she still found herself involved in the band's affairs, because new needs emerged as they progressed, for instance when Honus asked her to proofread their new website.

It was riddled with spelling errors and monstrosities of punctuation. "My goodness, you're supposed to be in college, Honus. Look at that. And that!" Holly tapped her finger on the screen. "Oh wow—*that!* You know how to write lyrics, so how in the world can you make that sort of mistake?"

"Jesus, Holly. I just wanted some help, not another sermon."

"I am helping."

"No, you're not. Let's drop it."

"Wait a second. You want it to look professional, don't you?"

This argument won the day. Honus might be an indifferent student, but when it came to Honeybunch, he cared. Since he didn't master HTML code, and since it was laborious for Holly to dictate the corrections for him to type, it was less trouble if Holly did it herself. Thus she became the band's webmaster. Honus showed her sites that he liked, and Holly downloaded templates for a booking calendar and sample contracts and adapted them for Honeybunch. Only two days later— she could hardly believe it—they were approached by a non-alcohol venue they'd never played before. Honus was elated. "It's happening, Holly! It's happening!"

"It's two-hundred and fifty dollars," she said. "Don't lose your head."

"Can you answer the guy for me? Be professional but make it sound cool, too. Say that we'll accept, but make it appear like he's lucky to get us. Write it with all the business shit."

"I think we should keep it simple."

"Well don't blow it. Don't make any mistakes!"

"You want me to do this or not?"

Honus had enlisted Jenn to edit performance videos of Honeybunch, and Holly uploaded excerpts and sound samples to the website. Supposedly to drive up rankings, Honus did repeated web searches of the band, but there was also something compulsive and self-gratifying in his pleasure. Googling himself blind. Holly also took care of business correspondence, though the majority of gigs still came through Honus's cellphone, from friends or friends-of-friends. The platform was up and running, and then Honus made an announcement.

"Had a meeting with the band and we've come to a decision. We want you to be our manager."

Holly chuckled. "Well, thank you, Honus, I'm flattered but I don't think—"

"We'll pay you! Ten per cent!"

"That's not really an issue," she told him, though in truth it was an issue, because Honeybunch was eating up a lot of her time.

"At first I was against the idea, too," said Honus. "No offense but it's kind of lame to be managed by your big sister. But the guys made me see it differently. We don't have to tell anybody you're my sister. We don't have to admit we're related."

"I'm a busy person, Honus."

"You won't have to show your face. It's mainly the website and keeping track of stuff. Come on! Are you on board?"

Holly thought for a moment.

"Twenty per cent," she said.

The email stunned her.

Subject: Dickinson correspondence

Dear Holly,

It has come to my attention that you might have made a potentially interesting discovery in the letters of our Civil War archive in Special Collections. I have conducted author, keyword and subject searches in our holdings but have not found corresponding references. Perhaps the materials in question have not been catalogued?

We would be grateful if you could relay to me, precisely, information about where these documents are stored, so that I can examine their contents and guarantee that they receive the archival and scholarly attention that they deserve.

Naturally your role in this discovery, if corroborated, would be acknowledged.

Sincerely,

Rosemary Muller

FOUR

MOAN AND SHOUT

Holly was mad. She couldn't remember the last time she'd been so mad. Why had Philip run to Rosemary like an eager puppy, spilling the news? *Why?* She'd been friendly with him lately, and he'd been nice in helping her to look for a job. But now, this betrayal. Had he been toying with her all along? Was it revenge because Holly had rejected him, not wanting to play giantess for his precious fantasy? Was he really that twisted?

And now she fumed. She shut down her computer without replying to Rosemary's email and stormed out of the house. Her next shift in Special Collections started in thirty minutes. She stalked down a sidewalk, feeling overheated despite the cool May morning. Her blood was pumping. She recalled a rally she'd attended as an undergraduate, sponsored by the Women's Resource and Action Center. A chubby girl in the dorm had encouraged her to go, and Holly was sympathetic to the idea, because the theme of the event was "Body Size Is Nobody's Business." (She knew a thing or two about *that!*) The rally, though, wasn't what she'd expected. It consisted of speakers grabbing the microphone and offering testimonies about how they'd been mistreated because of their appearance. The stories were heartfelt, some of them quite moving, all of them bearing witness to an issue Holly sincerely cared about. But, at the same time, there was an element that disconcerted her. An obese woman named Caroline offered a long, impressively articulate account of her mistreatment by insensitive people, mainly men but also women, a cringe-inducing litany of cruelties and humiliations and, near the end, she was shedding tears. Many of her listeners were crying, too. But she didn't stop there. Caroline's quavering voice rallied, became firm, and she declared how she had fought forward and managed to rise above the meanness, she was proud of herself, and of what she had accomplished in life, so now, as far as she was concerned, those people could kiss her fat ass. Her testimonial was in fact a defiance—a victory. "You hear me?" she said. "They can kiss my fat ass! Kiss my fat ass!"

And then the crowd began to chant: "Kiss my fat ass! Kiss my fat ass!"

Their voices rose to a crescendo, but Holly didn't join in, all the while uneasy that others might disapprove of her not expressing her solidarity. She *felt* it, all right, but not like this. Or, she might've crowed, "Kiss my giraffe neck!" but, aside from the fact that it wouldn't have the same satisfying ring as Caroline's slogan, it wasn't something she *wanted* to say. All this shouting, though the emotion behind it was entirely legitimate, felt somehow like another version of "strut your stuff." However hard-won, it still played up to another's gaze. Holly had hoped blindly for a way to embrace *nobody's* business. ("How dreary—to be—Somebody!")

But this morning, though, she pictured Philip Post and recalled the rally and its pitch of emotion and, this time, she wanted to act on it, and not just verbally: she wanted to reverse roles. Philip would be on the receiving end, and it wouldn't be a kiss. Holly wanted to *kick* his ass.

She required an explanation and more than an explanation, because there was no conceivable explanation that would be good enough. Yes, kick his ass. Wipe that grin off his face and shake his tie loose. Vandalize his stupid bicycle! Goddamnit! If he thought he could mess with *this* nobody, Philip was in for a lesson.

Steaming, she stopped at a shop along the way and picked up an extra coffee, and when there was a delay at the counter and as a consequence she would be late for work, she was glad. So what?! She had more important things on her mind. When she eventually strode into the Department of Special Collections, Merle stood up at his desk, bobbing his eyebrows.

"Inez wants to speak to you," he said.

"OK, OK. Just let me put my stuff down."

She went to her cubicle where she intended to leave her jacket and purse. To her surprise, the row of acid-free cartons was gone. Her shelf had been stripped bare.

In an instant, Holly's righteous indignation drained away. Oh my, she thought. They know, too! Am I being fired?

Inez was speaking on her telephone extension as Holly approached her glassed-in office and, when their eyes met, she beckoned for Holly to enter. A moment later she hung up the receiver. Holly had the uncanny impression that Inez had been talking about her.

"Sit down, sit down! My goodness. It seems you've made quite a discovery!"

To Holly's relief, she wasn't fired. Inez was excited, explaining that Professor Muller had called last night and was personally taking charge of the Donahue correspondence. "This is very encouraging. It's exactly the kind of faculty transversal interest in our collection that we need. This always comes up in our funding review."

"I'm glad to hear it."

"It would've been nice if you'd alerted us first, but Professor Muller tells me you're one of her students. I understand that you'd want to ask a specialist. She says her first look is very promising and compares closely to correspondence she's worked on in the Houghton Library at Harvard. She's already in touch with a colleague there. Professor Muller spoke of you in very friendly terms."

Holly felt a twisting in her gut. "I don't know what to say."

"Well, I do. Thank you, Holly."

Inez stood up, nodding, so Holly rose, too. Before she left the office, she said, "My stuff has been cleared away. What am I supposed to do now?"

"Just ask Merle. He'll set you up."

So she followed Merle with his jingling keys to the locked shelves and they loaded four new boxes onto a trolley, along with a fresh stack of acid-free cartons. "These are mainly government correspondence," he said. "Supplies for cavalry, leather goods, horse feed, that sort of thing. This information could have statistical applications." As Holly settled in her chair and looked at the new pile of work, her heart sank. It looked dreadfully boring.

Then her gaze shifted and she spied an edge of yellow paper peeping out from under her shelf. It was where she kept office supplies, her pencil jar, self-adhesive labels, a manual of preservation protocols. She recognized the paper instantly. It was Dickinson's. She'd been re-reading the poem two days ago, for pleasure. That's why she'd put it aside. It was the longest piece in the correspondence, and the only poem that had been copied out separately and wasn't part of a letter. It was the prize of the lot. Lately, considering the materials in their entirety, Holly had begun to wonder if it predated all the letters. Perhaps Emily had given Michael this poem when they were still seeing each other back in Amherst, and when he went off to war, he'd taken it with him. Holly looked over her shoulder. Merle was at his desk, on the phone, and he stood up, still talking, and began to shake out some fish food into his aquarium. He paid no attention to her. Quickly Holly put on her nitrile gloves, extracted the paper and spread it out flat. She already knew the words by heart.

> *Will you prepare—a sturdy box*
> *for my ravishing—mind—with holes*
> *allowed—so we can breathe*
> *in kind?*
>
> *A slot in front—where words—come*
> *Out into the light—you sense*
> *Within—one blink, my dear—*
> *the box will fall through skies*
>
> *Inside your head. Are you the same*
> *Apart—from me—I couldn't say*
> *since I'm not free—yet*
>
> *If you hear me—moan or shout—*
> *Please—ensnare my mind*
> *Keep me in—to let you out*

Another glance over her shoulder. Merle still wasn't looking her way. She slipped the poem into her purse.

By the time she reached the Crewe Building, she'd managed to get up a fresh head of steam against Philip Post. She didn't know what his office hours were, but in the end, it didn't matter, because she saw him in the hallway talking to Kenneth Swallow, the only other Brit in the department, a balding, jug-eared postdoctoral fellow who was working on a book about Smollett and the Scottish Enlightenment. He'd been elected to the faculty council and she'd heard Philip refer to him as a crashing bore. Now Swallow was saying, "Sorry, Philip, I'll have to get back to you on that."

"Excuse me," Holly interrupted. "May I have a word?"

Swallow turned, blinking at her.

"Holly!" said Philip. "I was hoping to see you. Did you get my message? I sent you an email about an hour ago."

"I was at work. I haven't checked my email. But I did get a message from Rosemary Muller. You little shit!"

Philip gave a high-pitched chuckle. "That's what I was writing to you about." He looked at Swallow, who was taking in every word. "Kenneth, could you excuse us for a moment, please?"

Swallow edged away.

Philip lowered his voice. "It's nothing to get upset about. I happened to have a conversation with Rosemary Muller. It was a chat between colleagues about research. Don't take it personally, Holly. I had no idea that she'd react so quickly. I was going to tell you. Sorry if it seemed abrupt! Listen, I have a class right now, I'm running late, but I have to ask: any news from Bordeaux? Packing your bags for France?"

Holly ignored his question. "But you don't even care about Dickinson!"

He frowned. "Did you have a project with the letters? I wasn't under that impression. What did you intend?"

"It certainly wasn't to go running to Rosemary Muller!"

"We'll talk, I promise. But I've got a class now. Sorry!" He strode off.

Kenneth Swallow, who'd been bending over a nearby water fountain, turned and came back to her. "What's he done this time?"

"Excuse me?" Holly was surprised by his directness. "I don't want to go into it."

"You're not the first."

It took a moment, but his words sank in. Oh God, she thought, he thinks I'm another Courtney Davies! Knowing how fast gossip travelled, Holly acted immediately to dispel

Swallow's assumption. "I don't know what you're talking about," she said. "Philip and I have a professional disagreement."

"Oh, I'm not insinuating anything nasty on your part."

"Then what are you insinuating?"

"Probably something nasty on his part."

"Didn't you hear me? It's a *professional* disagreement."

This didn't seem to dissuade Swallow in the least. He nodded gravely. "He's a fake, our Philip is."

His eyes were begging. Holly knew that she should walk away but there was something he wanted to share, and she succumbed. "What do you mean?"

"I hardly know where to start." Kenneth licked his lips and looked around as if to confirm that no one was listening, though it was obvious that they were alone, and he knew exactly where to start. "You know how he's always saying that he studied at Cambridge. I reckon he's mentioned that to you?"

Holly nodded.

A sickly grin split across his face.

"That is technically true, he started an M. Phil at Cambridge. Under what circumstances, I cannot say." Swallow clucked. "But he didn't finish it. And he certainly didn't do his undergraduate course there. He was at Hull."

"Hull?"

"Yes, Hull."

Swallow's grin now moved from side to side. He had a remarkably mobile jaw and unhealthy strawberry blotches on his chin. Most people looked more attractive when they smiled but that wasn't the case with Swallow. He looked like a masticating troll.

"I don't think that has any bearing on my situation, but thanks anyway, Kenneth. Excuse me, I have to go."

But where? Who could she talk to? Without premeditation, as if inexorably drawn, she followed the stairs to Robert Borden's office.

She knocked but there was no answer. As she turned to leave, he came shuffling around the corner, a stack of essays under one arm. He appeared more stooped since the last time she'd seen him, or maybe it was just a bad day.

"Ah," he said, nodding. "*Ah*. Could you hold these for me, please?"

She took the essays while he fumbled in his pockets for his keys to unlock the door. "Do come in, Ms. Winegarten. It's been a long time. I was beginning to wonder if you were snubbing me."

The personal tenor of this remark made her shy. Though it was true that for the last two semesters she'd avoided him, his words weren't entirely fair. Borden wasn't the kind of person you dropped in on casually, for a spur-of-the-moment chat. Their relationship had never been like that.

"Looks like a lot of marking," she said, putting the essays on the corner of his desk.

"Three sections of freshman composition this semester." He motioned for her to take a chair.

She recalled what the graduate assistants had told her, that because of his enemies in the department, Borden was the only senior professor to be stuck with such grunt work. Now he peered at Holly and guessed her thoughts.

"They have thrown me to the bottom of the well," he said. "So be it! All I have to do is look up. I can still see the light!"

Holly put on a smile. Again, the personal dimension to his remark felt peculiar. She ran a hand through her hair. "Professor Borden, I have something to show you."

"Yes?"

She removed the paper from her purse and began to explain, in fits and starts, her job at Special Collections, her discovery of a cache of Emily Dickinson correspondence, and the fact that Rosemary Muller was now in charge of the documents. As soon as he understood that the scrap lying on his desk was written by Dickinson, Professor Borden frowned and leaned forward intently, adjusting his glasses on his nose and, while Holly spoke, he reached into his jacket pocket and shook out a handkerchief and wrapped it around his forefinger before touching the paper. As she watched him become absorbed by the text in front of him, Holly wondered if he was really listening to her account about how she had been wronged.

"You are confident of the authenticity of these materials?" he asked. "Really?"

Holly nodded.

"The handwriting here is difficult." He began to read aloud, "*One blink, my love, the box . . .*"

Holly interjected, "Will fall through skies inside your head."

Borden looked up, smiling. "You do pay attention, don't you, Ms. Winegarten?"

"Well, I've been staring at it for weeks, trying to make sense of it. Months."

"Shall we take it from the beginning?" he asked, squaring the sheet in front of him, adjusting his glasses one more time. Holly recited from memory as he read along, confirming, with nods and grunts, her deciphering of the smudged portions. "Yes, that must be it! That's it!"

Now he looked up and chewed on his thumb and began to pepper her with questions, most of them centering on whether she'd seen anything like this poem before. "Ms. Winegarten, I don't know the entire corpus, not even close. But you've looked into this, haven't you? What do you think? There's nothing like this in the Franklin editions, or in the archives? There's no reference to this work?"

It was an unfamiliar experience to have Professor Borden defer to her like this, but the situation warranted as much.

Slowly, she shook her head.

He leaned back and let out a sudden yelp, showing the fillings in his teeth. "Nice! Nice!" He carefully inserted a piece of paper underneath the poem to flip it over to look at the other side but, finding nothing, flipped it back again. A pointless gesture but Holly had done the same thing, eager for more. But now his tone changed. "So you snatched this out of Special Collections? You've stolen this, do I understand correctly?"

"No! I mean . . . well, it was sort of an accident that they didn't take this one away. And there's something very unfair about the whole thing, isn't there? So I wanted to show it to you. I'm conflicted about this, Professor Borden. I don't know what to think."

He chuckled, shaking his head. "For some people this is worth a lot of money. Of course more than it would fetch at auction. This is *priceless*, you know."

For a second or two Holly wondered if he approved of her taking the document—he was delighted in her theft and now he was calculating what to do next, how to sell the manuscript for a handsome sum.

But no. He looked her in the eye.

"Ms. Winegarten, this is a very sensitive matter and you'd better take it back before you get into trouble."

He wasn't telling her anything she didn't already know. Holly met his gaze, and when his expression hardened, she nodded.

"Let me tell you a story," he said, rocking back in his chair. "I grew up in Kentucky. Have you ever been to Kentucky?"

"Yes." Years ago, Holly had attended a summer basketball camp for juniors in Lexington. She'd subsisted on beef burgers and popsicles. Her squad had come in second place to a team from Indiana. She didn't think Professor Borden would want to hear such details. "Nice place," she said.

"There is much to love, yes." He gave an airy wave, and once more it struck Holly as strange that he was sounding a personal note.

"When I was a child, one day I found a toad. An enormous toad! It was hiding in the shade and I spotted it when I was weeding my parents' garden. It was such a toad! A magnificent specimen!"

He paused, no doubt intending for her, at this moment, to picture the beast. (It was a teacher's trick, which she'd observed in his lectures about Ralph Waldo Emerson and the transparent eyeball.) Now she tried to oblige him, but her mind conjured up only a fleeting image of a toad before it gave way to a picture of Professor Borden himself, a jowly boy with chubby knees and glinting glasses and a book under his arm. Of course in some faraway epoch Professor Borden had been a child, but there was still something fantastic about the notion. Did he wear suspenders? she wondered.

"I didn't want to lose the toad. I didn't want it to get away. It was such a toad! Fortunately I had a big five-gallon bucket that we used for watering. I emptied it and circled round and approached the toad from behind, 'softly, softly,' as they say. I pounced and covered him up. This fortuitous toad! I ran back up to the house to tell everyone what I'd found."

This was beginning to sound nutty. Holly sat very still.

"But you know what? When I came back, with my big brother, to show off the toad, the bucket was lying on its side and the toad was nowhere in sight. It was *that* strong. It had knocked over a five-gallon bucket."

She thought about how to exit. Coming here had been a mistake. Professor Borden leaned across his desk.

"Don't try to keep this document for yourself, Ms. Winegarten. It is a toad. A magnificent toad. It must be respected."

He opened a desk drawer and extracted a green plastic sheath and, as she reached across to help him, they slid the poem inside. Then he slid the sheath inside a manila envelope and handed it back to her. "Do you agree?" he asked.

Holly nodded. "Sure. This belongs to the library." She excused herself and said goodbye.

Her conversation with Borden left her dissatisfied. She knew he was right, she should return the poem. But then what? Was that how it all ended—by trusting Rosemary and her ilk to run everything through the university career machine, the sausage grinder of ideas? Naturally there were legal concerns about the document, it didn't belong to her. She couldn't hoard it. And when Philip had asked if she had plans for her discovery, she hadn't been able to answer him. All that was true. But still . . .

OK, she thought. I'll return the poem. Tomorrow.

But the next day she put it off, and the day after that was a Saturday, when she didn't have to report to Special Collections but spent the morning chopping onions, tomatoes and stew meat for ten gallons of chili at Stoddard's Family Restaurant. While working she thought of a poetry website she'd stumbled upon in the course of her investigations called "In Defense of . . . Nothing." It was a useful site, though at first she'd misunderstood the title and found it off-putting. The source was a line from Auden: "Poetry makes nothing happen." This, initially, sounded to her like complete resignation, a claim that poetry was pointless. Might as well say, Fuck it, why bother? But, when put into context, she realized, Auden was suggesting something quite different, that there was more to life than grasping careerists and money-getters and politicians routinely allowed; some of the most powerfully felt human experiences were treated as if they were nothing, but this *nothing* mattered very much, often more than others' claim of lofty purpose. Poetry was the place where this *nothing* was permitted to happen. Holly wondered if Auden was echoing Dickinson by defending a place that would be congenial to the sentiments of a Nobody.

At the end of her shift, as she approached her Comet in the parking lot, her phone rang in her purse. Fumbling, she looked at the caller ID—an unknown number.

"Hello?"

"Hi. It's Roger. Hope I'm not interrupting."

"No . . . it's OK."

She shifted her purse to the crook of her arm. So she was right, after all. He was getting in touch.

"Would you like to have coffee with me?"

"Well, that depends. When?" she asked.

There was a silence. "I mean now. Since this is an all right time. You're off work."

She looked around the parking lot, wondering if he was nearby, if she was being watched. But she didn't see anyone.

"I made brownies," he added.

After a brief conversation she understood that he was inviting her for coffee at his apartment. "I just took them out of the oven. They smell great."

"Listen, Roger, I've got a lot of stuff going on. Maybe another time? Let's try somewhere downtown. Not your place."

"So it's OK if I call you again?"

"Yes, Roger. But some other place."

By the following Monday it seemed less urgent to return the Dickinson poem. She'd taken it out of the green plastic sheaf and reread it for the fiftieth time and now it lay on her desk at home next to her bills and junk mail. In the end, it was just a stained and faded scrap of paper.

Sure, Rosemary Muller could use it as fodder for another article to enhance her professional status. But did Holly really want to go to more trouble to enable *that?* After what she'd experienced in Rosemary's seminar? Oh, it was futile to hold a grudge. No good could come of it. But she also couldn't forget her frustration.

That same weekend she received an email from Ludovic Santraud, a two-line message, rejecting her application in Bordeaux. *Damn!* Holly slapped her palm down and reread the message. She'd allowed herself to get her hopes up, she'd been a sucker. *Damn!* It had been foolish from the start. Too easy. The job that Philip had talked about had sounded too good to be true—and, evidently, it was.

Maybe it's better this way, she told herself. I don't want to owe Philip Post.

Still, this was a setback. And now a sense of claustrophobia enclosed her as she wondered if she was ever going to get out of town. Saving money took time, and soon she'd have to start paying back her student loans. If she really wanted to travel for anything more than a brief vacation, she'd have to find work at her destination. There were agencies that advertised job search services, but they charged fees, and could they be trusted?

But pride made Holly stubborn, ready to stick to her plan, and this pride—or was it spite?—also kept her from returning the document to the library. She knew that her actions weren't a pure and disinterested defense of *poetry*. She wasn't being high-minded. When she reported back to work at Special Collections, she could look around the corner to the consultations area and see Rosemary Muller's mop of silvery hair as she poured over the Donahue letters. Busily scratching notes on a pad. Sometimes Rosemary reached beside her for a magnifying glass, bending closer to the scrawls. When Holly witnessed this, she was glad that she'd broken the rules. Broken the law. In her heart of hearts, she believed that this professor was a kind of hijacker.

Once Rosemary looked up and saw Holly watching her. Rosemary's expression wasn't unfriendly; she barely seemed to register Holly's presence. She was concentrating on something else. Holly smiled and tasted an emotion like a childish taunt. *Ha! I know something you don't know!*

"How're things, Holly? *Comment ça va?*"

This was how Philip addressed her. You would've thought that nothing had changed. This time, though, Holly had cornered him in his office, and he couldn't brush her off the way he had in the hallway in front of Kenneth Swallow. He stood by his window in a white button-collar shirt with nicely ironed creases. He wore chocolate-colored jeans and his pointy-toed cowboy boots.

"You owe me an explanation," she said. "You had no interest in those letters. All you knew was that they mattered to me. And what's the first thing you do? You go running like a little suck-up to Rosemary Muller. What in the world is that about? You don't even *like* Rosemary."

A flash of concern crossed his face.

"What do you mean? How dare you? I hope you don't go around repeating that to people."

"I don't talk about you to anyone. Don't flatter yourself. Just give me a straight answer."

"I told you, Holly. It was a collegial conversation and I just happened to mention it. I'm sorry you've taken it this way, but I had no idea that you were so proprietorial about these things. You said you were leaving town. Thinking about other prospects. Something more exciting . . . *comme la France! Tu as des nouvelles?*"

"Don't you patronize me, you—you phony."

This conversation wasn't doing any good. She hadn't mentioned her rejection letter from Bordeaux and it was foolish to think she could get a satisfactory explanation out of him about her problems here. She was on the verge of leaving and slamming the door, but she couldn't step away without a final jab.

"Philip," she said, "you were a student at Hull, right?"

She detected a trace of surprise around his eyes, but he answered blandly, "Yes, I was. There are excellent people in the English department there." He squinted and added in an old man's cackle, "The road to Hull is paved with goats' intestines."

"What?"

"You know, William Blake?" He snickered. "A parody that was published in *The New Statesman?*" He watched her. "Maybe you don't know."

"No, and I don't care. I'm glad that they have excellent people. But let me ask you. Why don't you mention Hull the way you always mention Cambridge?"

"I don't always mention Cambridge."

"Yes, you do."

"Hull has a top-notch English department and can compete with many colleges in Cambridge or Oxford, I'll have you know."

"Wonderful! And I'll have you know that I don't give a rat's ass. All it means is that you're even more of a pompous fake than I thought you were."

He looked back at her with a puckered, pensive expression. "You've been talking to Swallow, haven't you?"

She shrugged. "He talks to me."

"That little snob. He's a fucker."

"He's not a snob. For what it's worth, I've never heard him drop the names of his schools."

"Oh, *please*. Why do you think he dresses like he does?"

He waited expectantly, but Holly drew a blank. She had no particular recollection of the way Swallow dressed. It wasn't noteworthy in any case. If she thought about it, perhaps she had a vague impression that Swallow always looked a bit drab, even shabby.

"Those *shoes?*" Philip said helpfully.

"What about his shoes? I don't pay attention to Kenneth Swallow's shoes."

"There's not a pair of more beat-up shoes to be found in the entire university. Look for yourself. He *never* polishes them. Swallow was at Harrow and then went up to Cambridge. King's College, you see. He graduated with a first. He must be thirty-five years old and his mum and dad still fly him home for a Guernsey holiday. They have a place on the island. He doesn't think he has to prove a *thing*. Those shoes are part of his sartorial pose—of course he wouldn't wear them if he wasn't already posh and coddled. He's very insidious. Those shoes are a statement."

For a moment Holly wondered if Philip were making an elaborate joke, if his ironic mode was on full throttle. But he appeared to be dead serious, even petulant. "My goodness," she said. "*Nobody cares.* You should relax, Philip."

"You're a nice person, Holly, but people are always looking for an edge, one way or another. That's the way we are.
That's what Swallow's shoes are all about. He's a mincing little lord. I'll make a confession to you. You know Philip isn't
my Christian name?"

Holly shook her head.

"It's my middle name. My real name is Clive, which is
rather old-fashioned and farty-sounding but I had a grandfather named Clive, that's why my parents chose it, you see. And
when I was a child I certainly didn't board at Harrow, I went to
our local comprehensive school. Kids started calling me "Clive
Jive," or "Jive Clive," and they didn't say it in a friendly tone,
believe me. And then it got shortened to simply "Jive" once
they latched on to my surname, Post, which happens to rhyme
with "beans on toast," and they called me that for a while, till
the whole lot of it got shortened to a rhyming slang and I was
christened "Jive Beans." That's what everybody called me, for
years. Jive Beans. It was dreadful."

He crossed his arms and looked out the window as Holly
tried to process what she'd just heard. She had the impression
that this confession had cost him something; it was not in jest.
He was showing his scars. It was absurd, to be sure. But Holly
had her own memories of childhood mockeries and was reluctant to dismiss him out of hand, though it was not lost on her
that he'd turned around the conversation and cast himself as
a victim.

"You know what I think, Philip? We're surrounded by a
lot of silly noise, but it's only that, noise. Our real worth is
decided by how well we face the truth of who we are in our
private moments. Our public selves are over-rated."

"Lovely," he said, "I hear you. But sometimes it's necessary
to take measures to survive."

A warmth came to his eyes, an appeal to her sympathy. He had a point, but she remembered seeing this look on Philip's face before, the first night they'd gone out to dinner. It was easy to get drawn into those eyes.

But what were they expressing? A longing to share? Or a scheming desire for a standing O?

"Goodbye, Philip."

She left his office.

When Holly imagined Emily giving the poem to Michael, she saw them on the far edge of the garden at Homestead, near the orchard with its cherry and peach trees where they could not be seen.

Chock. Chock.

Someone was chopping wood. If another person came up the private path from Austin's house and encountered Emily and Michael, there was no cause for suspicion. In June a stand of Indian Pipes, Emily's favorite flower, bloomed here, waxy and white. She might've come to admire them. And Michael could be heading to the stable. There was nothing compromising about seeing them together, not like in the barn.

But here they couldn't kiss. For several seconds they watched each other. *Chock. Chock.* She was angry but she yearned for his mouth. How could she bid him goodbye?

She detected a movement in the corner of her eye and quickly turned her head. *Who?!* But it was only a cat, wandering in the rhubarb. It had followed Emily from the house, her only witness. She disliked this cat. Recently it had killed a bobolink and strewn bloody feathers beneath the washing line. She turned back to Michael. "What are you trying to prove?"

Chock. Chock.

"Many of us are going."

"But you don't have to go."

"Five hundred dollars is a lot of money," he said.

"That's not what this war is about."

He removed his hat and worked at its brim with his thumbs. "It's enough for your brother."

"That's not fair!" she said. "Don't make it about him."

"You think it's only about us?"

"I've never thought that. But I wish it was. I truly do."

The argument was fruitless and presently they became aware of a silence. The chopping had stopped. It could mean nothing. Or it could mean that they had less than a minute before someone came up the path. She looked around and saw only the cat, slinking away.

"What's fair, I don't know," Michael said, replacing his hat. "I don't have your way with words. But I'll be back."

She stepped forward and from her sleeve she slipped a piece of paper and thrust it in his hand. "*Finished* can never be said of us." Then she turned and went swiftly back to the house, her feet swishing in the tall grass.

"Carrot stick? Dip?"

Holly held out a plate.

"No thanks."

She circulated through the room. Beer and wine and sodas and cheese snacks. Chelsea was away for the weekend and it was just as well, because guests had taken over the house: Honeybunch and hangers-on before a "Battle of the Bands" competition at the Mousehole. Art and Anita had driven up for the event, arriving with Jack and Maria and their child Strapp. (Lately, it seemed, they travelled everywhere together, as a clan.) Jenn was there, and so was Lucy, Steve's latest girlfriend who rolled and licked joints for him. (So far, Holly noticed, they hadn't done this in front of the parents.) There was also a new young woman unknown to Holly who sat on the Yeti's knee, nuzzling his ear, evidently susceptible to his charms. In another corner stood Steve's mother, Gloria, a mulberry-scarfed lady who taught junior high somewhere in Indiana. She had a booming voice (Holly recognized the schoolteacher's powers of projection) and now she was talking to Art about standardized testing while Art boomed right back at her in his own schoolteacher's voice. Honus had put on some music for ambiance but it was too loud. Even the Troll was here, clutching a can of soda, his eyes darting from side to side, as if at any second he might leap out a window.

Amid the hubbub, Holly wished that she and Art could duck out for some quiet time together. She was confused and needed to unburden her heart. More than a month had gone by and she still hadn't returned the manuscript. She'd avoided Borden, not wanting to admit that she'd disregarded his advice. With every passing day the situation became more compromising. How would she explain her possession of the poem? Anyone would assume that she was a thief. It was impossible to sneak it back into the locked shelves without Merle's keys, and by now Rosemary would have inventoried every scrap of paper and she would be surprised, not to say suspicious, if a new manuscript appeared out of nowhere.

Other schemes played out in Holly's mind, like the scenarios she'd invented about Scott Nichols or Jérémy Ndao or to fill out unknown details about Emily and Michael Donahue. Only now, what bubbled out of her imagination was riskier. *What if I sold the manuscript?* She surprised herself with the thought, but there it was, a stark option. She hadn't felt like a thief when she took it (her gesture had been an impulse, she told herself, an act of self-defense), but if in the legal sense she was a criminal, well, what was the next step in this role? There were plenty of collectors out there and surely someone would put aside scruples if convinced of the manuscript's authenticity. The price would solve her money problems in a stroke: she could leave the country. Sweetest of all, the transaction wasn't an impersonal cash windfall like winning the lottery or some other lucky break—rather, it felt as if Emily had reached across time to *her*, Holly, in her need.

Her secret sister. There was a beauty in that.

Yet she barely had time to savor the beauty before her imagination took a lurid, humiliating turn: a fantasy of being hunted down by Interpol and carried off by *polizia* and Art asking plaintively on the phone, *"Is it true, Sweetie? Is it?"* In a holding cell, an overhead TV screen showed Rosemary's big fuzzy head being interviewed on CNN above the caption PROF. MULLER DICKINSON EXPERT. *"This is an act of a disturbed individual,"* she said, exposing Holly beyond the seminar room, beyond the university, to millions of viewers across the world, *"She pretended she was somebody she wasn't."*

"Holly, are you sure you can't join us?"

Interrupted in her reverie, she saw Anita smiling up at her. Before this weekend had mushroomed into an improvised family reunion, Anita had invited Holly to a Torrid Tangos competition where audience members voted on the dance contestants. Maria was coming too, and the outing would include a *"super fun lunch with the girls."* She was trying to be nice, to include Holly in their plans. But Holly balked at the idea, and promptly called the manager at Stoddard's Family Restaurant and begged for extra hours that weekend. The manager was glad to humor her, and that was why Holly wasn't available for Torrid Tangos tomorrow or for the Battle of the Bands tonight. "Sorry," she told Anita, "I can't get off work."

"Oh, that's a shame."

"Yes, it would've been fun."

Now Art was waving for Holly to come over.

"What can I get you?" she asked.

"Gloria hasn't had a chance to talk to you," he said. "Gloria, this is Holly. She manages the band. She runs the website and all that."

Gloria raised her glass as if to make a toast. "And you're in graduate school, right? That's what your father says. You must be very busy."

"That's right." There was no point in explaining that her enrollment was only a pretext. "We'll see how that works out."

"Well, your Dad says you're very serious. Good for you. This Battle of the Bands might be fun but we have to get these boys to *study*. That's what I think. How do you get your brother to study?"

Holly laughed. "I don't. Honus just does whatever he wants. Always has."

Art said, "Oh, now . . ."

Gloria was unsmiling. "Isn't that the problem, though? Steven needs more time for rehabilitation but there's no way around it. The university works with the V.A. hospital on a research unit. They have an independence learning program. But that won't last forever. It's important to have a plan."

They followed her eyes to the other side of the room where Steve wore sunglasses and bobbed his head to the music. Nearby Honus was horsing around with a balloon, punching it with his fist to keep it afloat (*"seventeen! eighteen! nineteen!"*), encouraging Jenn and Lucy to count along with him. An idea came to Holly, with a force of immediacy so strong that she felt Art and Gloria were thinking the same thing: you couldn't imagine Honus in a war zone.

"Twenty! Twenty-one! Twenty-two!"

It wasn't just that he seemed so young—he was, well, Honus. Acting all Honusy. Was this a mere indulgence? After all, how did Steve look to Gloria? Surely she could still see in her mind's eye an image of her unmaimed son, fresh, whole. And with a twinge Holly wondered: what about me? Nowadays many women served and they fought, too. She hadn't wanted to join them but to *assume* that someone else would fight for her, whatever the cause, wasn't a birthright. She didn't think so. Lines floated to memory:

> *Are we that wait—sufficient worth—*
> *That such Enormous Pearl*
> *As life—dissolved be—for Us—*

Dickinson was talking about the war, and those who could afford to wait. It wasn't only Austin who'd given war the slip. It wasn't just the spoiled brother. Emily had written "*we*." She hadn't spared herself in the questioning. The Enormous Pearl—life!—brought with it demands to make something of worth. Again, Holly wondered: what's my plan?

"*Twenty-three! Twenty-four!*"

The doorbell rang, and Holly excused herself and went to answer it. To her astonishment, it was Roger.

"Hello Holly!"

"Hey. What are you doing here?"

"I brought you a book."

They'd met at a coffee shop a couple of days ago. It was their first extended conversation. When she'd asked what he did in life, he told her that he was a neuro-science postdoc doing experiments on the striate cortical cells of monocularly deprived cats. She asked him to repeat himself, and Roger explained that his work involved inserting a device, like a black contact lens, into a cat's eye. The other eye was left untouched, and brain activity was monitored. Research on visual acuity could have analogous applications in humans.

"Don't you use gloves?" Holly asked, noticing the scratches on his hands.

"Well, sure, but I thought this cat trusted me."

This first meet-up hadn't gone badly, and Holly agreed to his suggestion to see each other again. She'd assumed that he'd call about plans for dinner or maybe a movie; she certainly hadn't expected him to show up unannounced at her door.

He handed her the book which was encircled by a red ribbon, tied with a bow. It had a library binding so she checked the title on the spine. *The Single Hound.*

"That's the author you mentioned, right?"

"Thank you Roger."

Her eyes dropped for an instant and noticed his feet, his tennis shoes, which were still spotless, as if freshly licked.

"It's a first edition."

"You didn't have to do that."

"I wanted to."

Holly removed the ribbon and opened the book, noticing the date on the frontispiece, 1914. She knew that this volume was compiled by Dickinson's niece from some inherited manuscripts; her editing was faulty and she'd naively imposed titles where there were none. Later editions had fixed these errors. This copy was battered, and had passed through many hands. Still. Still. She was aware of the music pouring out behind her, the sound of voices.

"Listen, Roger, I'd like to invite you in but I've got a bunch of people here. Family and stuff. I'm sorry but this isn't a good time."

"Oh, I don't want to intrude. Give me a call when you're ready." Then he fled down the steps before she could say another word.

In the living room, Jenn giggled. "Who was that?"

"Yes, who was that?" Anita asked.

They must've spied Roger from the front window as he hurried down the sidewalk. "Somebody returned a book."

"Must be special!" exclaimed Anita.

The ribbon dangled in plain sight.

"You should've invited him in," Jenn said. "I'd like to meet your gentleman caller."

This teasing from her little brother's girlfriend annoyed Holly. *From this kid.*

"Me too!" said Anita.

"Who was it?" Art called across the room.

Holly escaped to her bedroom and closed the door to get changed for work. When she came out, the others were putting on their coats to leave for the Mousehole. They'd already forgotten her.

Honus threw out his fist. "Off to battle!"

The next day Holly left Art the key to the house so he could have access while Anita and Maria went to the Torrid Tangos dance show. It was better than hanging around the motel. When she came back from work, she found her father and Maria's husband Jack sitting on the couch and watching television, their eyes glued to a golf tournament.

"Hey," she said.

"Hey," they replied, barely looking up. She noticed that the door to her room was open, and she heard music playing.

"Who's in my room?" she said quickly. "Is somebody in my room?"

Art scratched his leg and Jack turned his head, blinking. "It's Strapp," he said. "We're babysitting." Holly surged toward her bedroom and he called after her, "Don't worry. Honus is with him."

True enough, Honus sat on the edge of her bed while Strapp played at his feet, surrounded by a mess of papers.

"What are you *doing?*"

"Hey, Holly."

Honus reached for a big cup of soda and sucked on his straw, snorkeling loudly. A litter of paper bags and napkins and fast-food carry-out containers covered Holly's desk.

"Goddamnit, Honus!"

"What? He's not hurting anything, I promise. It's only stuff we took out of your waste-paper basket. He's helping me find lyrics."

Now, for the first time, she saw the situation clearly. Strapp held a pair of scissors, and slowly, because he gripped them upside-down, he cut off a strip from a discarded photocopy.

"Well, still! This place looks like it's been hit by a tornado. This is a private space. You can do that stuff out there!"

Probably it was her fatigue from having just completed a day shift after working the previous evening, but Holly found it unfathomable that they could be so invasive, so cavalier. Honus sighed. "Sorry Hol. We didn't want to bother Dad and Jack." He rose to his feet and coaxed Strapp from the room.

It was only when she was picking up the mess that she thought of her stolen Dickinson manuscript. It had been lying on her desk with her personal notes. Now it was spotted with several daubs of red goo.

"Oh my God!"

She stormed into the living room, holding the manuscript at arm's length.

"Look at this! Look at this! Don't you respect anything? Do you know what this is?"

"What happened?" Jack asked, standing up.

"He got ketchup on it! This is an *original* Emily Dickinson poem!"

"I'm sure it wasn't intentional," Jack said, reaching down to Strapp who, at the sound of Holly's angry voice, now clutched his father's leg, his eyes growing large.

"Not fucking Strapp! Honus! It was Honus!"

"Don't shout, Holly," Art said. "Don't talk like that."

Honus looked at his lap, while Jack glared at Holly. Maybe Strapp was off the hook, but that didn't change the fact that she'd referred to him as "fucking Strapp." Oh, he would remember that, and of course he'd mention it to Maria . . .

"It wasn't intentional," Honus said softly. "I'm sorry."

The doorbell rang and Holly went to answer it. She had a sudden vision of Roger, coming at the wrong time again. She would tell him to get his ridiculous shoes off her front steps—but it wasn't Roger, it was Anita and Maria, returning from their excursion. They bustled in, speaking in high, gay voices. It soon became evident that after the Torrid Tangos they'd enjoyed a long lunch and pitchers of margaritas. They stumbled into the middle of Holly's argument, and they seemed to find it amusing. They asked questions in an attempt to understand the problem. Holly explained that Honus had gotten ketchup on a unique, precious document, and when Honus peevishly interjected, "It's not ketchup, Holly, it's salsa," they found it hilarious. They laughed and laughed, while Holly paced and waited for them to shut up, and after they finally settled down and she resumed speaking, they broke into intermittent titters and giggles, setting each other off, till soon they were roaring, harder than the first time.

Strapp, seeing them, joined in. *"Tee-hee-hee."*

Exasperated, Holly turned her back on the group and returned to her room. She didn't slam the door: she made a point of closing it very slowly, with a trigger-like click.

The Soul selects her own Society—
Then—shuts the Door—

Later, Art was knocking. "Will you come out, please? I'm sure it'll be all right."

Holly was thumbing through Roger's book, because she couldn't bring herself to look at the soiled manuscript. When she emerged from her room, still angry but more composed, she expected apologies. But no one mentioned the incident. The conversation concerned their plans for the evening, and where they would all go to dinner.

"I wouldn't suggest Mexican," Maria said, and set everyone laughing again.

On Sunday afternoon, before the entourage returned to Sheridan, Art invited Holly for a stroll. Just the two of them. She was tempted to refuse, and make a stand, but a stand for what? Petulance? Nobody would be impressed. So she accepted and they met at the city park. She didn't ask what the others were doing, and Art didn't volunteer this information, either. He walked with his hands in his pockets, and Holly observed that her father was slightly bent, a stiffness in his shoulders. "They keep it up really nice," he said.

He was referring to the park, the green spaces and flowerbeds.

"Yeah, they do."

"It was your Mom's birthday yesterday, you know."

This came out simply and without further words, Holly instantly felt short of breath. She'd known. Of course she'd known. But she'd been so busy lately and it was true that yesterday—all her waking hours—it hadn't crossed her mind once. When she was small and it was someone else's birthday, her mother or father or Honus, it was understood that you were supposed to act very pleasant because it was *their* day, not yours, and you shouldn't distract from it. You owed it to the person to be good.

Holly's throat went tight. "I'm so sorry."

"That's all right. I know you still think of her." They walked a bit further. "You were pretty mad, though. What was that all about? I mean really?"

Holly didn't know where to begin. She'd already made herself very clear. What else was there to say? She sighed. "It's an original document. It might not mean a lot to everyone, but it matters, believe me."

"I get that," he said. "She's your favorite poet, right? She's the reason you stayed in school? Her words mean a lot to you, don't they?"

Holly nodded.

"OK. But that was just a piece of paper. It's not the words, is it?"

"Well, no, but—"

"You know the story of Bill Mazeroski and the home run ball?"

The sidewalk had led them past swing-sets and shouting children. This conversation was becoming embarrassing. Her father was a reasonable, intelligent man, capable of many types of discussion. So why did he return to his old baseball obsessions, these corny old stories? It was unworthy of him. "Sure, I remember you talking about it," Holly said. "He's the guy who hit the home run and won the World Series for the Pirates. It was in the seventh game. When we were kids you told us that story."

"You remember."

"Daddy, you told us a bunch of times."

"Beat the Yankees in the ninth inning."

"Right."

Holly wondered if he would ask her the year. 1960? 1961? It mattered to Art, a date you learned like the attack on Pearl Harbor or Kennedy's assassination. It was part of her indoctrination. But he said, "The thing is, do you remember what happened to that home run ball? That's my point."

Holly thought harder but she couldn't recall. Maybe she'd blocked it from her mind, as a form of resistance. She'd heard so many stories over the years. Trivia could be suffocating. "The ball?" she said. "I don't think so."

They kept walking. "So, Bill Mazeroski hits this historic homer, right? The ball sails out of the stadium and into the street. And some fourteen-year-old kid is walking by on his way home to supper. His name is Andy Jerpe. He couldn't get a ticket for the game. A ball falls out of the sky and rolls in front of him. He bends over and picks it up. Next thing he knows, cars are racing down the street toward him, reporters are flashing their cameras, and they stuff him in a car and take him back to the clubhouse where the Pirates are celebrating and spraying the champagne and Mazeroski autographs the ball for him. Andy gets his picture taken and the next day he's in all the newspapers.

"Of course, it was different back then. Nowadays, a ball like that would be worth thousands of dollars. Someone would jump in and there would be an auction for some crazy sum. But this kid Andy Jerpe—he just keeps his autographed Mazeroski ball on a shelf in his bedroom. It's his personal souvenir. Nobody bothers him.

"The baseball season is over, soon it's winter, life goes on. Till the following spring, one early warm day, his buddies come over. It's a beautiful day. They want to play. They want to hit some fungos. 'Show us your Mazeroski ball!' they say. At first Andy is reluctant to take it out, but the guys pressure him and eventually convince him and they go out in the sunshine and play catch and whack the ball around. They have a good time. Then somebody hits a slice to the side—and there it goes, the ball sails off into some weeds. They run after it, start looking for it, beating the weeds—but they can't find it. They keep looking till it gets dark and his friends give up and go home. This is a priceless, one-of-a-kind ball! But it's lost. Andy went back by himself to look the next day, too, but he couldn't find it. Not the next day, either. It was never, ever seen again."

Holly looked sideways at her father, knowing that she *had* heard this story, or at least part of it. It would've been long ago. She didn't see the point, but whatever it was, it was pure Art.

"So," she said, "we're supposed to grieve this lost ball, to this very day?"

He shook his head. "No, not at all! Because it's only a ball, right? Don't you see? What was special was what Mazeroski did. The blow he struck. And that wasn't undone when the ball got lost. It's his accomplishment, not some ball, right? Like your poetry. It has to be the words, not the paper they're written on. Right? That's what's really worth caring about, isn't it? A souvenir is a neat thing but in the end that's all it is, a *thing*. The meaning of an event doesn't reside in the object. I know you're more subtle than that."

He sat down on a bench and Holly took a place beside him. A fat robin hopped on the grass.

"Yeah, I know," she said. "It's only an object. You're right. But people I work with still take it pretty seriously."

Art was silent, but it was obvious what he thought. Just because they were foolish, it didn't mean that she should join them. It was the sort of thing you told a child—"just because Debbie jumps in a lake doesn't mean that you have to." She was grateful that he didn't bother to repeat it.

They remained on the bench, taking in the sun. Holly felt both comfort and remorse, sitting with her father. In truth she wasn't particularly sorry for yelling at Honus. That was just one of those moments. But she noticed that Art didn't ask *why* she was in possession of such a document. He trusted her. But, unlike Andy Jerpe, it wasn't something that had fallen out of the sky. Why didn't he question her? He had no idea of the schemes in Holly's head. It was inconceivable to him that she was a thief.

"Excuse me, do you have a minute?"

Rosemary looked up from her table, blinking, rubbing the fingers of her nitrile-gloved hands. Holly had been apprehensive about approaching while she worked in the consultations area, but there was no better place to give her the letter, to create the impression of spontaneity. Brazen it out, get it over with in one fell swoop. And, in fact, Rosemary didn't appear annoyed at the interruption. She smiled. "How *are* you, Holly? I have to say, you've put us onto some very interesting material here."

Us? Holly wondered. Who's *us?* This much she knew: it didn't include the likes of Holly Winegarten.

"I'm fine, thank you," she said. "Sorry to disturb you, but I might have something else for you. I think it belongs with your letters. I'm pretty sure the handwriting matches!"

Holly's voice came out tight and breathless, but she perceived that the effect was positive, because it made her sound innocent, not conniving. More than innocent: maybe a bit stupid? Rosemary sat up straight. "You think so, do you? And what might you have for me?"

Her tone was indulgent, almost as if she'd cut the phrase short—"And what might you have for me, *little girl?*"—but, of course, no one ever called Holly "little girl," and when Holly held out the letter, it was with the knowledge that if anyone was innocent here, it was Rosemary.

She studied it for a minute before speaking. She no longer smiled.

"This is a whole new poem! Where did you get this? Why wasn't it with the rest of the Donahue file?"

"Gee, I'm really sorry, but it must've slipped through the cracks when I was doing the initial sorting for cataloguing the cartons. It ended up with somebody else's stuff. But as soon as I saw it, I wanted to get it to you."

"Thank you, Holly." She held it up to the light, squinting and frowning at the salsa stain. "It's not in great shape but it's still legible. Are you sure there aren't any others like this? Could there be other stray pieces?"

"No, I don't think so."

"Well, keep looking. This is amazing stuff!"

Holly felt a tension released in her chest. Rosemary was buying her story, at least for the moment. The manuscript was out of her hands. Now she could look Art or anyone else in the eye. Rosemary readjusted the goose-neck of her lamp, and Holly moved away swiftly.

When her student status expired in May, Holly's job at Special Collections came to an end. She had no plans to register for further courses but, after all these years, it still felt peculiar to leave the cocoon of the university. Symbolically, at least, she was turning her back on the world of ideas, the search for knowledge, and high seriousness.

It was astonishingly easy. She was reminded of a basic fact: only people who inhabited the university environment cared about its workings. The rest of the world didn't give a damn.

For this transition Holly found a new job at a brightly-lit store called Buckley's, located in a sprawling mall near the interstate highway. Buckley's specialized in designer eye wear and accessories. After a week's training, Holly donned a white smock and sat behind an ersatz medical desk and greeted customers and applied a formula of nose bridge measurements for eyeglasses. In a stroke of good luck, she was soon promoted when a colleague was fired for watching Internet porn on the company system.

The increase in pay helped with her upkeep of the Comet. ("A rust bucket," according to the man at the body shop.) Holly invested in patches and a new paint job, choosing a sensual color called black cherry n° 2. ("You paint over a turd, it's still a turd," muttered the man at the body shop.) Holly thought the car looked very smart afterwards.

That summer she saw more of Roger, and sometimes Roger met her after her shift at Buckley's and they went skating at the mall's indoor ice-rink, a refreshing activity on a stifling summer evening.

"How do you keep your shoes so white?" she asked one night when he removed his sneakers and began to lace up his rental skates. "It always looks like you're wearing new shoes."

Roger nodded, embarrassed.

"I use swabs," he said.

"Swabs?"

"At the lab we have alcohol swabs everywhere, in these little packets? We need them for sterilization, because we handle the animals and do procedures. Well—I use them on my shoes, too." He shrugged and bit his lip. "It's sort of relaxes me."

"I see."

She'd noticed earlier that Roger was methodical but not always sensible in his behavior. His first invitations, his unexpected appearance at her door—were these bold acts or somehow clueless, or perhaps a curious combination of both? She peeked sideways at him as she bent to tie her laces. Recently he'd cut his hair shorter and Holly thought he had a nice profile.

When they got out on the ice, he moved with graceful, easy sweeps, skating backwards as well as forwards. Holly followed cautiously, careful of her knees, but it was amusing to watch him circle her with a slight grin on his face, cutting the ice and throwing out powdery crystals, showing off a little, but not too much.

Although Holly put in long hours at Buckley's and Stoddard's, it was the mellowest summer in recent memory, with none of the pressure of training for sport or the later years of assiduously reading and trying to improve her mind. She was spared the restless urgency of striving and driving herself to the next level. Now she had no such worries, and she enjoyed the change. Was this how most people lived? There might be something to it.

In July, after a period of uncertainty, she slept with Roger. Her hesitation wasn't because she found him unappealing; rather, she was nervous about complications at a time when she was seeking simplicity. But one night after a jazz concert in the park, she let it happen. She knew that he was interested and, from his perspective, he probably thought he was being patient. The question of sex hung in the air. To her relief, when she accepted his invitation to his place that night, it all went fairly well, aside from minor issues afterward, such as the startling jack-in-the-box way he bolted upright in bed and asked *Can I bring you a drink of water?* Roger also had a terrible alarm clock that ticked so loudly she got up in the middle of the night and took it to the next room, stuffed it behind a cushion. Inconceivable how he could sleep through that noise! Before returning to the bedroom, she paused, feeling her bare feet on the cool pine floor, still hearing the stifled clock under the cushion. She knew that she would come back to this place. She'd missed physical contact, and now wondered how she'd managed to go so long without it, how she'd kept herself distracted from this fundamental fact. This summer she felt as if she was becoming reacquainted with someone she'd always known, and strangely, that person was herself.

Holly avoided the campus, though once, rounding a street corner, she bumped into Inez from Special Collections, walking a big slobbering dog. Another time, in the supermarket, she saw Kenneth Swallow poking at the frozen foods.

In a town of this size, reminders of her previous life were impossible to escape. She even daydreamed, in the course of a long day at the mall, of spotting Emily. A little redhead at the earring counter or in the sporting goods store seeking a white tennis outfit. Look: there she was on the escalator! Such images came with startling ease. Well, as long as I don't start *talking* to her, Holly thought, I'm not crazy. She'll talk to me, in her poems.

September came, and unlike recent years she didn't scroll through the departmental website, scouring the course descriptions. Instead she investigated Yankton Associates, an employment agency that specialized in work abroad. Holly did grammar exercises in an Italian textbook and tried to improve her level by slowly reading an old paperback of Natalia Ginzburg's *Le piccole vertù*, which she'd found for fifty cents in the bargain bin of a used book store. Sometimes, when business was slow and Holly was alone in Buckley's, she sneaked it out of her purse and read. She labored over each piece, because her Italian wasn't effortless and the words impressed themselves on her mind as an almost concrete grouping, like reading poetry. One day, behind the counter, concentrating and silently moving her lips, she became aware of movement in front of her, and in a single gesture she closed the book and slid it behind her elbow and looked up with a smile to greet the customer, and found herself face-to-face with Courtney Davies.

"Oh! What are you doing here?"

"I work here, Courtney. How can I help you?"

"Well, I got this."

Courtney slid her optical prescription across the desk and Holly began to type the information into the store's database. Courtney went to inspect the display racks and tried on several styles of frames. As she typed, Holly stole a few glances, recognizing Courtney's fat book-bag, a lumpy blue monstrosity with zippers that she'd lugged faithfully to Rosemary's seminar. The mall sound system piped a string instrumental of an old Beatles song.

Eventually Courtney came back with a frame with turquoise temple inserts, priced at $239.

"Those are pretty ones," Holly said. "And they're hypoallergenic and nickel free."

"You don't think they look too serious?"

Courtney slid them onto her nose. Holly thought: *Kiddo, your seriousness goes way beyond glasses.*

"No, they're nice. Very nice."

Taking Courtney's nose bridge measurements, Holly explained that her prescription lenses for these frames would be ready in less than twenty-four hours, in keeping with Buckley's Quality Service Pledge. (This recitation was obligatory.) Courtney signed and initialed the purchase agreement, and Holly swiped her credit card. The transaction went swiftly. But, before she left the store, Courtney asked, "Have you dropped out of school? I haven't seen you around."

"Yes. The program wasn't really for me. You know you can get a second pair of frames for half price?"

"No, that's OK, thanks." Courtney lingered to chat a little longer, mentioning that she'd expanded her dissertation subject to include the question of less visible migrants whose voices were often silenced. "There's a paradoxical invisibility nowadays at a time when hypervisibility, institutionally speaking, can be interpreted as an epiphenomenon of growing differential visibility. Especially in today's media, you can't get away from it. There's awesome work being done recently that suggests visibility has become fractal."

"Well," Holly said, mentally translating what she'd just heard but running into a wall before she could reach the end. She smiled. "Go for it."

"I've had good news, too." Courtney smiled back. "My proposal to give a paper for the Modern Language Association has been accepted. The convention is in Chicago this year. I'll be the only graduate student on my panel, because everyone else is, like, full professor? This is so exciting!"

"Congratulations, Courtney."

"The department will be well-represented this year," she added. "Did you hear about Rosemary Muller's discovery?"

Holly had been treading water in this conversation, waiting for it to end, but now she froze.

"I . . . I don't think so. What discovery are you talking about?"

"Some Emily Dickinson letters, right here in our own library, apparently with new poems. She's giving a paper in one of the nineteenth century panels. Her co-author—get this!—is Philip Post. Can you believe it? I had to see it with my own eyes. It's on the official program."

Holly felt herself breathing quickly but she didn't say anything; she licked her lips and let Courtney go on talking. Courtney was appalled that Rosemary, whom she'd considered a mentor and an example for all the women in the department, could choose to collaborate with the likes of Philip Post. "What kind of message does this send? You have to wonder what—"

"Those letters?" Holly interrupted. "How did Rosemary find them? What does she say?"

"Some library employee stumbled across them and didn't know what he was sitting on, but then Philip spotted them and brought them to Rosemary's attention. Makes me gag. He's such a suck-up. If they'd discovered anything near his specialty you can bet he wouldn't have shared it. But of course he runs straight to Rosemary because he's coming up for tenure next year. He's scared to death that she'll block his career. Rosemary is on the review committee."

"That so?"

Courtney interpreted Holly's response as an interest in the minutiae of departmental politics, so she began to elaborate on the composition of the committee and the complications arising from Philip's inter-departmental status. What had once been his calling card could become his liability. Budget cuts were on the horizon. It was a complicated chess game with many variables, but one thing was certain: Rosemary's opinion carried a lot of weight in the liberal arts faculty. "I hope she's just toying with him, making the fucker jump through hoops before he gets the axe. You know, I'm not even sure that Philip has his green card yet. That would make it hard for him to apply anywhere else if they deny him tenure. His career could go up in smoke! They could kick his poncy ass all the way back to England!"

Courtney's face glowed with this happy thought. By now Holly could hardly listen. Under her desk, her fingers flittered on her knees. Mercifully the telephone rang and she was obliged to pick it up. She noted down information about a delivery from a supplier, repeating aloud invoice numbers and a tracking code while Courtney looked on and listened with an expression of concerned sympathy. When Holly put down the receiver, Courtney said, "Well, I'll leave you to your work. Thanks . . . and good luck!" Then she left the store.

These parting words were intended to be friendly, but Holly recoiled. How patronizing! *Good luck.* What was that supposed to mean? What was she really saying? Of course Courtney was judging her. In Courtney's eyes, Holly had left behind the World of Intellect and the Fight for Empowerment of the Marginalized and, when you got down to it, nothing less than What Mattered in Life. In their place, she'd chosen to work IN THE MALL. How pathetic. What a sell-out! She'd met the beast, and she'd embraced it. Holly might as well have dropped everything for a career as a pom-pom girl, if such a thing were possible; it was only a small step above standing on street corners and handing out leaflets in favor of female circumcision.

Holly wanted to run after Courtney and wag a finger in her face. Don't read me this way! she would say. Don't make me a character in your smug narrative. The mall was just a place and lots of decent people had reason to work there. What brought YOU here?

Ridiculous, she knew. Why care what Courtney Davies thought? She'd turned the page, hadn't she? The departmental rivalries and intrigues were just another version of the old schoolyard. Not her problem anymore.

Still, for the rest of the afternoon, Holly stewed. She couldn't put it out of her mind. Customers came and went, and she served them with a distracted air. The clock moved very slowly. When she had a free moment, she didn't return to

Le piccole vertù. She wouldn't be able to concentrate. Oh, this was exasperating!

Although it was forbidden to use her work station computer for personal email or searches, Holly couldn't wait for her shift to end. Less than an hour after her conversation with Courtney, she typed in a search for the convention of the Modern Language Association.

At first she was denied access to the program because she wasn't an M.L.A. member, but eventually she was able to parasite onto a link of someone who was. The program was huge, and rather confusing. There were many panels. But wait— there it was! A co-authored paper by Rosemary Muller and Philip Post, entitled, "Spatio-Topological Text(s): Toward a 21st Century Reading of New, Unpublished Work by Emily Dickinson."

Holly's temples throbbed.

"Come in!"

When she entered Borden's office, he was watering his ficus. There was a stack of essays on his desk beside some crumpled candy bar wrappers.

"The return of the prodigal," he drawled, putting down his plastic bottle.

"You probably know why I'm here."

He shook his head and motioned for her to sit down.

Holly had hurried up the stairs and was out of breath. Now she made an effort not to sound abrupt. "Have you seen this year's program for the M.L.A. convention? There's something surprising there."

Borden lowered himself into his chair and tried to cross one leg and then another before perching on the chair's edge. He reminded Holly of her Granddad Winegarten when he complained of hemorrhoids. She tried to put the thought out of her mind.

"I bid farewell to the M.L.A. years ago," he said. "Don't know about their program nor do I care. I've moved on professionally."

Holly rested a hand on the edge of his desk. Maybe Borden wouldn't want to hear about it, maybe he'd dismiss the whole thing. But who else could she turn to? Who else would understand? Now, while leaving out personal details about her contacts with Philip Post, as well as the fact that she'd dithered and delayed in returning the poem, she told him of her disappointment, her outrage that the discovery was being exploited in this manner.

"It's not right. You see my point, don't you? It's not right. 'Spatio-Topological Semiotext(s)'? What on earth is that?"

Borden shrugged. "I don't know. But we haven't heard their argument, have we? Perhaps you're being hasty. Putting aside the circumstances, I don't doubt that Professor Muller is a capable scholar." Borden grimly tugged at one of his ears. "Though I agree that their title is infelicitous. Is that what you're saying?"

His manner surprised her. She'd expected to get a rise out of him, a taste of something acid. After all, wasn't there bad blood between Borden and Rosemary? She'd called him on the carpet for his stupid remark about "clit lit" and had had him disciplined. Borden had never been one to shy away from controversy. But now he sounded bland, almost as if he was defending her.

"It's not just their title," she pursued. "Honestly, I don't *trust* them. They pounced on those letters, the poetry. Is there a good reason why? These manuscripts are a big deal and they're going to blow the whole thing." She heard herself speak and it was like listening to an exaggerated relapse of the old Holly—

as if, once she'd opened herself up again to those petty sentiments, she was going on a binge.

Borden blinked behind his glasses, exhaling deeply from
hairy nostrils. "Now you're being presumptuous. We can't
know what they'll produce. But let's back up: those letters
aren't yours and they never were yours. They belong to the
library. They belong to *everyone*. I can understand that you
might feel an attachment to them, and of course you should be
acknowledged for your discovery. The handling of the matter
might seem opportunistic and distasteful, but that's nothing
new, Ms. Winegarten. These maneuvers happen all the time.
Don't expect me to feign shock. In any event, all this has *nothing* to do with the more serious enterprise of literature, which
is a question of an entirely different order."

Holly thought: Tell me something I don't know, old man!

She hadn't come here to be corrected. He owed her something better than a lecture and she was determined to get it out
of him. It was like a desire to poke a sleeping bear with a stick.

"You know how they feel about us, Professor Borden," she
said. "Let's be frank."

He drew up his chin. "I'm not sure what you're referring
to. Frank about what?"

Careful now, she thought, careful. She couldn't say, *Everybody thinks you're a joke. A dinosaur.* Holly's breath hitched
and she shifted her tone. "I'm sure we agree that these materials are more important than anybody's career. But we can't
ignore how Rosemary and Philip operate. There are principles
at stake."

"I see. We are supposed to worry about *Rosemary*. With
Philip."

Holly sighed. "Professor Muller and Professor Post, yes. I
know them, maybe better than you do. And I'm not talking
for the sake of a career. I have no status here."

"But you imply that you know better. You think you could do a better job."

"Yes, I could."

Holly hadn't come to brag, but if he was going to take the conversation in that direction, she wouldn't back down. She had game.

Borden mused for a moment. "I confess that my memory is not as sharp as it should be. And you showed me the poem only once. That's the most important piece in the lot, isn't it? Do you still know it?"

Holly nodded.

Borden lifted a palm. "Please?"

Holly recited the poem slowly, feeling her way around its rhythms while visualizing its dashes and line breaks and turns of meaning. When she finished, Borden was silent, letting the words linger between them. Eventually he said, "Would you be so kind as to type up a fair copy of what you just said? I trust that you retained the punctuation, too? I should like a version, for my personal use."

She nodded.

"As for the rest—if you think you can do a better job, Ms. Winegarten, you should try."

"Try? How?"

"You should go to the M.L.A. convention and tell them what you know. Don't let others monopolize the conversation. I say in perfect confidence that they need people like you."

Holly laughed. "Yeah, right! I'm not a member of the M.L.A. I'm not even a student anymore. They wouldn't let me give a paper. Not in a million years. I couldn't get past the door."

"You're jumping to conclusions. I would be willing to help you, if you were interested. Have you heard of Hans Wo-erner?"

"No."

"He's a Thoreau specialist and has done very solid work on the transcendentalists. He's Swiss, we go back many years. Always was a bit of a hippie. A *Swiss* hippie." Borden sucked on his lower lip and chuckled at his own joke, and Holly waited for him to finish. Eventually Borden continued: "He's a great friend and is still very active in the game. He always has a panel on nineteenth century voices and I'm sure that, as a favor, he could find a slot for me. For *us*, Ms. Winegarten. For your views to be aired among serious scholars."

"Really?"

"We could give the paper jointly. This is your project and I fully acknowledge it as such. My role would be that of your guarantor. Since you don't have formal qualifications, I could be useful in that regard. To get you through the door, as you say. Upon which, you can make your case. What do you think?"

"You would really do that?"

"Of course. It would be refreshing to return to the fray!"

Holly felt herself shrinking; she was convinced of her rightness but she didn't want to perform in front of an audience of strangers, to make an argument and compete with specialists in a large arena. She'd come to Borden's office seeking . . . *what*, exactly? Merely a sympathetic listener, someone to join a bitching session? It hadn't occurred to her that he might raise the stakes. She said slowly, "All right then."

"I'll send Hans a message today and I'll let you know his reaction as soon as I hear from him. You'd better get busy, Ms. Winegarten. Now if you'll excuse me," he said, pulling an essay off the stack on his desk, "I have to get to work, too."

FIVE

SKIES INSIDE YOUR HEAD

"Fabulous! We're going to open for Spotz!"

Holly could hardly believe it, but it was true. Spotz! was a nationally known band, currently touring the U.S., especially college towns, to push their latest album. They'd recently enjoyed two hit singles. As a promotional gimmick for this tour, they'd set up a contest inviting regional bands to submit sound files to their website, and selected winners would perform as the opening act for a portion of the tour. The bands wouldn't get paid, but they'd receive significant exposure. And Honeybunch had been chosen!

True, they weren't the only winner—they'd have to share the stage with two other bands, and could perform only a short set—but they'd play for audiences of 2000 to 10,000 people. A year ago, when they were signing up for open mic on alcohol-free Mondays at *Dead Freddy's*, who would've dreamed that such a thing was possible?

"The Gash isn't exactly my style but there's a certain grit in his voice that's kind of cool," Honus said. "He has *something*. It's hard to put your finger on."

The Gash was lead singer for Spotz! He had dark curly locks and performed shirtless while wearing bullfighter pants. Holly was certain that a short time ago, Honus would've heaped scorn on The Gash, as an outdated rocker, a pop pretender. He was famous but not cool. To be cool you had to be known, but not famous, not in that way, unless you were much older, and then you might qualify as an icon. (Maybe.) It was complicated. Guys like The Gash were on shaky ground. But now that Honeybunch was going to share a stage with Spotz!, Honus had discovered some redeeming qualities. Maybe he and The Gash were going to hang out together. Different styles, to be sure, but they were bros in the same business.

"You gonna perform without your shirt?" Jenn teased.

"You never know. Will you join me?"

"You never know." She giggled. "You always have such thoughts."

"Well, you always give me such thoughts." Honus wiggled his eyebrows.

Holly interrupted, "How much is this going to cost?" She wanted to come to the point. Playing in a larger venue complicated matters. Although a stripped-down simplicity had always been a part of the Honeybunch sound, making a virtue out of low-budget necessity, Honus had been griping about equipment for a long time, complaining that Steve's drum kit sounded like shit, and you couldn't fix everything with duct tape. (Lately Honus had started wearing yellow duct tape wound round and round his T-shirt as part of his stage attire; he looked like a bumblebee.) Today he'd come to see Holly and brought her cupcakes. *Cupcakes?* Ordinarily Honus didn't pay her social calls. He never brought pastries. Holly suspected what this was about. A new microphone pre-amp, a power amp and who knew what else. Her brother wanted to borrow money.

"I've been thinking about this," he said.

"How much? Give me a number."

"Well, with a couple thousand we could—"

"Oh, come on. Be reasonable."

"Fifteen hundred! I've been looking on the Internet, I'm talking used gear, nothing new and fancy but equipment that isn't *shit*. You play with shit, you sound like shit, that's the problem."

"It's just a few shows. Couldn't you rent the equipment?"

"For chrissakes, we've gone over that!"

Honus found such questions insulting, because he planned for Honeybunch in the long run. New gear wasn't only for these upcoming shows. It would be an investment for future gigs, beyond Spotz! A future that was bigger, always better. To think only of the short run was to dismiss their prospects and undermine his faith. Instead of repeating all this, though, Honus reached for a cupcake and began to lick off the frosting. This was his usual procedure: a cupcake was always naked, shining, before he took the first bite.

Holly watched him. "I suppose you've already asked Yeti and Steve?"

"We've talked about it, sure. Yeti pulls his weight, he supplies the van, all the transportation. When was the last time we bothered you about that?"

Holly shrugged.

"And Steve doesn't have that kind of cash lying around. You know that. You know the deal."

And Jenn? Holly wondered. She was literally at arm's length, listening to the conversation, and Holly resisted the temptation to turn to her. She'd been told that Jenn's parents were both dentists who paid her tuition but sternly refused to indulge her with pocket money, expecting her to earn every penny herself while making good grades. And so far, Jenn had kept up her end of the bargain. Not long ago Holly had taken Honus aside and told him he should stand on his own feet instead of being on academic probation and relying so much on Art and Anita to pay for things. But this little speech had backfired. Because instead of turning to his parents, now Honus looked to his sister.

"What makes you think that I have that kind of cash lying around?"

"Hang on. You're always so touchy, Hol. That's not what I'm saying."

But it was what he was implying. She no longer paid tuition, she worked two jobs. In her spare moments, when she wasn't reading some nerdy book, she was probably closed up in her room, counting and stacking her money. What else would she do with it?

With her family, Holly had only vaguely alluded to her plans to move on, and hadn't mentioned leaving the U.S. She didn't want to answer a bunch of questions. (Though she was troubled by their lack of curiosity, by how easily they accepted her quitting the realm of ideas for the "normal world"—did they really suppose that her current situation was her future? How disappointing.)

Yes, Holly had saved money—but there were many everyday expenses, soon student loans would come due, and this crazy scheme of going to the M.L.A. convention to publicly challenge Rosemary and Philip would drain her savings. Until now, she hadn't realized how much you had to *pay* to join the conversation. The convention registration, hotel and transportation, plus the lost wages at work, easily came to a thousand dollars. So much for free intellectual exchange! It was a sport for the rich or for well-groomed darlings with a suitable sponsor.

Recently she'd sent an advance fee to Yankton Associates for an international job search. Included in the agency package were visa services but there was no guarantee of a living wage—it might only lead to giving private English lessons. She'd filled out the forms and tried to polish her CV, remembering what the man at the body shop had said about her Comet. That was how she saw her CV.

Honus swallowed his cupcake, avoiding her eyes. Waiting for an answer. She knew how much these concerts meant to him. Her brother was following his dreams, too—and why shouldn't he? She pictured him as a little boy in a baseball uniform, his nasty chafed skin from the catcher's gear, his bandaged, broken fingers. His quiet suffering. Holly wasn't feeling noble or generous—quite the contrary—but she mentally calculated how much money would leave her a minimum without abandoning her own projects. She still had a couple of months of earnings before the M.L.A. convention.

"OK—I can do a thousand. You'll have to make it work with that."

"Oh, thanks! You're my ace. I mean it!"

He held out the plate to her, and Holly served herself, thinking: *this is an expensive cupcake.*

Holly and Borden hammered out a strategy. She laid out the main points for the paper. Since the biographical aspect of the discovered letters was inconclusive, they would focus mainly on the extant poem, the finished creation. Although the situation felt like a deliberate showdown with Rosemary and Philip, they would not acknowledge it as such. They would remain aloof, above the fray, say what they believed and never mind the rest. Holly didn't *feel* aloof, but this suited her better than playing institutional tit-for-tat, and it might have the added benefit of disconcerting Rosemary more than a conventional confrontation. As for Philip, it was hard to figure out what was fitting, but since she couldn't toss him into an abyss of black fire, spinning and screaming, this would have to do.

Their paper was a late addition to the convention program but Borden managed to get his friend Hans Woerner to squeeze them into a panel early on Saturday, before Rosemary and Philip had their turn later in the afternoon.

"That way, Ms. Winegarten, you will be the *first* to have given a paper on this subject. No one can take that away from you."

"It's only a few hours before their paper. No one cares."

"We shall see, won't we?"

Sure enough, a short time after they were added to the program, Holly got a call from Rosemary Muller.

"Hello Holly. How *are* you?"

Holly was slow to answer, thinking: How did you get my number? But then she realized: Philip, of course. Mr. Weasel.

"Fine. I'm excellent. How are *you?*"

"There's maybe something you could clear up for me about our friend Robert Borden. I'm sorry to say this, but I'm afraid he might be using you. That paper you're doing: 'Some Remarks on New Work by Emily Dickinson.' What's that all about?"

Holly immediately resented this assumption. Borden using *me?* Do you hear yourself? Even if in the past she'd sought his approval, as well as Rosemary's, this time she was the one in charge. Was that so hard to imagine?

"Well, we're attempting something different from a spatio-topological approach of a semiotext thingy. I'm still thinking about it, though."

There was a silence that Holly savored, as Rosemary took in the fact that her work had been referred to as a "thingy." Eventually Rosemary said, "Why do you think a man like that put you up to this? Have you considered?"

"What are you talking about? Actually, I approached Professor Borden."

"Let's be frank. This all sounds like a rather misguided and desperate effort to attract attention. You might think you'll enjoy the spotlight. But this is no classroom, Holly. This is another level, an international forum, and it's not an appropriate setting for beginners or the inexperienced."

There it is! Holly thought. *There.* In a perverse way it was a relief to hear Rosemary's condescension come out in the open. It removed all previous doubt that maybe Holly had been imagining it, maybe she was too defensive. It gave her something to push back. Now Holly said, "I'm not a beginner and I'm not inexperienced. Don't worry about me. For my part, I look forward to hearing you speak. Philip, too! I'm sure he'll benefit from collaborating with someone as experienced as you."

Another silence. Eventually Rosemary replied, "We'll do our best. This was intended as a friendly call, I hope you understand that. I don't like scenes. You follow me? This kind of exposure might not suit you. Goodbye, Holly."

Later, when Holly recounted this conversation to Borden, he chuckled and tapped a cigarette. "What did I tell you? This really gets under their skin."

But a doubt gnawed at Holly, a regret at her tone with Rosemary. What had she meant by "exposure"? That was Rosemary's parting remark, and now Holly couldn't get the word out of her mind. Maybe it was a warning. Even a threat. Perhaps Rosemary had seen through Holly's duplicitous handling of the manuscript, its delayed delivery, and worst of all, the unpardonable fact that she'd damaged it. She might not dwell on these matters if Holly were out of the picture, since what was done, was done; but if Holly insisted on inserting herself into the conversation, Rosemary could call her out and demand an explanation. What was the meaning of such shenanigans? Holly swallowed and looked back at Borden. She hadn't told him the whole story and now it was too late.

"What is it?" he asked, eyeing her.

She swallowed again. "We need a better title," she said eventually. " 'Some Remarks on New Work by Emily Dickinson.' That's so bland."

"That vexes them all the more. Understatement can be a dagger thrust!"

Holly didn't answer. Borden inquired, "Have you come up with something better?"

"I don't know. 'Moby Toad?' "

He barked with laughter, showing his snaggly yellow teeth.

The day had started very well. They left town early, Holly at the wheel and Roger navigating the blue lines of the map. They explored country roads and then cruised on a winding blacktop along the river, the fall foliage of the trees magnificent—red and crimson and gold and orange, splashing the air, reflected on the water. Toward noon they picnicked, a simple meal of apples and cheese, followed by sticky slices of German chocolate torte bought along the way in a small town where old ladies had set up card tables for a fundraiser on the lawn of a Lutheran church. Nearby a wizened man deftly stacked squash into pyramids, their irregular, brightly colored shapes, speckled and striped, as bright as undersea coral.

"How beautiful!" Holly exclaimed. "Oh, I'd like some of those!"

The ladies shook their heads. "Tomorrow," they said, in a tone which suggested greater pleasure should be postponed as a matter of principle. "Those are for *tomorrow*."

But it was already a special day. As if the volume knob of Life had been turned up several notches. With the change of seasons, the sun went down early, which added a wistful note.

It was dark and growing chilly when they came back that evening, and Holly and Roger were reluctant for the day to end, so they went downtown to an Italian restaurant for dinner. They'd never been to this place before, but the meal felt perfect. In a rare pause in conversation, happy fantasies came unbidden. A few years from now, when she was established in Europe and Roger was a successful scientist attending a top-level conference in Rome, she would drive him around in her sports car and they would zip up to the Aventino overlooking the city. "The European Union is funding a new feline vision research center," he said. "Cats are the future. They've offered me a job."

Now he asked across the table, "What are you smiling about?"

"Everything," she said.

After dinner, their faces warm with wine, they went for a walk, hand in hand, along streets near the campus. They leaned in close.

Then a surprise: it was Jérémy Ndao, coming down the sidewalk from the opposite direction, holding hands with a young woman. Holly noticed his tall lean frame, the comfortable bob of his shoulders, and wondered if he might not see her if she looked straight ahead and kept on walking. It had been years since she'd spoken to him and she'd assumed that he left town.

"Hello, Holly."

"Oh . . . hello. What are you doing here?"

Her question sounded abrupt, but Jérémy smiled his slow, easy smile—oh, she hadn't forgotten that smile but seeing it again was a jolt. A pleasure that made her sad. He pointed upwards.

"I live here. Second floor. Moved out of the old place a couple of years ago."

The gentle sibilance of his accent. He was referring to a nearby brick building. Holly had walked past it many times.

"Jérémy, this is Roger."

"And this is Sophie." They exchanged introductions and shared remarks about the beautiful Indian summer's day. Under the streetlight, Holly noticed Sophie's shortly cropped hair, a tattoo on her pale neck, her diminutive stature—her forehead would press right about *there* on Jérémy's chest. It seemed safe to assume that she wasn't his wife from Senegal.

"Goodnight."

"Goodnight."

They walked on, and at first Roger said nothing about this encounter. He and Holly chatted about his plans to leave town for a few days to visit his mother, a meet-up at an interstate motel. Roger sometimes shared stories about his family, how his father had abandoned them long ago and his mother had supported Roger and his brother with waitressing jobs. Later, she'd married a long-distance trucker and acquired a commercial driving license and now they partnered on cross-country trips. Roger was proud of his mother and liked his step-father, but his family couldn't understand why someone with his abilities had chosen post-doctoral work on the neurophysiology of cats instead of becoming a "real doctor." Roger's younger brother, who'd spent two years at a community college, worked for a furniture outlet in the Twin Cities and made as much money as Roger. "My mother hasn't had the luxury of time," he said. "And in school that's what I've enjoyed. I put in long hours, but they're of my choosing." Holly thought he was going to say more about his research, but instead he asked, "Holly, would you like to meet her?"

She hesitated. "Uh, why not?"

She was willing to meet his mother, but in truth she was in no hurry to do so. And now, as they headed back to her car, Roger asked, "You used to go out with that guy, didn't you?"

She let go of his hand for a moment to button up the top of her coat, and then took his hand again.

"For about five minutes, a million years ago."

"I thought so."

Holly found herself in a mood to talk. It was better to be frank. Roger should understand. Sure, she'd been tempted to look over her shoulder a moment ago, to see if little Sophie had skipped upstairs into Jérémy's building. But Holly hadn't looked, and at bottom, she no longer cared. She hadn't thought of Jérémy Ndao for a long time. She didn't hold a candle for him, not seriously. But she wanted to talk.

"Funny about that guy. He's been a student here forever and I don't think it's about the research. Maybe it's a visa thing, his way to get away from home. I wonder if maybe I'm not so different. I'm trying to find a way out."

Holly had made no secret with Roger of her desire to go abroad. She'd told him an abridged version of her disappointment about the job in Bordeaux.

"You know where you're going to go?" he asked.

"Couldn't say."

"Holly, that doesn't sound serious."

Holly slowed her walk. This was an unfamiliar note. He hadn't spoken in this tone before. Was he judging her? Sure, in despondent moments, she'd told herself the same thing, that she ought to have a firmer grip on her life. But it sounded different from someone else. From someone who usually tried to please her.

"Well, I'll be the one to decide that, won't I?"

A peevishness entered her voice and now she realized that the evening had run its course, she wished she were at home, working on her Dickinson presentation. During their picnic an interpretation had occurred to her of a spatial metaphor, *skies inside your head.* She'd been mulling it over ever since. She needed to test it out while it was still fresh in mind.

"What about me?" Roger asked.

They stopped walking and Holly thought: Oh God, I shouldn't have opened my big mouth.

"Listen, Roger. Do you see yourself in Italy?"

He didn't answer.

"When you finish your post-doc, where are you going to go? Where are you going to live?"

He remained silent, his hands thrust in his pockets. Just a short time ago, he'd figured in Holly's fantasy. But how could she share it now, if he doubted even her first step? She took him by the arm and pulled him along, continued down the street.

"You don't know, do you?" she said. "Depends on where the jobs are, right? On the science foundation grants. It's a roll of the dice to find a place to pursue the specialty you love. I get that. But do me a favor. Don't tell me I'm not serious. You're just as uncertain about the future as I am."

Holly felt that her words were true. But in saying them, she also felt that she was being bloody-minded and ruining their day. A lovely day. Maybe their best day ever. What had happened, really? Please, I have to go home, she thought.

As they approached her car, Roger said, "My specialty isn't the only thing I love." He looked at her. "Or the only one."

She let this statement go unanswered as she drove him back to his place. What could she say? Of course she cared and she wanted love. But if he didn't believe in her hopes, how could he expect her to declare her love in return? First, he'd have to understand her better. This kind of talk now made her feel flustered, it confused her heart. Holly was driving fast and when a light changed, she braked abruptly, skidding to a stop.

"Oops," she said.

"I'm sorry," Roger said, looking down at his feet. "I didn't mean to do that."

She reached over and stroked his arm. She felt a wave of tenderness. "Oh, honey. It's all right."

"I'm sorry 'cause I broke your floor."

At first she didn't understand but then Roger lifted the floor mat beneath his feet. The light turned green and she drove on, the Comet's muffler blatting.

"I'm not kidding, Holly. I can see the pavement moving."

This wasn't good. Holly remembered that there had been a rust hole down there, over which she'd put some of Honus's tape. She'd also layered on an extra mat, for insulation. That had been in April or May, she'd had time to forget about it. But a moment ago, when she'd stopped suddenly at the light, Roger must've pushed down hard with his foot, and broken open the spot.

"This thing isn't safe," he said. "You shouldn't be on the road."

"It's OK. I get where I'm going."

"That remains to be seen."

His voice was snappish. Their goodnight kiss was brief, even perfunctory. Holly drove home, unhappy about this conclusion and stressed about the moving ground below her, the fragility of her Comet.

The next evening Chelsea called a house meeting. Odd, this time of the month. They usually met at predictable intervals to sort out their utility bills. But on short notice she summoned Holly and the Troll, who now sat expectantly on the couch, waiting to hear what she had to say.

"Listen, I've decided to sell this place. My other places, too. I'm leaving town and starting a new business in Portland. It makes sense for me to liquidate everything here. Of course that means you'll get a month's rent free, those are the terms. But I wanted to warn you as soon as possible—I hope to be operational in Oregon by the New Year. Frankly, the sooner you leave, the better."

"Portland?" said Holly. "What are you going to do there?"

"Same as I do here, pretty much. But bigger. It's a better place for me. More opportunities."

The Troll's face crinkled. "Is this really necessary?"

Chelsea half-smiled. "Come on, Wayne. You can't ask that question."

"I mean, you could sell the place with us still in it. The next owner will want to rent it out. That would work, wouldn't it?" Chelsea was already shaking her head, and he added, "I got all my *stuff* here."

He was visibly upset and Holly wondered what kind of stuff the Troll kept in the basement. His shirt was frayed and his jeans were ripped, not fashionably so, just ripped. He looked like a shipwreck survivor.

"In all likelihood the buyer will knock down this house and put in apartments," Chelsea said. "You can make more money with more units. If I stayed around I'd consider it myself, though that's not really my line of business."

"What about your house on Audubon Avenue? That has a cool basement. I could go there. Kick those suckers out."

"Sorry. All my renters have to go. In order to do this now, it's costing me on my end, you know."

That might be so, Holly thought, but the sale of so much real estate was going to leave Chelsea with a serious pile of cash. And with that, a ticket to a new life of her choosing. I should learn from this, she told herself. Be independent like Chelsea. But how? She respected Chelsea, but she didn't see herself operating in her kind of world. In the end, they didn't speak the same language.

The next day, the Troll resurfaced in the kitchen while Holly was preparing her dinner. He didn't make small talk.

"We could live together," he said. "What do you think?"

"Excuse me?"

"Where are *you* going to go?" He tilted his head and peered at her, as if she was hiding something from him. "It's always worked with us, right? There's no reason to change. We should look for a place together!"

"I don't think so, Wayne."

"But at least tell me. Where are you going to go?"

He was probably 28 or 30 years old, she reckoned, but this was how Honus had spoken when he was twelve and he wanted to accompany her to the movies.

"I'm leaving the country, if you must know."

"Really?" He shook his shoulders, as if he'd never heard such a preposterous alibi. "Leaving? The *country?*"

"That's what I said."

As ridiculous as this conversation was, it steeled Holly in her resolution. Yes, she would be as bold as Chelsea. She would confront Rosemary and Philip and stand up for herself, and then she'd take control of her life in a new place. She sure as hell wasn't going to be another dropout stranded in this town, living a trollish existence.

He pouted. "That's not fair."

Apart from her conversations with Borden, Holly never set foot in the Crewe Building, and when she went to the university library to confirm a source, she kept a low profile, slipping down the side stairs and avoiding Special Collections. It was irrational behavior because she had every right to be here. This was a public university and the library was open to all state residents. Unlike students, she couldn't check out materials, but she knew where to look in the PS1541 section on the fourth floor. Although she didn't exactly *miss* Merle and Inez, she wouldn't have minded a friendly chat.

But she couldn't cross the threshold. And the reason was simple and sheepish: she didn't want to bump into Rosemary Muller, in the event that she was in Special Collections to consult the Michael Donahue materials. She didn't want to face any questions.

One day curiosity overcame her, though, and squeezing her fingertips hard against her palms, she climbed the stairs and walked straight to the Special Collections entrance. Through the glass wall she had a clear view of Merle at his desk, typing into his computer while his aquarium bubbled. She could see her former work cubicle. She could even glimpse the top of Inez's head in her office. It moved slightly from side to side: she was talking on the telephone. Holly sensed that she was gazing into a larger aquarium where she, too, had swum.

Rosemary was nowhere in sight. Still, instead of crossing the threshold, Holly turned around and walked away.

A short time later, she was sitting in the food court at the mall with a co-worker named Paula. "Who's that guy?" Paula asked. "He keeps looking over here and now he's waving."

Beyond the food court, people waited for tickets at the Cineplex. Standing in line was Philip Post. Holly didn't wave back.

But now Philip saw that she'd noticed him, and he waved more vigorously. Holly stared back coldly. She made no sign. He grinned and adopted a pugilistic pose, threw a few punches in the air. As if their rivalry was a game, one big joke, and even if the world didn't know it, they were privy, they shared the joke.

"What's that about?" Paula asked.

"It's supposed to be very smart."

"Well it's stupid. Even if he is kind of cute."

"That about sums it up."

"What's taking so long?"

"Come in here and help me," Holly said.

Thanksgiving this year had taken an odd turn. Shortly before it was time to sit down at the table, Art and Anita had disappeared behind their bedroom door. The turkey was out of the oven, and Holly was basting its caramelized skin. Anita had done most of the preparations but Holly had made a grilled pepper salad and a platter of deviled eggs, and now she took care of the finishing touches. She looked at the clock and popped the bread rolls back in the oven. "Put some butter on those spuds and start mashing," she told her brother.

With a martyred air, Honus sighed and set to work, throwing in a big lump of butter. He gave the potato masher a ceremonial flip, then bent over the bowl and began pounding.

Jenn entered the kitchen. "Can I do something?"

"No, you're company," Honus said. He worked faster, adding a swirl of his wrist. Now he was showing off.

Holly had invited Roger to this meal, but he'd declined. They'd seen each other several times since the night he'd told her she wasn't serious, but things were no longer the same. The stakes had been raised. It would've made perfect sense for Roger to come today, since his parents were on the road for the holiday, but instead of joining her in Sheridan, he'd accepted an invitation from a lab colleague.

He was asserting a distance, even though she strongly suspected he wanted to be with her. When she telephoned him, he sounded pleased and was never the first to say goodbye. He inquired about her life. Not long ago, Roger used to brush her hair—Holly enjoyed that, found it soothing. Roger liked Holly's long hair and while he brushed, they chatted. These conversations could be more relaxing and intimate than talking in bed. Wasn't that the sort of thing they should be doing now? she wondered. They needed more time to understand each other. If he cared, then why stay away?

Tonight she would call Roger to tell him that she'd missed him, and she hoped it wouldn't make things worse. Recently she'd updated her job search with Yankton Associates. So what if she didn't get her first choice? It didn't have to be Italy. She ticked all the boxes: France, Germany, Spain, Slovenia, Austria . . . everywhere. She was in charge of her destiny. If Roger could understand that, then he *did* truly love her.

"What are they doing, really?" Honus panted before a golden, airy mound of potatoes.

He was referring to Art and Anita, but Holly hesitated to answer in Jenn's presence. Then she thought: Oh, why pretend? She's part of the family now.

"They're having an argument."

"What about?"

"I don't know," Holly lied. "But they'll be out in a minute. Let's make today a good time for them."

Earlier, as she was transferring her grilled peppers onto a china serving dish, she'd listened to Art and Anita bicker about Florida. Apparently Jack and Maria had rented a condo at Pondaro Beach in order to spend the holiday in the sun with Strapp. They'd even made arrangements for Grandma to join them, which was why this would be the first Thanksgiving without Grandma in many years. "We could've gotten a condo right next to theirs and spent the holiday together," Anita said. "Instead we're stuck up here and it's going to snow tomorrow."

"But what about Holly and Honus?" Art said. "They don't have time to run off to Florida, not with their schedules. Right Holly?"

Holly acted busy and didn't reply.

"No, you're just cheap," Anita said. "We never go anywhere. Holly's too polite to say it to your face."

Both of them were right. Holly didn't have time for some goofy family jamboree. And, of course, Art *was* too cheap. But she didn't like being invited to take sides. "Leave me out of it," she told them. "I'm just a tiny and impressionable child."

Art and Anita left the room to continue their argument and they didn't reappear until Holly and Honus had put out all the food and called them to the table—a reversal of roles, a family first.

After they settled in, the conversation revolved around Honus's fevered plans about his gig with Spotz! He spoke of fresh tunes spawned by their new equipment.

"My mic has resistance to feedback and the pick-up on the percussion is crispy, so we hear ourselves better. New stuff just comes out. It's almost magical."

"Like 'Shovel Face'," Jenn put in. "That one's terrific."

"We're louder now," Honus said. "There's so much more of me."

"Holly, you haven't said anything about yourself," Anita remarked. "What's new with you? How's your young man?"

Referring to Roger this way was intended to sound playful, carefree. Holly shifted the subject to her plans to attend an academic conference after Christmas.

"You're going to Chicago with a professor?"

"Yes, that's right. We're sharing a slot."

Anita threw her a look—sizing her up, in a way that had nothing to do with Holly's height. Was this trip to Chicago a pretext for a romantic weekend?

Oh my, Holly thought, picturing Borden. How to explain? "You said you were finished with school," her father added.

Faces blinked. Somehow their tolerant expressions made it worse. Stop it! she thought. Why couldn't they understand? Not about Borden, but about the importance of her passion for literature. Honus gave a little smirk and then chugged some milk. Art and Anita busied themselves with the food on their plates. These people loved her. They were the toughest critics of all.

My breast not covered with the Bed-cloaths

Lying in her childhood bedroom on Thanksgiving night, Holly's mind drifted between sleep and waking . . .

You rubbed my stomach.

Holly rolled on her other side. Then she opened her eyes into the dark. How long till morning? She was awake, waiting for light to creep in the window. Or in this gauzy consciousness, was she dreaming? In the dim barn Emily and Michael reached out, fingering buttons. It was so warm. Holly pushed down the blankets and tweezed her legs.

"Is there time?" Emily asked.

Her hand slipped in his shirt, the delightful muscled smoothness.

He pulled open her blouse. Her hard nipples, tips pebbling, signing air—

The five hour drive to Chicago traversed barren winter fields. There were occasional patches of snow and a few flurries in the air but mainly it was an unending stream of dull shades of brown. Holly had been uneasy about this trip, the daunting prospect of being trapped in a small space with Borden. A mere thirty minutes in his office could be exhausting. But it was cheaper than flying and she'd been grateful for his offer. Her Comet was chancy for this trip and he'd picked her up in a boxy, mud-spattered Buick. The journey went well as they read through their talk and made minor editorial changes, which Holly typed into her laptop while he drove. "You sure you don't want to put the poem on a PowerPoint slide? It would be easy. That way the audience can see it all at once."

"I made fifty photocopies," he said. "People are fine with a handout. You can *scribble* on a handout. With PowerPoint, people just snooze when the lights go down. It's as bad as television."

"They can still take notes."

"Shall we change the subject?"

It was a rhetorical question, so Holly didn't answer. (A rhetorical question was a well-suited technique for a bully, she thought.) The rest of the trip was uneventful, aside from occasional stops for Borden to use the toilet, and an awkward moment when he turned to her and said, "I'd like to thank you. The truth is, and I suspect you know it already, I've become rather distanced from many of my colleagues. There are reasons for this, it's a source of difficulties. But now, by dint of your efforts, I feel like I'm returning to what really matters. It's putting aside the noise in order to hear the music. This means a lot to me."

Holly shifted uneasily. One minute he was bossy, and the next chummy? And worse—considering Rosemary's warning about coming to the convention, her threatening undertone—

was she setting Borden up for an ambush? "You're welcome," she mumbled.

"I remember that day you showed up in my office and told me you wanted to go to graduate school. I fear you felt insulted by my answer but my intention was the contrary. You see, I've observed many young people and nowadays, with grade inflation and boosterism of all kinds, there's an endless stream of students with outstanding grades and letters of recommendation that praise them to the skies. Predictably, these kids believe what they've been told about themselves. They are tender babes but ignorant. But you were different, Ms. Winegarten."

"I certainly didn't have outstanding grades."

He shrugged. "Remember when I asked if graduate school was ready for you? I should've explained myself. It's because I had high expectations. People like you can avoid the academic *quadrille* dance. And this improves the institution. Professional life turns so many teachers into caged, timid creatures, running on a hamster wheel. I do not see you on a hamster wheel."

"A *quadrille* on a hamster wheel?"

Borden snorted. "Mixed metaphors have a long and respectable history, my friend. Your presence transforms the university by finding ways to connect the love of literature with people outside the cage."

"Well, thanks, but I can't fight that fight. I'm no longer at the university. And it's far from easy to connect on the outside, believe me."

"You're young. You've got plenty of time."

They rode along in silence. Presently Holly entertained a fancy that there was a third party in the car, sitting in the back seat, eavesdropping on their conversation. A steeplechase quilt covered her legs and she wore a winter bonnet, which curved and partly obscured her luminous face. Holly didn't turn around or expect her to say anything, but she was glad that she'd come along for the trip.

Traffic thickened as they approached the city. Holly had printed out directions for their freeway exits and she read them aloud. The convention was being held at the downtown Hyatt Regency. In order to save money, they'd already skipped the first day and a half of events and they'd booked cheaper rooms at the Abbott Hotel, only a few blocks from the convention center. They found it without difficulty, parked the car in a ramp and rolled their suitcases into the front lobby. Standing in line to check in, Borden spoke of plans to have dinner with his old pal Hans Woerner. He didn't invite her to join them but that was fine by Holly. She wanted to claim her room and have some quiet time to herself. "See you tomorrow morning!"

"The hounds of hell couldn't stop me," he said.

Holly ate a salad at a nearby steakhouse, choosing a well-lit booth where she could read as she ate. She distracted herself with a Barbara Pym novel (this was no time for reading research material) but she was aware, during the meal, of a growing pressure in her chest, a tension she used to experience back in her playing days, the night before a championship game. She studied people at other tables and realized that many of them were convention attendees, too. Some still wore ID lanyards while others were recognizable for their body language, the way they leaned in to listen and then leaned back to *comment*, folding their arms; it was the seriousness of their faces or the measure of their laughter; it was their age, no one truly young; their eyewear, which was minimalist or oversized and ironic; it was many things, not one image but a sum of details, quietly amassing into a portrait of the tribe. She didn't even have to overhear a conversation, though at one point Holly caught the phrase, "Forget that trope, dude!"

Before returning to her hotel, Holly took a walk along the lakefront. A cold scrub of wind on her face. It cleared her head. Multi-colored Christmas lights shone on buildings and quivered as blotches on the water. Above the Chicago skyline she saw moving lights—jet airliners—and imagined them on their way to Madrid, Paris, Lisbon. *How long before my turn comes?*

On the corner next to her hotel a neon sign advertised Windsor's Tavern. Passing the fogged window, Holly peered inside. She couldn't say why she did this—perhaps an idle wish to see Emily again?—but she saw Borden standing at the bar, talking animatedly to a tall man wearing a long white scarf. Borden's mouth fell open, guffawing. Out on the street it was a soundless image, and there was something grotesque about it. His arms swam the air, and he silently guffawed again.

Holly pushed through the tavern door and approached the bar. She plunged her fists in her coat pockets. A jukebox played loudly; Borden noticed her and called out "Holly!" above the music. "There she is!" he shouted to the man next to him. "She's the one I was telling you about. Holly sweetheart, this is Hans! Hans, Holly!"

Holly sweetheart?

"Everything all right?" she asked, ignoring how Hans Woerner lifted his chin, marking her height in the usual way.

"Splendid!" said Borden. His face was flushed; the corners of his mouth glistened. "Come and join us for a drink!"

"No thank you. We've got a full day tomorrow. We start early."

"We shall *slay* them, my dear! We are Samson amongst the Philistines! Two Samsons! We shall reach out to the pillars of the temple, and by our force alone the entire edifice will come crashing down!"

Hans Woerner laughed. "Didn't Samson perish in the process?"

Borden gave an exaggerated shrug, and then his jaw tightened, suddenly he was troubled. "Excuse me. Back in a minute." He scooted off, and Hans called after him, "Robert! Robert!"

"What?"

Hans pointed. "That way."

"Yes. Of course."

Borden turned and hastened towards the men's room.

"Robert says you've done very interesting work." Hans gestured toward a barstool. The word came out "*vork*." He adjusted his scarf. "Please have a seat, Holly. What are you drinking?"

"I can't stay. And neither can he. Listen—this is very important. Can you get him back to his room? *Soon?*"

"I can try."

Holly didn't like his diffident tone. Polite, but unconcerned. "Maybe you don't understand. He *really* has to get to bed."

Hans cleared his throat. "Maybe you don't know Robert."

"Please. You're his friend."

Holly buttoned up her collar and went out into the night.

Back in her hotel room, she started to peel off her coat when her cellphone rang.

"Holly, it's me. You've got to help me. Some bad stuff has happened."

"Honus?"

His voice sounded altered; there was a background echo or maybe it was just a bad connection. Holly still had one arm in the sleeve of her coat.

"Can you come get me? I've been arrested."

"What? Oh my!" She shook off her sleeve and her coat slipped to the floor. "Where are you?"

"Where do you think? I'm at the police station! Melbourne Drive. There's gonna be bail to post, it's $8000. But there's a bail bondsman right across the street. That's what they say, he works with the station all the time and we pay only 10% up front. I'm sorry, Holly, I know it's late, but could you come and get me?"

"My God. What happened?"

"It's a long story, I can explain later, but—it's Jenn—she—" Suddenly there was a silence and Holly thought they'd been cut off but then came a gasp, muffled, halting breathing. Again, an echo, like a sound in a swimming pool. Honus was sobbing.

"What *happened?* Oh no. Is Jenn OK?"

"We broke up. She left me. There's someone else. I can't stand it. It hurts so bad, Holly. Oh, it hurts."

This was followed by more crying and hiccupping into the phone. Holly sank onto the edge of her bed, her mind racing while she spoke calmly to settle him. She told him to slow down, to take it easy, she was listening, he wasn't alone. She was sorry he was sad—but why was he arrested? "Honus, was anyone hurt?"

"*I'm hurt!*" he shouted. "Aren't you fucking listening? Don't you understand? All I did was smash a TV at the motel after the concert when she told me, and she called the desk and the motel manager called the cops and they showed up and acted like a bunch of assholes. They got me for vandalism and criminal mischief. I busted the mirrors too and they claim I was resisting arrest but a guy was yelling right in my face. Now are you going to come and get me? You want me to spend the night here?"

"But Honus, I'm not even in town. I'm in Chicago. I have my conference, remember?"

"Oh shit."

There was a silence. "Surely there's someone local who—"

"What am I supposed to do, Holly? I got only one phone call and I was counting on you. Yeti is pissed about the motel bill and Steve doesn't drive. Oh, man. I couldn't call Mom and Dad. Don't you tell them, Holly, please. Can't you do your conference another time? Please?" He was crying again, and she could no longer understand his words. She was filled with a mixture of pity and disgust. She wanted to tell him to stop being a big baby but now wasn't the time, he was incapable of listening; she would have to save that conversation for later. "Holly, they're gonna make me hang up!" he exclaimed. "I've gone over time! You'll fix this, OK? Holly? Holly?"

"All right! I'm on it!"

"Don't tell Mom and Dad."

"I told you I'm on it!"

"Thanks."

And the line went dead.

Pacing the narrow strip of carpet, Holly considered her options. Could she leave her paper in Borden's hands? Could he be trusted to do it right? This would be a perfect excuse for her to flee and escape the convention. She didn't belong here, anyway.

But that was cowardly. She'd come this far and she would have to stick to her commitment. She couldn't entrust her case to Borden. That would be folly. Tomorrow morning, could he even be trusted to get out of bed? Holly didn't have her car, and even if she rented one, it would be four a.m., at the earliest, before she arrived at the police station. She'd promised Honus not to contact Art and Anita, and though Honus was being hysterical if he believed that he could censor this escapade—their parents would find out, sooner or later—she couldn't break her word to her brother. Not now. She'd said that she would cover for him. So what did that leave?

Chelsea was in Portland this weekend, setting up affairs before her final move, and there was no one at Buckley's or Stoddard's Family Restaurant to whom she could turn for this errand. And, well, there was the Troll, but he would be working. She couldn't call and ask him to pick up Honus at the police station while he did his pizza deliveries, could she? Really, there was only one choice. She punched her phone.

"Hi, Roger, I'm sorry it's so late but—"

"What a nice surprise," he said.

The next morning when, as agreed, Holly went down to the hotel lobby at 7:30 to meet Borden, she was relieved to see him standing by the window, sucking on a large coffee.

"Good morning, Professor Borden!"

"Good morning, Ms. Winegarten."

She couldn't repress a big smile, she was so happy to see him out of bed and dressed and ready to go. She resisted an urge to clap him on the shoulder or offer him a high five. (Had Robert Borden ever, in his entire life, performed a high five? It was difficult to conceive.) His suit was rumpled but then Borden was always rumpled; as they exchanged a few pleasantries, she noticed a hoarseness to his voice, a tiny dab of shaving cream visible below his left ear and a waxy, cadaverous pallor to his face; even so, there were no signs of the social incontinence of the previous evening. Perhaps he was accustomed to morning-afters like this one, only she hadn't had the occasion to observe him closely.

As for herself, Holly had slept badly and awoken early with dark rings under her eyes. She'd showered and washed her hair and discovered that the hair-dryer in her room expelled only a weak, tepid flow of air—she imagined the last breaths of a dying robot—so the process of drying her long mass of hair was slower than usual and erased the time gained by her early rising. She pulled on her best black trousers and a black dress top. She applied only a small amount of make-up, using a cover stick for a few spots, while having the impression that her morning moisturizing cream made the circles under her eyes shine more conspicuously.

I look like a Goth raccoon, she thought, inspecting herself in the mirror.

Borden took another pull of coffee and reached for his briefcase. "Shall we?"

During the brisk walk to the Hyatt Regency, they didn't speak, and Borden let his coat hang open despite the cold and didn't seem to notice when its belt dragged on the ground. At the reception center they picked up their registration packets and ID lanyards, and then filtered into the crowd in the vast exhibition space adjoining the ballrooms. Booths for scholarly quarterlies and university presses and technological services displayed their wares; there was a table to sign a petition against American torture and further on a man in a silver denim vest thrust a leaflet in her hand (*"Please support our Radical Caucus resolution for critics of Zionism . . ."*); conventioneers mingled in groups or spoke into cellphones, casting furtive looks around them. In some ways the atmosphere was probably no different from a trade fair or a baseball card convention, but there was also a palpable sense of people appraising each other, intimations of a pecking order. The sheer mass and ambient buzz, though, were reassuring to Holly. She didn't know her way around but it wasn't a problem. She felt like she'd slipped under the canvas and entered the big tent of a circus.

She was definitely one of the younger people—there was a visible gerontocracy, no doubt full professors, who wore well-cut jackets and leather accessories and attracted gazes of pornographic intensity from their juniors, mainly adjunct teachers or graduate students, Holly supposed, salivating for a job. Despite their comparative youth, these aspirants appeared more worn and weary than their sleek elders.

"One, two, three . . ."

A clarinet squeaked, a trombone belched. On a small raised stage a quartet of Gertrude Stein lookalikes began playing jazz. A banner above them read *The Tender Buttons*. Borden frowned and looked at his watch. "Shall we?"

They still needed to scout out the location of their panel discussion. Leaving the exhibition space, Holly wondered about Courtney Davies. According to the convention program, she'd given her paper yesterday. Despite her misgivings about Courtney, she hoped it had gone well. She knew how much Courtney wanted to make an impression. But it might not be easy, amid so many acrobats and fire-eaters.

Their meeting room wasn't large but it was already packed. Hans Woerner greeted them warmly and led them to their seats on the dais which they would share with other panelists. "A very good crowd!" he said. "You must've brought them in." He glanced over his shoulder. "I know most of the people who turn up for these sessions, and today we have some new faces."

Holly took her seat and in seconds spotted Rosemary and Philip Post in the audience. Rosemary was in deep conversation with people in the row behind her. A coterie of Dickinsonians? Had they come especially for her paper? Philip sat quietly and when he lifted his eyes toward the dais, Holly looked down at her notes.

She and Borden were scheduled second on the morning's program. Hans Woerner introduced the first speaker, a burly fellow from Penn State, who angled his shoulders toward the audience like an offensive lineman and, at the signal, charged through a dense discourse about Henry David Thoreau and his family's pencil factory. Holly couldn't bring herself to listen, her nerves were too jangled. The presentation was followed by questions, mainly about the writer's journals and Native American graphite mines. Finally it was finished, and Hans Woerner turned to Holly and Borden. "And now, it is my pleasure to introduce . . ."

Their microphones crackled—they were on!

Borden was the first to speak. Though he had a face like chalk—truly, he looked ill—and, visible to Holly, beads of sweat rolling down his jowl, he was utterly composed and, as he finished the preliminary remarks and warmed to the subject, he began to grin and elongate his pauses, for effect. "Genius is allergic to groupthink and resides in . . . *particularity*." Holly wished he would rein in his attitude, but the gaze of the audience clearly affected Borden. "The individual may appear to sever herself from society even as she engages with it more *in-ti-mate-ly*."

Just make the points! Holly thought. Stop hotdogging!

As arranged, an assistant to Hans Woerner passed the handouts around the room, and Borden announced that they held in their hands a previously unknown and unpublished poem of interest not just for Dickinson studies but for insights into reading practices. "It was discovered a short time ago by my colleague, Ms. Winegarten."

The claim of discovery caused a few faces to look up abruptly, a crossing and recrossing of legs. Some people frowned at the handout. "Let's look at it together, shall we?"

Borden turned to Holly. This was her cue.

She was flushed, her heart pounded, but her voice came out steady and firm. She recited from memory, following the rhythms and breath pauses, and soon members of the audience left off reading their printed texts to stare at Holly but this didn't last, either, as she approached the end of the poem and the attention of the entire room rushed as if in a shared stream of thought away from her to the words themselves, which seemed to hang in the air, as if the "skies inside their heads" were suddenly communicable:

> *If you hear me—moan or shout—*
> *Please—ensnare my mind*
> *Keep me in—to let you out*

When Holly finished, there was a silence. Not even a cough. She could hear the whistle of her own lungs. Borden asked: "Are words, instantiated in one body simultaneously a heritage and potential creation in another body?" Borden bobbed his brows. "Isn't this the very core of language?"

He went on in this manner and Holly wanted to shut him down. She agreed with everything he said—after all, she'd written most of it—but again, his delivery was an unnecessary distraction. It went against the spirit of the poem, its affectionate discipline. When he finally finished, he turned to Holly.

She elaborated on the Donahue correspondence, how it challenged received ideas about the author, and how this poem was not only an intensely personal document but one which enacted the very process of literature. Desire was laid bare. The future of literature wasn't beyond us, but in us. A potential awaiting discovery. She affirmed, "Modesty needs no apology. Emily Dickinson, a so-called recluse, wasn't hiding; she was making a space where she could do what she did best. Constraints are a way to freedom, to *enable* the self, to share with another and to go beyond the self. The text can't create meaning without the soulful attention of the reader who, in this example, is both a real and a virtual lover. The giver is taking and the taker is giving. *This* is ravishing."

When she finished, the immediate reaction of the audience was muted. Scattered applause, tentative but genuine; mainly, people seemed to be mulling over words, still pondering. Many didn't look to the dais but stared at their handouts. Holly felt gratified and relieved, though it was very different from the roar of a basketball arena.

"Thank you very much," said Hans Woerner. "Most interesting!" He turned to the audience. "Are there any questions?"

There was an immediate movement, and Holly wasn't surprised to see Rosemary's hand in the air. Here it comes, she thought.

"Could you tell us more about the context of the source, and how you came to share the poem with us? I'd also like to ask a follow-up question."

Borden breathed into his microphone. "Are you sure that our first answer won't suffice?"

This elicited a few chuckles and before Holly could speak, Borden went on to say that when his colleague, Ms. Winegarten, discovered the original document, she was immediately struck by its importance, and it wasn't long before it was brought to the attention of a pre-eminent expert in the field—"*yourself*, Professor Muller, as you already know! Time constraints haven't allowed us to dwell on circumstantial details. Ms. Winegarten, is there anything you would like to add?"

Holly had a sinking feeling. Either Rosemary was going to follow up with a pointed question about the Civil War period that she would be unable to answer—she didn't possess that kind of expertise—or she'd go straight for the jugular, and denounce her physical abuse of the manuscript. Holly said softly, "My focus is on reading. Of course I welcome insights about the historical context, too."

"That's not the context I'm talking about," Rosemary said. "You're not affiliated with a university, are you? You're not an archivist, are you?"

Holly bent closer to the microphone, knotting her hands in her lap. Her vision swam and a figure in white, seated in the back row, stood up. A sound of soft laughter. The figure in white exited the room. Holly inhaled.

"I work in a mall," Holly replied. "I'm here as a guest."

"That's right," said Hans Woerner, smiling. "As organizer of this panel, I requested a waiver from the executive director, to enrich our program. There is nothing amiss."

"You marked her as an archivist," Rosemary said. "And just now, she said she wasn't an archivist."

Woerner sighed. "I simply checked the box on the form that corresponded most closely to the situation, since the subject concerned a manuscript."

Borden's tapped on his microphone. "What's your purpose? Is this just an *ad hominem* attack? Are you defending some kind of closed club?"

"On the contrary," said Rosemary. "All my career I've fought for inclusiveness. When I started out, these gatherings were very different—very much an old boy's club. My purpose is to defend professional standards."

Holly could feel Borden seething beside her, but she didn't want him to be her interlocutor. He'd talked too much already. She said quickly, "Well, all right. Is there anything about my interpretation that doesn't meet these standards?"

Rosemary brought her hands together. "Your interpretation . . . that's not what I mean, Holly. I'm referring to the poem itself. This work belongs to Special Collections and university policy forbids unauthorized use of its materials. Dickinson manuscripts have a sad history of being misrepresented. This has caused a lot of grief. You know about that, I'm sure.

The version you've passed out today looks very much like the original. In fact I'd say it *is* the original. It's never been published and it's not in public domain. Did you get permission to photocopy or scan this manuscript?"

"The Civil War collection relies on crowd-sourced transcribers," Holly said. "It's all in the public domain. Ask my colleagues Inez Ramaro or Merle Pritchard. They'll confirm that."

Rosemary smiled. "They're my colleagues, too, and perhaps you're not aware, but this selection is now under contract for a book with Princeton University Press, and it will soon be copyrighted material. I'll repeat my question: did you get permission to photocopy or scan this manuscript?"

Holly shook her head. "I didn't do either. I just read the poem and learned it."

Rosemary hesitated for a moment, slightly thrown off. "That's a lawyerly answer. I think you understand the spirit of my question."

"I'm not trying to be lawyerly. It's the truth."

"So. In the end, you're just relying on something inside your head."

"In the end, doesn't everybody? It's only eighteen lines. That's not hard. But I'm respectful, if that's what you mean."

Rosemary shifted on her feet. "Please don't tell me what I mean. All right. It's not a prodigious feat of memory. Granted. But—"

"How many follow-up questions does she get?" Borden interrupted, turning to Hans Woerner. "She's monopolizing the time."

"No, let her go on," said Holly.

"Thank you," said Rosemary. "Just one last question. Or, rather, observation. You seem to dismiss the importance of the

medium. This is a precious document and you appropriate it
for your purposes."

"I don't dismiss the medium," Holly said. "But language
is its own sturdy box. I'm not stealing from the *author*." Suddenly Holly no longer felt defensive. She bristled at the suggestion that she was profiting from the situation, when it felt like
exactly the opposite, when she considered the hefty convention
fee and the price of the hotel and all the rest, though mentioning such details would sound petty and irrelevant to this crowd,
in their warm little pond. She looked out at the faces and spotted, once more, Philip Post. She continued, "Material versions
are only of anecdotal interest. They belong to the lucky. Or the
grasping."

Holly heard a hitch in Borden's wheezy breathing and
a tired, sad expression washed over Rosemary's features. Instantly Holly felt a stab of regret. Rosemary assumed the barb
had been aimed at her, not Philip. Holly didn't agree with Rosemary about many things but she didn't believe that she was
unscrupulous. Holly pictured the fragile manuscript that she'd
wrongfully removed from the library and hoarded at home.
She *had* stolen it, for a while. In a way she'd even vandalized it.
She'd also lied. Everything was messy. Now she added, "I look
forward to hearing what you have say about these new materials. You're speaking this afternoon, right? Two o'clock?"

Rosemary stared, as if wordlessly asking: *What are you up
to?* Eventually she answered, "Yes. Two o'clock." And then
she sat down.

"Well played!" Borden said afterward. "Slay her with sweetness!"

He was in high spirits and wanted to go out to lunch to
celebrate. Holly didn't share his mood. She was relieved that

they'd avoided outright denunciation and had made a decent impression, but she didn't want to *play,* still less to *slay.* Not any longer. Plus, she was exhausted. After their presentation, they'd sat through two more papers and long-winded Q & A. So she declined his lunch invitation. The prospect of listening to Borden crow over a hamburger was unappetizing.

"I have to make some phone calls," she said. "See you this afternoon."

Holly bypassed the exhibition space and ballrooms and went to the Hyatt Regency atrium, a glass firmament revealing a blue winter sky. She found a calm spot away from people beside a fountain and an olive tree. It was a mature olive tree, maybe 100 years old, and as she took out her cell phone she wondered at its uprooting, how it came to this unlikely place. At the center of the fountain were two sculpted *putti* with plump naked bottoms and wings, guarding the water that slipped and slupped over flat rocks. The effect was peaceful, almost hypnotic. Holly blinked, remembered herself and pressed her phone.

Honus answered after five rings.

"Hey," she said. "You home now?"

"Yeah. I was sleeping."

"Roger come get you?"

"Yeah."

"What did he say?"

"Not much." Honus's voice was scratchy, and now he coughed. "That guy never says much. There were lots of papers and shit. He cosigned for me. It was 3:30 in the morning before we got out of there."

"Did he seem pissed?"

Silence. Then: "Jesus Christ, Holly! I'm living a nightmare and you just wanna talk about him."

"That's not what I meant. I'm sorry about what happened, Honus. I really am."

"Let me go back to sleep. I want this all to go away."

The line went dead.

Holly sighed and rested her phone on her knee. She watched the fountain for a few more minutes. Then she took a deep breath and called Roger, but got only his voicemail. She left a message of thanks, and then stood up and walked to the end of the atrium before she realized that she wasn't particularly hungry and didn't want to go anywhere, so she turned around and came back to her olive tree. She would stay here until it was time to attend Rosemary and Philip's presentation.

What had they concocted? she wondered. Maybe Rosemary was waiting until she controlled the floor before launching an embarrassing attack on Holly. This morning she'd just been laying the groundwork. Nothing obliged Holly to attend her talk, but not attending, after this morning's discussion, would be feeble. Worse, it would be a public retreat, as if conceding everything Rosemary might say. Holly couldn't do that.

No. She would wait by the olive tree till two o'clock, and then finish this damn business.

Holly took out her lap top and used the Wi-Fi code supplied in her convention packet. She checked the weather conditions for the drive home. Then, opening her email, her eye immediately lit upon a message from Yankton Associates. *Oh my my! Was this her ticket to Rome?* She clicked on the message and read it once, twice. She rolled her neck and shifted her shoulders, and leaned toward the screen again. She read the message a third time. It said that a job awaited her in Ho Chi Minh City.

Although both Rosemary Muller and Philip Post were listed for the panel devoted to "Dickinson and Her Descendants," from the outset it was clear who was in charge. Philip hung back. In his dark jacket and a white shirt buttoned at the collar, he had the air of a young cleric. He followed Rosemary onto the dais. She'd changed her outfit since the morning session. Now she wore an austere but elegant olive green pant suit—silky and understated, as if she'd shown up to speak in pajamas but they were such exquisite pajamas that they didn't seem inappropriate. You could only wish you had a pair yourself.

"Greetings!" she told the assembly. "Delighted to be here." The room was full, a different crowd from this morning, women a clear majority. That aspect of Dickinson studies hadn't changed. Holly and Borden had arrived ten minutes early but they were lucky to find seats in the next-to-last row. Holly's thoughts moved in many directions. She imagined a globe, an expanse of blue Pacific and Vietnam, whose curled territory unexpectedly appeared like a beckoning finger.

"Clearly Emily Dickinson doesn't lack for admirers," Rosemary continued, "and today, she has something new to tell us." The lights went down and a PowerPoint slide snapped on, a towering headshot of Dickinson. "In my entire career, and I dare say for more than a century, there has been nothing in our field as surprising and significant as what we are going to share today. That might sound like a rash claim, but this poet continues to defy expectations. I'll begin by giving credit where credit is due. My colleague Philip Post was the first to call my attention to manuscripts that recently came to light in our library's collection of Civil War letters. I'll let him provide the background. Philip?"

His face winsome, he leaned toward his microphone and paused, as if he were shy and unaccustomed to others' attention. He briefly described Special Collections' mission to dig-

itize its archives and reminded his audience of Michael Donahue's situation in America and of complications with wartime
correspondence. He spoke more slowly than usual, with a
back-of-the-throat English drawl. Holly had expected something more theoretical, with more sparkles, but Philip was re-
strained, accepting the role of water-carrier. Or maybe for him
this speech was a meta-discursive parody that only the initiated
could appreciate. (What a treat!) After a couple of minutes,
Holly thought: My goodness, he's not even going to mention
me! She wondered if she ought to be relieved, even pleased—
but still it was shocking. Then Philip remarked, "A few of us
got a foretaste this morning on this subject but most of you
weren't present, so I have the enormous pleasure of making a
special introduction." He looked over his shoulder at the PowerPoint slide of Dickinson's face and asked, "Will you excuse
us for a moment?" The face disappeared.

This got a laugh. He must've pressed the remote control,
but he'd distracted everyone with his gaze, so no one saw him
do it.

"Today I'd like to call your attention to another name,
without whom we wouldn't be here today. She was the first
to spot something extraordinary in the archive. Holly Patricia
Winegarten! I see you there. It was so kind of you to come and
listen! Could you stand up, please?"

Philip looked straight at her, and people in the audience
began to turn and crane in her direction. Holly froze, feeling
her neck go hot. *No!* she thought. *I'm not going to perform
in your show.* She didn't stand up, hoping he would desist and
continue his presentation. But Philip asked again, and now Borden nudged her. "Come on. Don't play hard to get."

So Holly rose, her knees creaking, careful in the narrow
space, before a pool of faces, eyes moving up and down her.
As if expecting her to tell her name again, confirm that she

was a Somebody. From his seat Borden began to clap and a few others joined in but most people didn't bother, waiting for what came next. She sat down.

Philip continued his presentation, referring to the new materials, but Holly didn't hear much of it, distracted by irrelevancies. *Why did he say Patricia? Did he snoop around and find out my middle name?* She rarely used or even thought about this name, but Philip's introduction felt like a presumed intimacy, acted on in public. She felt a stickiness on her back, an unpleasant clinging of her blouse. Her ears were ringing. By the time Holly could focus again, Rosemary had reclaimed the microphone and was clicking through slides, detailing the letters, comparing handwriting samples. She described recent trips to the Houghton Archives at Harvard and to the Dickinson Museum in Amherst. She'd also unearthed a faded daguerreotype of men from the 28th Massachusetts Regiment. One of those indistinct faces, which she slowly scrolled across on screen, was Michael Donahue. Rosemary announced a hypothesis that there had been a passionate love affair between Emily and Michael and that Michael had taken her brother Austin's place in the army after she'd jilted him in order to pursue her life as a poet.

Although Holly had reached a similar conclusion (though she also wondered if Rosemary underestimated the importance of religion, notably Michael's Catholicism and Emily's ambiguous if not agnostic Congregationalism, among the obstacles confronting the lovers), she was impressed by Rosemary's research. It was sharp, to-the-point; her enviable access to other resources hadn't been wasted on her. *I couldn't have handled this background as well,* Holly thought. Professor Muller was truly in her element.

"The letters are an invaluable testimony," Rosemary said, "but the prize of the lot is a long poem, written out in fair copy, predating the letters. It will have a deserved place in the canon. And this is where things become even more fascinating. First, let's consider the text."

Words flashed on the screen, a typed transcription: "*Will you prepare a sturdy box . . .*" No written copies were handed out, perhaps to protect Rosemary's impending copyright, so for the moment, the poem was safely contained. And how would Rosemary interpret it? After a few general remarks, she said, "Philip?"

He pushed a trolley on squeaking wheels across the dais. It bore an object draped by a white cloth.

"Michael Donahue was a carpenter and woodworker who executed many practical jobs around Amherst. Perhaps his greatest legacy is this."

Philip whisked away the cloth, revealing a small chest, a ruddy mini-wardrobe with little drawers.

"With thanks to the Dickinson family collection and a grant from the Spalding Trust, which provided funding for transport and insurance, I'm honored to show you, for the first time with positive identification, Emily and Michael's box."

Philip moved his hand above it with an air caress.

"For more than one hundred years, this piece was displayed in the Amherst museum but misidentified. The box was in the poet's bedchamber where she did most of her writing. It's made of cherry wood, with mahogany veneer and boxwood stringing. The bottom drawer held hundreds of Emily's poems, discovered by her sister Lavinia after her death. It was the poet's memory storage device and much, much more. Historians incorrectly claimed that the box was constructed several generations earlier, circa 1785-1810. But my research, which has been corroborated by Aubrey Pitcher from the Smithsonian, dates the nails used here to one hundred and forty years ago—that is, during the American Civil War. I repeat, this is the box in which so much of the poet's work was found after her death. This box was made personally by Michael for Emily. This is a labor of love. Commissioned by Emily, it became the matrix of works that would forever change the course of American literature."

Several people came forward to take photographs. They had professional-looking cameras, no doubt media who'd been notified in advance of the event. Other members of the audience pointed their cell phones.

"And let us go back to the poem," Rosemary continued. "History is often an unhappy process even when it is retold as heroic. We sing of 'arms and the man'—and I will add, of course, of the woman. Let's look at the original fair copy. Here's an enlarged Jpeg photograph." Words filled the screen, each letter a yard tall, this time not a typed transcription but in the poet's distinctive sinuous handwriting. Rosemary scrolled down the page. "You'll notice this rust-colored smear? As we said earlier, Michael Donahue tragically fell at Chancellorsville. He carried this poem into battle. A love poem from Emily, now stained with his own blood."

Silence—the atmosphere in the room was electric. Holly glanced at Borden and saw him watching her with a quizzical expression. When Rosemary finished, barely a minute later, there was a clap, followed by another clap, and then a rush of applause. Holly looked again at Borden who shook his head as if to say, Well, she pulled it off, didn't she? Some people rose to their feet, to demonstrate their approval, and they were followed by others. Borden laughed and tugged at Holly's elbow. "More sweetness! Pile it on! Pile it on!" So they stood, too, and everyone joined in the ovation.

They loaded up the car and left that same afternoon. Tomorrow was another day of panel discussions and guest speakers, but as far as they were concerned, it was over. Holly volunteered to drive, since she wondered if Borden had imbibed at lunch, and he acquiesced with barely a word, so maybe her suspicions were justified. On the way out of the city, traffic was dense and required close attention, so it was only when they were an hour down the road that they were able to talk about what they'd witnessed.

"You have to hand it to her," Borden said. "Who would've dreamed that you could bring down the house with an empty box? A 'matrix of American literature.' A womb of one's own!"

Holly changed lanes to pass a truck. "Please don't be a dick," she said.

Borden chuckled. "Is that some of your ballplayer trash talk?"

In all the time she'd known him, they'd never spoken of her past, of her basketball days. Evidently he'd informed himself.

"Let me reformulate," she said. "Forget the 'please.' The rest stands."

"Oh, don't get annoyed." The highway hummed beneath them. A moment later Borden added: "please."

"I'm not annoyed. But I'm not your student anymore. This afternoon wasn't all bad, I learned some things. Rosemary did some interesting digging, you have to admit."

"Mmmmh." Borden took out a handkerchief and blew his nose with a honk. They passed frozen fields and the shadowy outlines of silos. He replaced his handkerchief in his pocket. "I'm wondering something. You showed me that manuscript, and I recall that it was yellow, and there were lots of folds. But the blood stain got by me entirely. When you saw it, what did you think it was?"

Holly saw no reason to lie, so she told him the truth about Honus and his salsa. Borden made no reply, and eventually Holly took her eyes off the road and looked at him. He was staring at her.

"Promise me you're not making this up."

"It's all true."

Borden brayed, an enormous horse-laugh, his palm slapped the dashboard. "Oh dear me! If the lad were here, I'd shake his hand! Bravo, you Winegartens! This is delicious. Bravo! Say, could you pull over at this exit? I need to use the facilities."

Holly eased onto the ramp and they made a stop at a brightly lit convenience store, glowing like a gumdrop fire on the dark prairie. Borden flung open his door and trotted off to the men's room.

She cut the engine and got out to use the women's room. When it came time to wash her hands, she was startled by the face in the mirror. This young person looked just like her mother, in an old photograph, taken in California before she'd left the West to make a new life with Art. Water was running. Holly blinked and it became her face again. She turned off the water. Maybe it was an effect of poor lighting. She reached for a hand towel, bent to the mirror. She wondered what Anita would tell her now. "Mommy," she whispered. "What do you think? Should I go away?"

Returning to the car, she noticed Borden at the convenience store's cash register, buying a six-pack of beer. He carried it out in a paper bag and put it between his feet in the front seat. As Holly re-entered the freeway, he popped open a can.

"Listen," she said, "an open container is illegal. I don't want to get a ticket."

"Don't worry. If we get pulled over, it'll be empty before anything happens."

Brilliant, she thought. A road trip with Bobby Borden.

A short time later, she heard the pop of a second can.

"You want one?"

"I'm *driving*."

"Yeah, but you know . . ." They rolled along for a while, and he sipped. "So," he said, as if picking up the thread of an ongoing conversation, "back to the grind, eh? A new year."

Holly was silent. Back to . . . what? She'd have to check up on Honus and speak with Roger, see what needed to be done. She'd have to come to a decision quickly about Yankton Associates. She'd have to look at a map, for God's sake! Ho Chi Minh City. Didn't that used to be Saigon? There was so much she needed to find out, and fast.

"Yeah, back to work," she told Borden.

He sniffed. " 'All is seared with trade; bleared, smeared with toil.' "

Holly knew he was quoting someone but it wasn't Dickinson. She'd have to look it up. A few minutes down the road, she said, "This has been one strange weekend. It wasn't what I wanted. But maybe I shouldn't have wanted what I wanted. I was wrong."

"How's that? What do you mean?"

"I wanted to have it both ways. To repudiate and yet impress those I was repudiating. If I were smarter I shouldn't have cared about impressing, I shouldn't have come here. I already *knew* that, really. It wasn't mysterious. But I couldn't stop myself. Or I didn't stop myself. Somehow the university makes it easy to forget."

"Don't blame education. Good lord!"

"That's not what I mean. I guess I'm talking about the trappings. The preening. The whole heart of dorkness. You know . . ." Holly searched for a moment, then blurted, "Philip Post!"

Borden sighed. "Ah. The whore. The whore."

He popped another can.

She gripped the wheel and said, " 'We will be known by our secret deeds. Not by name—but by our dreams.' I think that's how it goes."

"Is that Emily, too?"

"Yeah. One of the letters."

"Sort of like the biblical injunction to pray in your closet," he said. "Tough for us Pharisees." He thought for a moment, tapping the can with a fingernail. "Actually, we might've been able to fit that in your paper."

"Let's give that a rest, all right?"

By the time they stopped for gas and another toilet break, Borden had finished his cans. Holly was concerned to see him approach the beer coolers but this time he didn't take another six-pack, he settled for a tall boy bottle. In the car he fiddled with the radio; they didn't speak much. Eventually he leaned back and mumbled, "Keep going and enjoy the signs."

Holly squinted against oncoming headlights. It began to snow, which wasn't good. Borden had fallen asleep, breathing deeply. He snorted once, but didn't awaken. When she glanced over at him, his head was tilted back, his mouth open, his lips puttering. Maybe he was lecturing in his dreams. "Keep going and enjoy the signs." Was that some kind of homespun Emersonian koan? Or just old guy drunken talk?

Winter light rubbed the curtainless windows. Last night's snowfall had already started to melt; the street was full of slush. Holly called Honus and suggested that he come over for breakfast and they could talk about his situation, but he said he didn't want to talk and he wished she would stop calling and waking him up every goddamn minute when he'd finally managed to fall asleep.

"When is a good time?" she asked.

"Not now." He hung up.

Holly exhaled. The little jerk! Next she called Roger and this time, she didn't get his voicemail. "Hey Roger!"

"Holly? How are you? Where are you?"

Nervously she thanked him again (why was she so nervous?) and invited him to come over for coffee. "If you don't have obligations at the lab . . ."

"Sure. I can be there in half an hour."

"Good."

"See you then."

After this conversation, Holly stared at the phone in her hand. She'd already showered but now she went back to her room and made her bed neatly and picked out a better top, an aqua-marine wool sweater. But then she noticed that it was covered with little fuzzy balls from its last washing, so she wondered if it was a good choice while feeling foolish for acting this way—why did it matter? It shouldn't matter. She pulled on the top and started picking at the fuzzies with her fingertips, which was therapeutic, in a way, calming, better than thinking about questions in life. Then she went to the kitchen and arranged the coffee items and a bowl of fruit. The doorbell rang. He was early!

When she opened, it was Honus. On his head was a winter hat with dangling earflaps.

"What are you doing here?" she asked.

"You asked me to come, didn't you?"

"I thought you didn't want to."

"Once you woke me there was nothing else to do. Holly, I can't fucking sleep. You gonna let me in or what?"

He entered and, aside from his hat, he wore only a pair of voluminous khaki shorts and a thin sweater. He looked around the bare living room. "Where's all your stuff?"

"It wasn't my stuff, it was Chelsea's. She's moving out to the west coast. She's selling the house."

He plopped into the only armchair and looked silently out the window at the bare trees. He wasn't really curious about the situation with Chelsea. Holly folded her arms. "How are you?"

"I told you."

"You hungry? You need to fill me in on some details."

He scratched his arm and said nothing. It was as if he hadn't heard her. He still hadn't taken off his hat.

Holly retrieved a chair from the kitchen and brought it over and sat beside him and invited him, gently, to describe what had happened. He brusquely told her that it was pointless but she prodded, asking, why did he come here? Eventually a garbled account emerged, about how Jenn had dumped him for Yeti's big brother, a guy who'd been coming to the shows not to hear the band but, he discovered, to spend time with her. This had been going on secretly for months, and Yeti had known about it all along. After the show with Spotz! there had been a party and Jenn was drunk and confessed the truth and Honus had ordered everyone to leave and then he trashed the motel room. That was how the police got involved. That was why he'd ended up in jail. "It's second degree criminal mischief and vandalism and resisting arrest and interference with official acts. I have to enter a bunch of pleas on Wednesday."

"What do you mean by 'interference'? What's that about?"

"I was just trying to explain myself to those cops and they wouldn't listen, they got no respect at all. They wouldn't hear me out. Fuckers pushed me around."

He was belligerent, convinced he was a victim, and Holly changed the subject. "Have you spoken to Jenn?"

"What about? She doesn't give a flying fuck for me and you can't know how that feels. You *can't!*"

His bluster grated on Holly and she didn't want to reinforce it by giving him other opportunities to vent. So they sat quietly for several minutes. Eventually, though, when they resumed talking, there was something else in his manner that she couldn't reconcile and it was more troubling. She told him that she didn't pretend to know exactly how he felt, but she knew what it was like to have her heart broken. It was horrible but time changed things. Time.

"It's already happening," he said.

"What do you mean?"

"There was something odd in the person I was," Honus said. "Who I am now doesn't feel the same." His voice went higher, his eyes squinched as if he was crying, but there were no tears. "It's like madness, this . . ." He searched for a word, but when it didn't come he suddenly laughed, a joyless, hollow bleat. He was hunched over, puffy-faced between the flaps of his hat. He looked like a crazy pilot.

The doorbell rang, and Holly let in Roger. He smiled shyly and though they didn't kiss, his greeting was warm. He unzipped his coat and then stopped short when he saw Honus slumped in the chair.

"Oh. Am I interrupting?"

"It's OK," said Holly.

She was mortified that Honus didn't stand up or acknowledge Roger. She was on the verge of berating him like a child, obliging him to say something. *Show some respect! This guy got your ass out of jail!* But before she spoke, Roger said, "Hi Honus."

"Hey," Honus grunted.

"How you doing?" Roger asked.

"Fine."

"Would you like coffee, Roger?"

"Sure."

Holly hurried off to the kitchen. She'd intended earlier to start the machine brewing but Honus's arrival had thrown off her timing. "Ready in a minute!" she called. She returned to the living room with the bowl of fruit, which she placed on the floor, and then Roger helped her retrieve another chair, though maybe this wasn't a wise arrangement because forming a small circle in the bare room contributed to the mourning atmosphere. What were they supposed to talk about? It was time to put Jenn out of the picture. "Honus doesn't drink coffee," she began, as if it were a subject of general interest, and then, still groping, added: "Honus, you haven't said anything about the show. What was it like sharing the stage with Spotz!? I hope you got some photos. We can put them on the website. That would be cool, wouldn't it?"

Honus rubbed his face. He coughed and didn't cover his mouth. "There was a big crowd but it was hard to hear yourself. The sound blows back at you and it's disorienting. Everything went by fast. I don't know if we were any good, to be honest. Anyway, people came to hear Spotz! Not us."

Holly reached for an orange and the room was so silent that when she began to peel it, the breaking of its skin was audible. Its fragrance wafted over them.

Roger asked, "Holly, how did your paper go in Chicago?"

Holly thought for a moment, pulling off a slice. "Sort of like Honus's show, I guess."

"Really. Did you smash things up afterwards?"

Now Holly laughed, and even Honus gave a snort.

"No, I was in too big of a hurry," she said. "Roger, how much was the bail bondsman? What do we owe you?"

"Oh. It was eight hundred dollars."

"Eight hundred twenty-eight dollars," said Honus, fishing in one of the many pockets of his shorts and pulling out a tissue of blue paper. He read the total: "Eight hundred twenty-eight and sixty cents. They tack on fees. I'll get it to you as soon as I can, man."

Holly avoided her brother's eyes. This would come up in a later conversation, no doubt.

Roger pointed to dents on the carpet where the couch had been. "So where's your furniture? What's with the minimalism?"

She'd already told him about Chelsea's plans, so this question was partly disingenuous. Holly had a strange feeling that he even knew what she would say next. "Well . . . I got word from Yankton Associates."

"So. Italy. You're really going?"

The question sounded like a challenge.

"Not Italy. Vietnam. I'm supposed to start in three weeks."

There was another silence.

"You're joking," Roger said. "This is official?"

Honus looked up. "No shit?"

Holly nodded. Why did he say "joking?" Nothing was official till she showed up, and she hadn't yet called a number mentioned in the email or checked out airfares—it had been less than twenty-four hours since she'd gotten the offer, and she felt conflicted and confused—but she certainly wasn't "joking." Roger and Honus gawped as if expecting her to explain herself. She didn't want to explain herself. Why should she?

"Well, Hol, you'll blend right in there," said Honus.

"You're going to teach, right?" said Roger.

She'd already told him her intentions, hadn't she? Didn't that count? It wasn't only Roger, probably everyone else would share this incredulity. But she wished Roger were an exception, capable of making this allowance for her, wanting to be a part of her world. He seemed like the sort of man who could, if he tried harder. Just a bit harder! Don't look at me like that, she thought.

"Yes, teach," Holly said. "But mainly . . . I'm going to learn. What else would it be?" Her words came out softly but something inside her clenched like a fist. She could no longer worry about impressing anyone. Rosemary and Borden, even Honus and Roger, now seemed far away. The old arrangements were shattered.

The doorbell rang, and Holly got up quickly, eager to distance herself from this conversation. She opened to a woman who was reaching to push the bell again, and when the woman stopped mid-motion and looked up, her face was familiar. A middle-aged Black lady, stocky at the shoulders, wearing a blue hat. Her manner was grave. "Excuse me, Holly. We were introduced about a year ago? I'm Gloria Wells. I'm looking for your brother."

"Oh—yes. I remember. You're Steve's mother. Come on in."

Gloria didn't move, and now Holly noticed a car parked at the curb, the engine running, and sitting in the front seat, Steve.

"That won't be necessary," Gloria said. "I'm looking for Honus. We stopped by his place and he wasn't there, so I want to know where I might find him. I gather he's been out of jail since yesterday? Maybe you know about that? I'd like to have a word with him, face to face."

"He's right here." Holly called over her shoulder, "Honus!"

Cold air poured into the house but Gloria remained planted on the front step, and Holly called again. Eventually her brother appeared. "*What?*" Then he saw Gloria, and he stood up straighter. "Oh, hi."

"What the hell is the matter with you?" Gloria demanded. "Huh?"

"Why'd you do that to Steven? That's how you treat your friends? What kind of gutless little shit are you?"

"What are you talking about? Is there a problem?"

"Damn right there's a problem. Not a word to Steven. You would've left him to rot. You abandon him and get somebody else to clean up your mess. He wouldn't call me and I found out he was in jail only because there was an emergency with his medications and some other guys in the lock-up raised a fuss and got him some help. How could you leave him behind?"

"I don't know what you're talking about," Honus said.

"Oh, *please*."

The conversation see-sawed confusingly but it emerged that Steve had been arrested, too, and had had a rough time while awaiting processing. He was subject to severe panic attacks with hyperventilation and black outs. That's what eventually got him some attention. Honus claimed ignorance of all this. He hadn't crossed paths with Steve at the police station. "I was with Jenn back at the motel and we had a fight and I did some stuff and the management called the police, but by then Steve wasn't even in the room. I assumed he cleared out with the Yeti. Steve didn't do anything."

"They charged him with underage drinking. You probably know about that."

"Huh? We were drinking but that's freakin' ridiculous."

"Not the way the law sees it. He has enough on his plate without this extra trouble."

Holly said, "*Him?* Underage?"

"His twenty-first birthday is in February. This is his third offense."

"I didn't know," Honus said. "Really. I was distracted by other things. Let me talk to Steve."

Honus started toward the door, but Gloria blocked his way. "You're not talking to him. He's not talking to you. We got a doctor's appointment this morning and then we got to see a lawyer. That's all I care about right now. You got your own troubles, you deal with them, but he's given enough and he's not doing anything else for you people. That's what I came to tell you to your face. We're *done*. Hear that?"

"We're very sorry," Holly said. "We didn't know."

Gloria grunted. "Yeah, there's a lot you don't know."

She turned around and walked back to the car. Steve sat very still in the front seat, facing straight ahead. The car rolled away. The air was cold in the vestibule and after they drove off, Holly closed the door.

Epilogue

QUÁN NÉT

"Meet you back around eleven?"

"Sounds good," Brigid said.

They stood in front of the bright red storefront where Holly would have access to the Internet. She didn't start work till the afternoon and mornings were the best time to call home, considering the time zone difference. With a slap of flip-flops, Brigid continued down the sidewalk.

Holly parted beaded curtains and went inside and greeted the owner, a young man who was there at all hours. He wore a ballcap and ate from a bowl with floating dumplings. He nodded, letting her choose her own place.

She selected a computer near the fan and took a moment to inspect the headphones. The light was dimmer in here than on the street, the air stickier. The fan rotated, *tik-tik-tik*.

Before making her call, Holly quickly logged on to her email. Her inbox showed a backlog of messages, most of them without interest, but one jumped to her attention, sent only yesterday, from Roger. Well well! She pressed her hands together and stared at the name, letting the moment sink in. He was getting back in touch.

When she'd first left the U.S., they'd corresponded regularly. Holly enjoyed writing to him about her new life, putting her experience into words, and Roger told her how much he missed her and attached photos of himself and a squinty laboratory cat called Oliver. They'd agreed that Roger should get a cheap flight at Christmas, when the rainy season was over, and they could share a tropical holiday. She would take him to the Củ Chi Tunnels and the War Museum and other local attractions. Holly pictured them walking with hands clasped near the river, the novelty of being together in a new setting.

Then one day she opened a message in which Roger announced, in excessively formal terms, that he'd started seeing someone and he wasn't coming for Christmas and he felt that it wasn't appropriate for him to engage in the same kind of personal correspondence that they'd previously conducted—but he wanted her to know that he thought highly of her and would always be available as her friend, if she needed him.

This email left Holly shaken. The tone annoyed her but the larger significance was obvious and she should've been ready for something like this to happen. Her mind swam with questions. So Roger had given up on her? She'd had her chance, but he'd decided to move on. Her control of her life suddenly seemed a flimsy, vain thing. Was it merely a wishful illusion?

"Am I fool?" she asked her roommate Brigid, her throat burning, her eyes red. "Maybe I didn't understand what I wanted. I'd like to talk to him, face to face. Make him reconsider. You think I should go back?"

"Give it time. Don't do anything rash."

"Time? I don't think so. Sounds like it's already too late."

"Listen. If it was only about him, you wouldn't be here in the first place. You came here for a reason and that reason is still part of the picture. You're upset, sure, but don't spite yourself. Besides, maybe you're not hearing everything. He says he'll be available. You've marked this guy. He's still figuring himself out."

"Oh, come on. He's found someone else."

"For now, Holly. There's always a price and it's rarely what a person expects. Or wants. Just wait a bit. Hold on."

That was three months ago. On several occasions she'd called his number and hung up before he could answer; she'd lacerated herself with such impulses. Sometimes she took down the thin volume of *The Single Hound* which she'd brought overseas. It had been a private joke to herself to think the title referred to Roger. But now when she saw it on the shelf, she thought: *No. I'm the hound.*

Still, she'd weathered her initial panic, absorbed herself in daily life, because this was how it had to be. Yes, she was in charge of her future. And now, seeing Roger's name in her in-box, Holly thought: Look who's back! You've changed your tune!

She decided to wait before opening Roger's message, because she would require time to figure out a thoughtful response. First, though, she needed to call home. Ho Chi Minh City was twelve hours ahead of Sheridan, and her parents went to bed early. You had to call at the right moment. She pictured their old land line phone on the kitchen wall, and clicked out the number on her computer.

"Hello?"

"Happy birthday!"

"Holly? Is that you?" Anita asked.

"Who else would it be?"

"Well, just saying. *Good* to hear from you."

If there was an implied reproach in her words, it was a gentle one. Holly had sometimes forgotten or been lackadaisical about Anita's birthday. Just last year she'd waited until the day itself before putting a card in the mail, thereby guaranteeing it would arrive late; she hadn't bothered to call, either. "It's Holly!" Anita shouted, so that Art could pick up an extension and join in the conversation.

"Hey!" he said.

"Hey Art. Did you go crazy for her birthday?"

"We went out to dinner," Anita said. "And he cleaned my car."

"That's a start," Holly said.

"Tell us about *you*. How's Brigid?"

It was curious how her parents always asked familiarly about her roommate, a total stranger, but maybe they didn't know how else to address her present situation. When Holly had first arrived, she was reluctant to accept the housing arrangements made by her employer; she'd wanted to have her own place, and not share with another foreigner. She thought that in a duo, she would stick out even more, and it would complicate matters when Roger came to visit. But now she was grateful for Brigid. She'd arrived five months before Holly, and she'd shown her the ropes, helped her adapt to the job. Vietnamese students were pleasant and easy to get along with, but class sizes were large, and Holly was tired and hoarse by the end of the day. Walking down the street with her roommate, the pair were conspicuous, indeed—Holly for the usual reason, Brigid because she was copper-haired, her Irish skin as pale as mozzarella, her face strikingly pretty with plush lips. She and Holly got along well and trusted each other. A few months ago, not long after the break with Roger, Holly had fallen ill and lay curled with cramps, sweating into the sheets, with delirious nightmares that flickered nauseatingly with a blue light like a PowerPoint presentation. Brigid had stayed by her side, cared for her, literally held her hand. It was the commonplace initiation of her foreign stomach to a new continent, probably made worse because the food here was wonderful and Holly had grown cocky and careless in her habits. The sickness quickly passed, and she'd been fine ever since, but she'd mentioned the episode to Art and Anita, who now regarded Brigid as a necessary big sister, her live-in guardian angel, which was hardly the case. For her part, Holly had helped Brigid in delicate situations with her many boyfriends, who presently included a Canadian businessman who took her to drink ristrettos on top of the Bitexco Tower; a rather serious medical student named Hai who showed up at unexpected hours with chè desserts; and their shared tutor for Vietnamese lessons, a patient, smiling fellow named Thanh, whom Holly favored. Other men were constantly popping up, too. When Brigid went to a window of their apartment to smoke a cigarette, there might be a fellow she didn't remember waiting below on his motor scooter, hoping for a glimpse.

"We're going to visit some temples this weekend," she told them. "We're renting a mini-bus with a couple of guys."

"Well be careful!"

She'd told them many times how safe it was, but it never seemed to stick. She changed the subject. "How's Honus?"

"Oh, he's the same, but more so. He's sticking it out for another semester."

"Good for him," Holly said. "Does he have a girlfriend?"

"How would I know?" Anita said. "He doesn't tell us much. He's taking piano lessons. Says he wants to start another group if he can find people who aren't silly."

"I believe 'assholes' was the term he used," Art said.

"Whatever," Anita said.

Holly pictured her brother and remembered the loneliness of college life. She resolved to write to him. She would tell him to keep singing.

They chatted for a few more minutes, and Holly promised to call again at Thanksgiving. After her goodbye, she removed her headphones and lifted her arms high in order to stretch. She glanced beside her and saw the shop owner watching her. He looked back down at his bowl of soup.

People had been very friendly but it wasn't a free country for the locals; she didn't know what his parents or grandparents had lost or what he might really think of a person like her. Sometimes it felt like the longer she stayed, the less she knew.

Everything was beginning; there was so much to find out. The world was big and she was small. Holly took a deep breath and logged back on to her email and opened Roger's message.

It wasn't what she expected. Terse and impersonal, he'd written only three sentences:

Dear Holly,

Your friend died and I don't know if you know. Here's the link.

Sorry about the news,

Roger

Holly blinked and reread the message. She clicked the link, whereupon she discovered an article from the university paper.

Professor Robert Borden was found unconscious in his office early Thursday by a custodian who immediately called emergency rescue services. He was pronounced dead on the scene. Natural causes are suspected.

Professor Borden taught in the English Department for 27 years. Prior to his appointment he was on the faculty of Bowling Green State University. Rosemary Muller, current chair of the English Department, praised Professor Borden for his "long career and tenacious dedication, which made a lasting impression on everyone who knew him. We will not see the likes of him here again."

Holly pictured Borden's cramped, low-ceilinged office. He would've wanted to go out in a blaze of glory, performing in front of an audience, but he'd died alone at his desk, probably while marking a stack of papers. Natural causes, indeed. Maybe one comma splice too many had finished him off.

Out of curiosity, she checked the departmental website, but there was no notice or statement about Professor Borden. Perhaps it was too soon. She clicked the faculty profile for Philip

Post—yes, he was still there, a tenure survivor, now sporting a black turtleneck. Working under Rosemary Muller might actually suit him, Holly speculated. It was another way of getting spanked. A click on Rosemary's profile announced the upcoming publication in December of a volume with new work by Dickinson including editorial notes and commentary.

Holly hadn't thought about this for a long time. She'd been busy, living her life. Once she'd glimpsed a small figure in white lace on the back of a *xe ôm*, one of the local motorbike taxis that zipped around the city, defying traffic. But that was months ago. Now she supposed it wasn't a bad thing if other people got to read Professor Muller's research. They would make of it what they could.

But why wait for Rosemary's version?

Holly clicked away from the university portal and sought out a preferred site, "In Defense of . . . Nothing." She scrolled through the menu. Yes, this was a reasonable place to start. It could fit here. A labor of love.

Not for the first time she pictured Michael Donahue lying on his back in a field by a muddy creek in Virginia. Clouds drifted in a remote sky. Was he thinking, as he died in the weeds, of a woman many miles away whose words, even now, pressed next to his body? He hadn't allowed himself to be parted from a brain on fire.

Holly opened a talk thread and began to type from memory, moving her lips at the same time, respecting the rhythm, the words and dashes.

She hoped she had it right. The idea that this action was unauthorized didn't trouble her in the least. In fact, she felt as if Rosemary's edition gave her permission, even if that was contrary to Rosemary's intention. The moment felt ripe with possibility. Words didn't solve the sorrows of love and war but

they persisted beyond them. They could reach unexpected, un-
dreamed of places and persons. They unleashed new yearnings.

Holly reached back and lifted her hair in order to allow
the air from the fan to caress her warm neck. Ah, just like that.
Who knew what would happen to all the nobodies? She clicked
send. It was their shared secret.

Charles Holdefer grew up in Iowa and is a graduate of the Iowa Writers' Workshop and the Sorbonne. He currently teaches at the University of Poitiers, France.

His short fiction has appeared in many magazines, including *New England Review*, *Chicago Quarterly Review*, *North American Review*, *Los Angeles Review*, *Slice* and *Yellow Silk*. His story "The Raptor" won a Pushcart Prize.

He also writes essays and reviews which have appeared in *The Antioch Review*, *World Literature Today*, *New England Review*, *The Dactyl Review*, *The Collagist*, *l'Oeil du Spectateur*, *New York Journal of Books*, *Journal of the Short Story in English* and elsewhere.

ALSO BY CHARLES HOLDEFER

NOVELS

Bring Me the Head of Mr. Boots (2019)
Back in the Game (2012)
The Contractor (2007)
Nice (2001)
Apology for Big Rod (1997)

STORIES

*Agitprop for Bedtime: Polemic, Story Problems, Kulturporn
and Humdingers* (2020)
Magic Even You Can Do: By Blast (2019)
Dick Cheney in Shorts (2017)

CRITICISM

George Saunders' Pastoralia: Bookmarked (2018)

CPSIA information can be obtained
at www.ICGtesting.com
Printed in the USA
LVHW071502230623
750091LV00002B/77

9 781952 386350